I0587336

Whispers in the Wind

A Journey Through Time and Destiny

Patrick Timm

Coastal Tides Press

ISBN: 978-0-9910205-2-2

Published by Coastal Tides Press

Contents

Part I The Calling

Chapter One

The First Whisper

"Listen to all the teachers in the woods. Watch the trees, the animals, and all living things—you'll learn more from them than from books."
— *Joe Coyhis, Stockbridge-Munsee*

The river ran swift and cold, its voice steady as breath. Across the water, the far bank waited—still, untouched, and strangely expectant. Footprints from another age slept beneath the soil. When the wind rose, it carried faint cries that drifted like spirits through the September sky.

Branches swept low, heavy with red and gold leaves that brushed the earth like warriors guarding their fallen king. The air smelled of cedar and rain.

Jack Bellard stood at the water's edge searching for a way across. A fallen log, a scatter of stones—anything to bridge the restless current. Why cross at all? he wondered. To touch something forbidden—or to see what calls my name?

The wind answered with a cold swirl against his face. It nudged him downstream to a bend where a gray log, half-buried in moss, spanned the river. Ferns dangled from its bark, dancing above the churning water. Jack tested its surface with one boot. Slippery. Still, the pull of the other side was stronger than caution.

He drew a breath and stepped onto the log. No birds. No clouds. Only the hiss of water and the hammering of his own pulse. Halfway across, he dared a glance up—the sky an empty blue dome. Then the world tilted; he slipped, caught himself, and crawled the rest of the way.

The moment his feet touched the far bank, he lost balance and tumbled through a tangle of salal and ferns, landing hard but unhurt. The forest above closed in, branches knitting so tightly the daylight fractured into narrow spears. Jack brushed dirt from his jeans and checked his old pocket watch: a few minutes past noon. Strange—it felt later.

He adjusted his pack and started along a faint trail, the ground dry and brittle beneath his boots. Twigs snapped like distant gunfire. Each sound repeated itself until the forest seemed alive with echoes.

For a long time he walked beneath that green canopy, until a thin brightness appeared ahead—light spilling between trunks. The scent of wildflowers reached him, fresh and impossible this late in September. He quickened his pace.

The trees thinned, and he stepped out into a meadow glowing with impossible color. Grass shimmered emerald. The air misted cool against his skin. At the far end, a waterfall dropped from a hidden ridge, scattering diamonds of spray that drifted on the wind.

Jack let his pack fall, stripped off his boots, and sat on a bleached log. The water's sound lulled him. For the first time in months he felt peace rise through him like breath after a long dive. One man, now in a world of his own—drawn here by a world he left behind.

He leaned back and stared up at the bright sky. It wasn't just calm; it was different. The sun seemed fixed. The colors too sharp, too new. The season wrong. But the strangeness was gentle, not frightening. It felt like being remembered.

Jack's thoughts drifted. Work deadlines, half-finished copy, constant noise—the city seemed far away now. His body gave in to fatigue, and before long, he slept.

***

Two weeks earlier, the idea for the hike had come out of exhaustion. Portland in late summer hummed with busyness, and Jack was running out of breath. A freelance copywriter, he juggled clients, drafts, and revisions until every day blurred into the next. His home office faced the Willamette River, but he rarely looked up from the screen long enough to notice it.

That afternoon he'd been on the phone with Lisa Willows, production coordinator for one of his biggest accounts.

"The manuscript's coming along," he said, rubbing his eyes, "but without better source material, I'm stuck."

"I know," Lisa replied. "I've been chasing down the updates. Let me see what I can pull together. You always manage to make something out of thin air."

Her voice carried that quick brightness that always steadied him.

"Maybe so," he said, "but even thin air needs a breeze to move it."

She laughed softly. "How about lunch tomorrow? We can regroup before my manager breathes down both our necks."

"McNulty's? Eleven-thirty?"

"Perfect. And if you get there first, grab the back booth by the window."

***

He'd arrived early, as usual. The restaurant's hum wrapped around him like a familiar song. Outside, September sun washed the sidewalks; people moved with purpose and early-autumn energy. Jack caught his reflection in the glass—tired eyes, too many late nights—and looked away just as Lisa's voice broke through.

"Hey, dreamer. You look miles away."

"Just parking my brain in neutral," he said, smiling as she slid into the booth.

They talked shop first, trading ideas and quick notes, then the conversation drifted to lighter things—travel, movies, the end of summer. She told him he needed a break. He agreed.

"Maybe a hike," he said. "Mount Hood, maybe even Lost Lake. Just me, a thermos of ice tea, and no deadlines."

"That sounds perfect."

Something flickered in her eyes then—concern, maybe curiosity. He wondered if she'd ever come with him, but the thought felt fragile, unspoken.

When lunch ended, she left him with a smile and a yellow sticky note tucked beside the check: Don't forget to breathe.

***

Now, standing again at the forest's edge, Jack stirred awake to silence. The meadow lay unchanged, the waterfall still whispering—but his pocket watch showed the same time as before. He tapped the glass. The hands refused to move.

Shadows had shifted though; the sun lower, the air cooler. A quiet unease crept in. He slung his pack, pulled on his boots, and started back toward the river.

Under the canopy, the light dimmed quickly. He flicked on his flashlight. The beam felt swallowed by the dark. When he reached the fallen log, the water below looked heavier, slower—black instead of silver.

Crossing took longer this time. Every creak of the wood echoed like a voice. When he finally reached the far side, night had already claimed the forest. His watch still read a few minutes past noon. The clock on his dashboard, two hours later, would read eleven-thirty p.m.

Jack exhaled, gripping the steering wheel before starting the engine. The forest behind him was utterly still. As he drove away, wind pressed against the windshield in a long low sigh—almost like someone whispering his name.

Chapter Two

The Whispers Return

*"Certain things catch your eye but pursue only your heart."—
Old Indian saying*

Lisa Willows was running late. Her alarm hadn't gone off—her phone battery had died overnight—and now the morning had dissolved into a blur of hair, coffee, and misplaced keys. The mirror reflected someone more ordinary than the confident production coordinator she was at work: sweatpants, hoodie, ponytail.

No time for second looks. She grabbed her bag, dashed to the car, and fired off a quick text before pulling out of the driveway: *Call me when you can.*

The freeway was crawling. Between brake lights and the muffled hum of radio traffic, her mind wandered to Jack Bellard — his hike yesterday, his restless energy. Something in his voice the day before had stayed with her, like a note that kept playing after the song had ended.

***

Jack tossed beneath tangled sheets, resisting the sunlight pushing through his blinds. When he finally checked his phone, Lisa's message glowed on the screen. He smiled, thumbed a reply — Just woke up. Call you after a shower — lots to tell.

He cracked eggs into a pan, phone pressed between shoulder and ear when her voice came through.

"Hey there, sleepyhead."

"Morning, Lisa. You sound bright and early."

"Barely," she said, laughing. "Rough start. No alarm, no coffee. Typical Monday."

Jack chuckled. "I've had worse. Listen, you're not going to believe what happened on that hike."

He told her about the river, the forest, the open meadow — the sunlight, the wildflowers that shouldn't have been there in late September. And the waterfall.

"It was like walking into another season," he said. "And my pocket watch stopped. Dead. When I got back to the car, it was running again, keeping perfect time."

Lisa hesitated. "That's... eerie. And kind of amazing."

"Yeah. I can't shake it. I'm going back tomorrow."

"You're serious?"

"Absolutely. Want to come?"

A long pause, then a small smile in her voice. "Sure. I need the break."

"Perfect. I'll pick you up at seven. Text me your address."

"Done," she said. "And Jack?"

"Yeah?"

"Be ready to explain the part about your time-traveling watch."

"I'll bring charts," he laughed.

***

That afternoon, Jack drove downtown to the jeweler's — a narrow shop with an old clock ticking in the window. The air smelled faintly of oil and silver polish.

He placed the pocket watch on the counter. Its surface was worn, the engraving faint but somewhat legible: JB.

The old jeweler adjusted his spectacles. "Interesting piece. Mid-eighteen hundreds, I'd say. You said it stopped?"

"For hours," Jack said. "Then started again, right on time."

The jeweler turned it over, squinting. "Strange. Looks like it's been through more than time. And these initials — they yours?"

"They are. But the watch already had them when I bought it."

The man raised a brow. "Well now, that's something."

Jack smiled faintly. "Yeah. It's something."

***

He hadn't told Lisa the strangest part.

Months ago, he'd dreamt of an old woman handing him a carved box — sun, moon, and stars etched into its sides. Keep this, and give it to no one, she'd whispered. When he woke, the dream had faded like fog.

Two weeks later, at the coast, he'd wandered into an antique shop. Near the back, behind a cluttered display, he'd seen it — the box from his dream.

He bought it without a second thought. Inside, he'd later placed the pocket watch — silver, tarnished, and already engraved with his initials. At first, it was just curiosity. But over time, it became a ritual. He wound it every morning. The sound comforted him, a heartbeat of another era.

***

Lisa waited on her front porch, backpack beside her, a flash of morning light on her hair. For a moment, Jack just stared — this wasn't the office version of her. She looked real, grounded, alive.

"Hey, Lisa," he called, stepping out to grab her pack. "Let me get that."

"Thanks. How'd you sleep?"

"Barely. Couldn't stop thinking about what we might find."

She buckled her seatbelt, glancing sideways. "You really think there's something out there?"

Jack hesitated. "I don't know. But I can't stop hearing it — that sound in the wind. It's like it's calling me back."

Shortly after sunrise, they were on the road heading east, thermos of tea steaming in the console. The city fell away behind them as the Columbia River Gorge opened wide — walls of green, waterfalls tracing silver lines down basalt cliffs.

The highway curved along the river, the world outside gliding by in streaks of mist and sunlight.

"You know," Jack said, "I looked up Google Maps of the area. No meadow. Nothing like what I saw. Just forest."

Lisa frowned. "Then what did you walk into?"

"That's what I need to find out."

They left the main road near Hood River, turning south toward the mountain. Pines thickened, the air cooled, and the scent of moss and rain grew strong.

At the trailhead, Lisa tugged at her new boots and laughed. "Guess I should've broken these in."

Jack knelt to help. "You have nice feet," he teased.

"You're ridiculous."

"Probably," he said, still grinning.

For a moment, they stayed like that — too close, unsure what to do with it.

***

The river sounded louder this time. Jack pointed across the current. "That's where I crossed. I heard the wind... almost like words."

Lisa tilted her head. "I just feel the chill. Nothing more."

"Keep listening," he said. "It's there — faint, like voices."

She tried. There was only the murmur of water and the rush of wind through the trees. But she saw the look in his eyes — something between fear and longing — and she believed him.

They made their way downstream to the old log bridge. Moss slick under their boots, hands steadying one another, they crossed.

On the far bank, the forest swallowed them again.

"It should open into the meadow soon," Jack said.

"Lead the way," Lisa replied, brushing a strand of hair from her cheek.

They followed the narrow trail until the light grew brighter. But when the trees thinned, the sight that greeted them made Jack stop cold.

No meadow. No wildflowers. No waterfall. Only a logged clearing — stumps, mud, and silence.

He climbed onto a stump, scanning the distance. "This can't be. I swear it was here."

Lisa touched his arm. "Jack... I believe you. I felt it too, even before we came."

The words hit him harder than disbelief. He turned, searching her face.

"Something's calling," she said quietly. "I can't explain it, but it's real."

Jack exhaled, his voice low. "Thanks for believing."

The wind rose suddenly, circling them. He closed his eyes, hearing faint whispers carried on the air — indistinct, haunting, almost like a name.

"Did you hear that?" he asked.

Lisa shook her head. "Only the wind."

They sat on the stump, silent as the sun dipped behind the trees.

"We should head back," he said finally.

"It's strange," Lisa murmured. "Everything feels... alive. Like it's waiting."

They made their way through the woods, crossed the river, and reached the truck as twilight turned to night. The drive back to Portland was quiet — the kind of silence that holds questions too big for words.

Later, alone in bed, Jack stared at the ceiling, listening to the faint hum of wind beyond the window. It rose and fell, rhythmic, almost human.

"Jonnnn... Jonnnn..."

The whisper trembled through him — soft, mournful, and impossibly familiar.

He closed his eyes, thinking of Lisa's warmth beside him on the trail, and let the sound carry him into sleep.

Chapter Three

The Name in the Silver

"I do not think the measure of a civilization is how tall its buildings of concrete are, but rather how well its people have learned to relate to their environment and fellow man."— *Sun Bear, Chippewa Tribe*

Sunlight crept across Jack's kitchen table, painting everything in a gentle gold. He had always preferred tea over coffee, and the rising steam from his mug wrapped him in quiet warmth. With his notebook open, he tapped his pen thoughtfully against the waiting page. At the top of his list, he'd written: pick up pocket watch.

A songbird fluttered onto the windowsill, its feathers fluffed against the crisp September breeze. Jack's lips curled into a smile as he thought of Lisa and fired off a quick text.

Morning. Strange dreams again. Picking up the watch today.

He slipped his keys into his pocket and stepped out into the day.

***

The jeweler's shop carried the faint scent of brass polish and aged wood. Somewhere in the back, a clock ticked with steady patience, each second whispering across the glass counters.

Jack handed his claim ticket to the clerk, who returned with the watch wrapped in a square of velvet. "Here you go," the man said cheerfully. "Good as new."

Jack turned the watch over in his palm. Silver caught the light, and the gears inside purred in flawless harmony. Then he froze.

The engraving that once read only J.B. now bore words that hadn't been there before.

To J.B., with love — Lawitha.

He stared, pulse pounding in his ears. When he'd first bought it, the back had been so tarnished he could barely make out the initials. Now the words were perfect, etched deep and clear as breath.

He sat in his truck afterward, the watch heavy in his hand. The sound of rain on the windshield softened to a steady hiss. His dream, the carved box, the meadow, the whispers — all tangled around this one object like vines around a stone.

He closed his eyes. And then the memory rose, faint and insistent, as if the watch itself were reminding him.

The bell above the door had given a tired jingle as he'd stepped into a narrow antique shop near the waterfront. The place had smelled of oiled wood and rain-damp wool — a museum of forgotten things. Glass cases lined the aisles, crowded with relics of other lives: maps, coins, knives dulled with age.

He hadn't meant to stop. The Antique Emporium sign had caught his eye from the street, swinging in the coastal wind. Maybe he'd only wanted to get out of the rain for a while.

The clerk, a stooped man with thick glasses, barely looked up. "Everything's tagged," he'd muttered.

Jack drifted toward a case at the back. Among the row of tarnished watches one caught the light — as if it had been waiting for someone to notice. When the clerk set it on the counter and wound it, the second hand began to move, steady and sure.

"Came out of an old Portland estate," the man had said. "Box of river-family heirlooms from the 1880s. Still runs."

Jack turned it over, the initials J.B. clear enough, the faint script beneath unreadable under the tarnish. He smiled faintly — same as mine, he thought. The coincidence gave him a small, uneasy pause, but he let the feeling drift away.

Something in the small weight of it — the heartbeat tick — unsettled him. He bought it without thinking.

The present returned with a soft gasp. The watch gleamed in his palm, catching the last gray light through the windshield.

Who were J.B. and Lawitha?

The initials were his, but the name was not.

19

He rubbed the metal gently, tracing each letter. Outside, the wind rose and sighed against the truck's glass — cool, deliberate — as though urging him to listen.

Could it be the watch that carried me there?

The thought flickered and would not leave.

***

Downtown, Lisa was already deep in work — coffee steaming beside her keyboard, yellow sticky notes blossoming around her computer monitor. The hum of the office blurred into the background as she stared through the window at the gray Portland skyline.

Her mind kept circling back to the hike.

There had been something in that wind, something she couldn't name.

And something about Jack — the way he'd looked at her, as if recognizing her for the first time.

Lisa wasn't used to that kind of connection. She'd grown up in foster homes, her early years spent in the blank hallways of an orphanage until she was twelve. Friends were rare. Family rarer.

Work had become her safe place, the only world she could shape. But now, she felt something stirring beneath that order — a pull she didn't understand.

Her phone rang. She almost dropped it.

"Hey, Jack!"

"Morning, Lisa. You won't believe this," he said, voice tight. "The engraving on the watch changed."

"Changed? What do you mean?"

"It used to just say JB. Now it reads 'JB with love, Lawit ha.'"

There was silence, then a soft intake of breath.

"Jack... that's incredible. Who is Lawitha?"

"I don't know. But I think she's part of it — the box, the dream, everything. When I had the watch with me, the meadow appeared. When I didn't, it was gone. I think the watch connects it all — maybe even time itself."

"You're going back, aren't you?"

"Tomorrow morning. Alone this time."

"Are you sure that's safe?"

"I have to know. I'll call when I reach the trailhead, and when I return. I'll take a sleeping bag and stay overnight."

Lisa hesitated. "What do you want me to do while you're gone?"

"Research. The name Lawitha. It sounds Native — maybe from the Columbia River region. See what you can find. Maybe old maps, tribal names, anything."

"I can do that. I have a friend, Wakanda — Yakima tribe. She works in Spokane for the Tribal Affairs Office. I'll call her tonight."

"That's perfect," Jack said, his voice softening. "Just... be careful what you tell her. We don't want to sound crazy."

"You're already crazy," Lisa teased. "But I'll keep your secret."

Jack laughed. "Good. And, Lisa?"

"Yeah?"

"I'll miss you tomorrow."

Her smile faded to something quieter. "I'll miss you too."

***

After work, Lisa curled up on the couch, phone in hand. She stared at Wakanda's number for a long time before pressing call.

"Lisa!" came the warm voice. "My silly one — it's been ages."

Lisa laughed. "Still calling me that, huh? I've missed you."

"So many moons since our last talk. How are you, my friend?"

"Busy. Lonely sometimes. But good."

"You need more than work, Lisa," Wakanda said gently.

"I know," Lisa said. "Actually, that's why I'm calling. I met someone — a friend I've worked with for years. We went hiking a few days ago and... strange things happened. I don't want to say too much yet, but it's something I need your help with."

"Strange things?"

Lisa hesitated. "Not bad. Just... otherworldly."

"Then yes, you need me," Wakanda said with a laugh. "I'm traveling to Yakima next week for the salmon festival. Let's meet up. Tell me everything in person."

"That would be perfect."

They talked for a while longer, slipping back into easy laughter.

Before hanging up, Lisa asked, "Hey — have you ever heard the name Lawitha?"

"Hmm," Wakanda said thoughtfully. "Pretty name. Let me check."

The sound of typing filled the pause. Then:

"It's Chinook — from the lower Columbia tribes. Means elegant and beautiful."

Lisa's throat tightened. "Beautiful," she whispered. "That fits."

"Why do you ask?"

"It's just part of what I'll tell you when we meet," Lisa said. "And your name, Wakanda — what does it mean again?"

Wakanda laughed. "Possesses magical powers. Though I'm still waiting to see them."

"I think you already have them," Lisa said softly.

"Maybe," Wakanda replied. "But I think the real magic's following you, Silly One."

Lisa smiled through a sudden warmth in her chest. "Then I hope it leads me somewhere good."

"It will. Sleep well, Lisa. We'll talk soon."

"Good night, my magical friend."

Lisa ended the call, set her phone on the table, and leaned back. The hum of the city outside faded as she thought of Jack — and the word still echoing in her mind.

Lawitha.

She whispered it once, quietly, as if the name itself might open a door.

Outside her window, the wind stirred, gentle but insistent, carrying something ancient and unseen.

Chapter Four

The Chief's Awakening

"When you are in doubt, be still, and wait—when doubt no longer exists for you, then go forward with courage. So long as mists envelop you, be still until the sunlight pours through and dispels the mists—as it surely will. Then act with courage."
— *Ponca Chief White Eagle*

The foothills rose gently from the valley floor, climbing toward the steep, snow-capped shoulders of Mount Hood. Summer grasses trembled as the wind swept across the bluff in wandering gusts. Aspens flickered pale green against the darker stands of fir, giving way to an open field that stretched north toward the distant mountains and the wide Columbia beyond.

A small stream threaded along the eastern slope, whispering over stones as it wound its way down from the high places. Wildflowers dotted the meadow like paint splashes—violets, oranges, yellows, soft blues swaying in quiet clusters.

Jack stood at the edge of a bare patch of earth, the scene spreading out before him in ways both familiar and otherworldly. Hours earlier he'd texted Lisa from the trailhead, telling her he was starting his solo return. Everything unfolded exactly as before: the crossing, the deep woods, the strange shift in the air. And now he was here again—in the meadow that didn't exist in his own time.

Jack crouched near the trampled ground. Charred wood lay scattered in shallow pits. Eagle feathers rested in the grass. Rawhide strips, smoothed stones, and carved wooden sticks were arranged in patterns that didn't look accidental.

"Well," he whispered, "if this isn't an Indian encampment, then nothing is."

Once again, his pocket watch had stopped the moment he crossed the river.

He checked it—motionless hands frozen at the same time as before.

The geography was the same—Mount Hood rising like a sentinel above the land—but the world felt stripped of modern noise. No contrails. No distant engines. Only the steady breathing of the earth.

He sat on a stump overlooking the meadow, looking north toward the clean silhouettes of Mount Adams and the cone of Mount St. Helens—perfect again, untouched by 1980.

Jack huffed a shaky laugh. "Well... that narrows things down."

He listened. Silence pressed close around him. No birds, no insects, no nearby animals.

He was alone.

***

Jack settled beside his small fire as evening gathered, the warmth touching one cheek while the mountain's cool breath brushed the other. He checked his pocket watch again—still stopped. A strange calm seeped through him, the kind that made him wonder whether he was trapped in time or held here on purpose.

He stared into the flames until the logs collapsed, sending sparks spiraling upward. Exhaustion washed over him. He crawled into his sleeping bag, slid his knife close, and drifted into uneasy sleep.

His dreams weren't dreams so much as impressions: a silhouette in the mist, a hand brushing his, a name spoken inside his chest rather than into his ears.

Lawitha.

Dawn spilled pale gold across the meadow. Jack emerged stiffly from his tent, blinking at the world around him—and froze.

Yesterday the meadow felt paused and empty.

Today it hummed with life.

Birds called from the brush line. A woodpecker hammered. Squirrels chattered among the cedars.

"How...?" he breathed.

Movement caught his eye. At the far end of the meadow, a thin column of smoke curled upward.

Someone was here.

Jack strapped on his knife and walked downhill through dew-soaked grass. As he crested a small rise, he stopped cold.

A blanket-draped figure sat before a fire, unmoving, facing away.

The blanket was woven in ceremonial colors—unmistakably Native.

Jack approached carefully. When he circled around the fire, he drew in a sharp breath.

An elderly Native man sat cross-legged before the flames, features lined with age and wisdom, long braids falling down his chest. Feathers and beads adorned his blanket like quiet armor. His eyes were focused on the fire, as though waiting for something... or someone.

The man lifted a long-stemmed pipe, drew a breath, and extended it toward him.

Hands trembling, Jack accepted it and inhaled. The smoke burned his throat and sent him coughing. The elder's lips twitched in mild amusement.

They sat in silence until the old man finally spoke, voice deep and steady, shaped by an accent older than any map.

"Nah' sikhs, kahta' maika?"

Hello, friend. How are you?

Jack stiffened. He didn't understand the words, but he understood their welcome.

"My name is Jack," he said.

The elder shook his head gently. "No. Kwah-ne-sum Jonathan. Always Jonathan."

Jack's breath faltered. "I... I'm not Jonathan."

The elder studied him with long, unhurried eyes. "Jonathan," he repeated. "Mahsh... to return in secret."

Jack swallowed hard.

"What is your name?" he asked softly.

The elder pressed a hand to his chest. "En-tee-tee-ueh Watlala. Chief of the fish. Chief of the Watlala people."

Jack nodded, his voice rough. "I'm honored."

He hesitated, then took out his pocket watch and showed the engraving.

"Lawitha," he whispered.

The Chief's eyes tightened with recognition. He touched the watch reverently.

"Yes. Lawitha."

Jack's throat tightened. "Who... is she?"

The Chief drew a long breath. "My daughter. Whose heart once lived in your chest."

Jack felt the words like a blow.

He sank to his knees.

***

Running Horse appeared through the fog—tall, confident, eyes alight with shock and joy. Before Jack could speak, the man threw his arms around him in a fierce embrace.

"Ah, Jonathan," he said warmly. "Blood brother comes home."

Jack barely managed a nod, overwhelmed.

Running Horse grinned. "He looks like Jonathan. But no dress like him."

Jack laughed shakily. "I'm... trying my best."

They spoke briefly in Chinook, the Chief explaining that Jack believed himself to be someone else—that he came from another time, another world.

Running Horse shrugged. "Spirits clever. They send him back strange."

Jack wasn't sure if he should be offended or relieved.

"I want to help," Jack said. "I just need to understand what's happening. Who I was. Who your daughter is. And... where she is."

The Chief motioned uphill. "Come. I show you."

He could barely remember.

The wind rose behind him, carrying a whisper he almost recognized.

Jonathan.

He tightened his grip on the pocket watch and stepped forward.

His journey had only begun.

Chapter Five

The Silence Between Worlds

"O' GREAT SPIRIT— help me always to speak the truth quietly, to listen with an open mind when others speak and to remember the peace that may be found in silence." ~ Cherokee Prayer

Lisa began to worry. Two full days now, and still no word from Jack. He had told her not to fret — that he had enough supplies and knew what he was doing — but the quiet felt heavier tonight. If she didn't hear from him by morning, she'd drive up to the trailhead herself.

At her desk, the soft glow of the office lights made her yellow sticky notes stand out like little petals around her computer monitor. She picked one up — the note where she'd written "Ask Jack dinner?" weeks ago — and remembered how nervous she had been then. She smiled faintly, then crumpled it and tossed it away. She didn't need that question anymore. She already knew the answer; she'd felt it in the way he held her out there in the woods.

Another sticky note read: Meet Wakanda next week — call tonight. She slid that one into her purse.

A third note: Get a pedicure. Lisa rolled her eyes. "Well... probably time again," she muttered, chuckling softly.

Outside the window, the sunlight was thinning out, sliding down the building like melting gold. She wondered what Jack was doing right now — if he was watching the same sunset from another world, or another time entirely. The thought made her chest ache with a mix of worry and something tenderer, deeper.

The office was silent, everyone long gone. She shrugged on her jacket, turned off the lights, and walked out alone.

***

That night, curled on the couch with dinner and the warm flicker of the fireplace, Lisa dialed Wakanda. After several rings, the familiar voice message chimed through her speaker:

"Hi, this is me. I can't take your call right now, so blow smoke my way and I'll get back to you. Wau'-wau — speak."

Lisa laughed softly. "Hey you, Silly One here. Just checking in... Monday works for me. Lots to tell. Love you."

She hung up, then stared down at the book resting on her lap — reading not even remotely possible tonight. Her mind stayed fixed on Jack. On his smile. On the feel of his arms around her when the forest grew quiet and strange.

She tried calling him again ring after ring. Voice mail. She left another message.

Then another text.

Eventually exhaustion pulled her under, and she drifted to sleep on the couch.

***

A few hours later her phone chirped loudly. She bolted upright.

"Jack?" she whispered.

But the text was from Wakanda:

"Lisa, since it's after midnight thought I'd text. Yes, Monday works — I'm leaving in the morning for Yakima. Tribal council tomorrow night, salmon bake Sunday. I can sneak away Monday/Tuesday. Hope Jack is back safe. Love ya"

Lisa didn't reply. She called Jack again instead. No answer.

Her worry settled deeper. Tomorrow she was driving to the mountain. No question.

She made her way to bed.

***

Saturday came bright and sunny — the Pacific Northwest still holding onto its streak of early fall perfection. Lisa drove east through the Gorge, knuckles tight on the steering wheel as strong winds pushed against the front of her car. The highway felt longer today, every mile a tug on her heart.

All the way, she kept calling Jack. Still nothing.

At last she reached the trailhead. Jack's truck was parked exactly where he'd left it. Relief and dread knotted together in her stomach.

She walked down toward the river, retracing their steps to the spot where they'd stood before crossing — where Jack had first heard the whispers.

Lisa sat on the large rock and listened.

Her hair whipped across her face in the wind. She tied it back, then closed her eyes listening.

The rushing river. The wind through the trees. And then — faint, fragile — something else.

A whisper. Soft. Comforting.

"Jonathan is well... no worry. The spirits guide and protect him. He will return."

Lisa's breath caught. A tear slipped down her cheek.

She believed it. Every word.

She sat taller, feeling the same strange current of energy she'd sensed in the clear-cut meadow with Jack — that charged stillness, like the world was holding its breath.

Finally she stood, returned to her car, rolled the windows down, and pulled out the little photo of her and Jack perched on the old log from their first hike.

She held it gently. And she waited.

Chapter Six

Discovery

Humankind has not woven the web of life. We are but one
thread within it. Whatever we do to the web, we do to ourselves.
All things are bound together. All things connect."
— *Chief Seattle*

Jack walked beside En-tee-tee-ueh and Running Horse toward
an old cabin, a strange pull tugging at him. He didn't know if
it was a memory or something deeper—like muscle memory
of a life he didn't recall living.

The cabin came into view: a simple lean-to roof, a tiny
porch, one dusty window, and weather-beaten boards silvered
by time.

"Here is cabin you write words," En-tee-tee-ueh said.

Jack stepped onto the porch. A few planks creaked softly beneath his boots. He ran his palm along a support post,
feeling every groove in the ancient wood. Something in him
stirred.

Inside, a shaft of sunlight sliced through the dusty air. The
one-room cabin held a writing desk beneath the window, a

small stone fireplace on the side wall, a narrow bed in the back, and a tiny stove beside pantry shelves. A square table sat near the door, two mismatched chairs tucked beneath it.

Jack wandered toward the desk. The chief came in quietly and sat at the table while Running Horse lingered outside, keeping watch.

A quill, dip pen, and inkwell rested neatly on the writing surface. In the cubbyholes above were loose papers—lists, notes, scraps of writing. Jack opened the drawer. Beneath a stack of blank sheets lay a folded newspaper, yellowed and brittle.

He opened it.

The Willamette World — Portland, Oregon

June 23, 1867

Jack's heart kicked hard. His eyes scanned the articles until one byline froze him in place:

By Jonathan Butler

He sat slowly, the realization crawling up his spine. The chief was right. Jonathan wasn't a ghost or a misunderstanding.

Jonathan had been real.

Jonathan had lived here.

And Jack carried his watch.

He sifted through the papers again: supply lists, landmarks, and one sheet covered in Indian words he couldn't yet decipher. Then he found a handwritten poem—raw, emotional, aching for someone unnamed.

He copied it carefully into his own journal.

When he finished, he didn't notice En-tee-tee-ueh had moved to stand beside him until the chief spoke softly.

"Kla-how-ya, Jonathan?" the chief asked. How are you?

Jack looked up. "I... I don't recall any of this. But it feels familiar."

"You remember with heart before head," the chief replied. "Cloud in mind not forever."

Jack rubbed his face. "I think this newspaper puts us around 1867. When I return home, I can research... maybe find where I fit in all of this."

En-tee-tee-ueh nodded kindly. "You no worry now. You listen to spirits. More remembering come."

Jack followed, looking once more at the cabin—at the life he'd apparently lived.

The chief stepped out to speak with Running Horse, who returned from the trees with a shake of his head.

"Daughter not back yet," En-tee-tee-ueh said. "She gathers food with others. Maybe morning."

Jack nodded, part relieved and part disappointed. "Then I'll stay the night."

"Kloshe," the chief said. Good.

They left the cabin and followed the narrow trail through the underbrush. Jack's thoughts tangled together—Lisa... Lawitha... the watch... the impossible pull of two worlds. The forest darkened as they climbed toward the higher camp.

When they emerged, Jack saw small shelters, threadlike smoke rising from several fires, and only a handful of tribal members—families in hiding.

"Yuk-wa," En-tee-tee-ueh said, pointing to a shelter. This way.

Jack dropped his backpack. "Thank you. What now?"

"We rest, eat, and wait for Lawitha," the chief replied. "Running Horse make place for you sleep."

Jack sat with the chief by the fire. A woman brought bowls of fresh berries and strips of dried meat.

"Eat, Jonathan," the chief said.

Jack nodded and tasted the food, flavors simple but comforting—the sweet burst of berries, the smoky salt of the meat.

"Your tribe... are they safe?" he asked.

"For now," the chief said. "Half with Wirsham across Nichi-wana. Others hide here. White soldiers come soon. Want us move to reservation behind mountain. Land is barren... unforgiving. We do not want leave."

A hollowness opened in Jack's stomach.

"I'm just one man," he whispered. "I can't change history."

"You not change history," the chief said. "You speak truth. You buy time. Spirits bring you back for reason."

Jack swallowed hard. The weight settled on him like a cloak.

"You remember first white men I meet?" the Chief said suddenly, eyes softening. "Journeyers who come from Great White Leader. Had Indian woman with them."

"Lewis and Clark," Jack whispered. "Sacajawea."

The chief smiled faintly. "Yes. She strong. Wise."

Night fell around them, a blanket of darkness pierced by firelight. Jack drifted in and out of thought—visions of Lisa mixing with images of this world, this tribe, this responsibility. He wasn't sure where he belonged anymore.

The chief prayed quietly in his language, head bowed, hands still.

Later, Jack was shown his place to sleep. A shelter, warm blankets, a fire's fading glow outside. He lay awake awhile, thinking of Lisa's eyes, her trust, her kiss on his forehead in the clearing.

Morning crept slowly across the mountain. Women carried water, children wandered sleepily from shelters, men spoke in low voices.

Jack found En-tee-tee-ueh at his fire again.

"Good morning," Jack said.

"Good morning, Jonathan."

A pause.

"No word yet from Lawitha. But she return soon. No worry."

"I have to go," Jack said. "I promised someone I'd be back today. I'll return. I swear it."

The Chief nodded. "Running Horse take you to trail. Spirits will guide you after."

Jack stood and offered his hand. The chief gripped it firmly.

"Go in peace, white brother," the Chief said. "We wait for your return."

Jack followed Running Horse through the trees. Halfway across the meadow, the young warrior stopped.

"Jonathan, my brother," he said, placing a hand against Jack's chest. "Journey safe to your world. Great bird above watch over you. Kla-how-ya."

Jack turned as Running Horse vanished into the mist.

Overhead, a bald eagle circled once—slow, deliberate—before drifting toward the forest where Jack's path home began.

Chapter Seven

Spirits Never Sleep

"And while I stood there I saw more than I can tell, and I understood more than I saw—for I was seeing in a sacred manner the shapes of things in the spirit, and the shape of all shapes as they must live together like one being."
~Black Elk, Black Elk Speaks

Jack followed the river upstream, the trailhead finally coming into view through the soft morning light. A cool breeze drifted along the water, carrying faint whispers that curled around him like familiar breath. He remembered that first strange moment when he stepped off the main path and let the wind draw him deeper into the forest. Those whispers had been the start of everything—his calling.

He stepped into the gravel of the parking lot—and Lisa saw him instantly.

She flung open her car door and ran toward him. Jack dropped his backpack, arms wide as she collided with him in an embrace meant for long-lost lovers.

"Oh Jack, I missed you," Lisa breathed.

His heart hammered. He held her close, forehead against hers. "Lisa... while I was gone, I realized something. I love you. I always have. It's been buried inside me this whole time."

Her eyes softened, shining in the morning light. Their lips met—slow at first, then deeply, a release of everything pent up inside the both of them.

"I was so worried," she whispered against him. "I knew you were safe somehow, but what would I do without you?"

Jack laughed gently, brushing his thumb along her cheek. "I have so much to tell you."

They returned to the picnic table between their cars. While Jack changed into clean jeans and washed up, Lisa unpacked a bag full of sandwiches, fruit, and bottled drinks. When he joined her, she nodded toward the spread.

"A surprise lunch by my... boyfriend?" she teased.

Jack grinned. "I'll gladly be that, if you'll be my girlfriend."

"Deal," she laughed.

They settled across from each other.

"Well," she said, "did you see anyone over there?"

"Oh yes. Lisa, I met an old Indian chief. He thought I was someone named Jonathan." Jack ran a hand through his hair, remembering the campfire smoke, Running Horse's embrace, the fog-shrouded meadow. "There's a lot going on back in that time. More than I even understand yet."

Lisa leaned in. "Tell me everything."

"I will," he promised. "But maybe over dinner? Back in Portland?"

"I'd like that," she said softly. "I'll swing by my place and freshen up."

Jack smiled. "Lisa... did I tell you I love you?"

"You can say it again," she whispered.

"I love you."

She kissed him once more before getting into her car. They drove back to the city with Lisa trailing behind him, both wrapped in the warm glow of a brand-new beginning.

***

That evening, Jack set his table with candlelight and fresh flowers from his English garden. He'd showered, napped, and lost a good ten minutes just thinking of Lisa walking through his front door. When the knock came, he nearly jogged to answer it.

Lisa stood there in a soft blouse and jeans, cheeks flushed, eyes bright. Jack pulled her in, kissing her lightly before stepping back.

"Welcome to my humble abode," he said with a flourish.

"Something smells amazing."

"It's just a little something I threw together. Chicken fresco, asparagus with olive oil, wild rice, mushroom pilaf."

Her eyebrows shot up. "Jack. That's not dinner. That's a date."

He laughed. "Cooking for one gets boring. Tonight is a treat."

"And you baked an apple pie?" she added, catching the scent drifting from the kitchen.

Jack sheepishly shrugged. "I make them in batches and freeze them."

She nudged him playfully. "You're full of secrets."

Dinner turned warm and easy—shared stories from childhood, memories from the office, little things they'd never asked each other before. After cleaning up, they curled together on the couch. The fire cracked gently in the hearth, and Jack poured two small glasses of Whidbey Port.

"To new adventures," he said.

Lisa clinked her glass to his. "New adventures."

He told her everything then—from the silent Indian encampment to the moment the world "woke," to En-tee-tee-ueh and Running Horse, to the cabin filled with Jonathan's papers. Lisa listened, eyes wide, capturing each scene.

"Jonathan was a writer," she murmured. "Same initials. Same watch." She shook her head. "Jack, this is unbelievable. I really wish you could've met Lawitha."

"Me too," he said quietly. "But maybe I will. There's still so much left to uncover."

She reached for his hand. "Wakanda is coming Monday. You'll love her. She'll help us understand it all. She knows so much about this history."

"That would be great," Jack said. "Tomorrow, I want to dig into research—compare everything I saw with the historical timeline."

"I'll bring my laptop," she said.

Firelight flickered across their faces as silence slipped comfortably between them. Jack wrapped an arm around her; she rested her head on his shoulder. Outside, trees brushed the windows as the night wind drifted through the yard, whispering softly against the glass.

The spirits watched over them. The future leaned forward.

And the clock on the mantel kept its steady, gentle tick into the unfolding night.

Chapter Eight

Restless Peace

"Peace and happiness are available in every moment. Peace is every step. We shall walk hand in hand. There are no political solutions to spiritual problems. Remember: If the Creator put it there, it is in the right place. The soul would have no rainbow if the eyes had no tears. Tell your people that, since we were promised we should never be moved, we have been moved five times." ~An Indian Chief

Portland woke to gray skies and wind-driven rain on Sunday morning—a fitting goodbye to September. By Monday, October had rolled in with its usual damp chill. Lisa and Jack had fallen asleep curled together on the couch, and when Lisa stirred awake, she found herself wrapped in a quilt and the soft scent of Jack's home drifting around her.

She stretched, smiled, and followed the smell of breakfast into the kitchen.

"Good morning, Jack," she said, leaning against the doorway.

He turned from the stove with a grin. "Hey, Lisa. Hope you're hungry."

She slid into a chair. "Is there anything you can't do?"

Jack laughed as he flipped pancakes. "It's hard to be humble. I guess we fell asleep last night."

Lisa sipped the coffee he poured. "I didn't plan on spending the night... but I'm glad I did."

"Me too. Good company after a journey back in time." He set plates on the table—pancakes, sausage, fresh fruit, and his favorite steaming cup of tea. He reached for her hand, holding it gently across the table. For a moment, neither of them spoke. They just smiled, letting the quiet fill the space.

After breakfast they retreated to Jack's den. He read passages from his journal—details of the dreamlike fog, the cabin, En-tee-tee-ueh, Running Horse, and the strange familiarity he couldn't explain. Lisa listened closely, asking gentle questions as she pieced the story together.

Eventually the two turned their attention to research.

Jack pointed toward his desktop. "See what you can find on the Watlala tribe. I'll look into Jonathan Butler and the newspaper."

Lisa sat forward eagerly. "Wakanda's going to flip when she hears all this. I hope she believes it."

Jack exhaled slowly. "Whether we figure out the past or not, we still have this—whatever this time travel is. And I still don't know where you fit into it."

Lisa paused, fingers hovering above the keyboard. "I get this strange feeling like... I was there too. Maybe in a dream. Maybe something else."

Jack nodded. "En-tee-tee-ueh thought I was Jonathan just by looking at me. Then the watch. Then the cabin. It's all too much to be coincidence."

They both returned to their screens.

"Here," Jack said after a few minutes. "Jonathan Butler. A reporter from Portland—Willamette World, same newspaper I found in the drawer. British-born. Wrote short vignettes. Worked with someone named Richard Shively... but nothing about Chinook tribes."

He leaned back and stared out the rain-streaked window, wind sweeping the branches.

Lisa frowned at her own findings. "Jack... the Watlala tribe did get moved. Just like the Chief told you. Some crossed the river with the Wirsham, the others got relocated to the reservation. Exactly as you described."

She paused, her voice growing emotional. "They were here long before us. Forced to move, sometimes more than once... look at this quote."

She read softly: "This war was brought upon us by the children of the Great Father who came to take our land without a price..."

Jack watched her eyes moisten. "I saw no anger in the camp," he said gently. "They didn't want a battle. They just wanted to stay on their land. I told them I'd try to help, even though I know I can't change history."

Lisa brushed her cheek. "It's heartbreaking. Everything I'm reading... it all matches what you saw."

Jack nodded. "We'll see what Wakanda says. And I want to talk to George Lawson at PSU—he's a physicist and a good friend. Maybe he can help me wrap my mind around this time travel thing. But until we know more, we should keep everything quiet. At least for now."

He took her hand, leading her into the living room. They curled together on the couch, letting the steady patter of rain soften the room into silence. Both had fallen into deep thought when a text alert buzzed on Lisa's phone.

She blinked awake. "Wakanda will be at my house late tomorrow morning—maybe noon. I'll call you and we'll come over." She smiled warmly. "You'll like her. And we'll finally get to spend some real girl time together."

"Can't wait," Jack said, wrapping her in a hug. He walked her to her car under a break in the clouds. The moon shone through a drifting patch of silver light.

"Drive safe," he said. "Text me when you get home."

"I will. Sweet dreams."

She drove off, taillights glowing against the wet pavement. Jack watched until her car disappeared, the cool breeze brushing against his face. The wind rustled the trees overhead—soft, indistinct whispers slipping through the night, familiar as memory.

Inside, he locked the door, feeling the weight of the day press upon him. He collapsed onto his bed, mind racing with fragments of the past and the faces of the Watlala tribe. Exhaustion finally won. He fell into a deep sleep while Lisa's I made it home text waited unread on his phone.

Chapter Nine

Mystery Man

"Give thanks for unknown blessings already on their way." ~
Native American saying

Jack lived two blocks from the University of Portland, overlooking the Willamette Bluff. The neighborhood streets were
named after colleges, and he'd grown up just a few blocks
away. Most mornings started the same: a five-mile walk before
breakfast to clear his head and get his mind ready to write.

Today was no different. The streets still glistened from
Sunday's rain, but the sky had broken into patches of blue and
drifting cloud. Before heading out, he sent Lisa a quick text:

'Fell dead asleep after you left last night. Hope you had a
good night. Call me when Wakanda shows up'.

He slipped his phone in his pocket and set off toward the
university.

As he walked, his thoughts drifted back to the mountain.
He'd hiked that area many times over the years and always
stuck to the main trail upriver—a steep climb into Elk Meadows. On clear days, Mount Hood rose so close it felt like you

could reach out and touch the snow. The return route was always tricky; by afternoon, glacier melt turned the river milky and fast, the kind of water that swallowed your ankles and hid the rocks underneath.

But he had never followed the river downstream until the day the whispers in the wind drew him there.

Colored leaves skittered along the sidewalk as he passed the university. They crunched and rustled under his shoes, an autumn rhythm under the sound of distant traffic. He couldn't keep his mind from circling back to the Indian camp, the cabin, the desk, the supply list, the notes in Chinook. And the Willamette World newspaper.

He'd seen all of it before. Not just in the last few days—but somewhere deeper. It was a strange kind of remembering that wasn't quite memory and wasn't quite imagination. Jack lengthened his stride, letting the wind push at his back and swirl leaves in the air around him.

***

Across town, Lisa was just finishing her shower when the doorbell rang. She smiled instantly—Wakanda.

She wrapped her hair in a towel, grabbed a robe, and hurried to the door. When she opened it, Wakanda stood there grinning, arms already open.

"Hey there, Silly One, how are you?" Wakanda said, pulling her into a hug.

"I'm great, my dear friend. Get in here," Lisa laughed. "How was the drive from Yakima?"

"Oh, easy. Little headwind in the Gorge, nothing serious."

They walked to the den, the old comfortable rhythm between them sliding right back into place.

"I am dying to hear this story about you and Jack," Wakanda said. "Last time we talked, he was just 'handsome coworker Jack.' Now I hear he's also 'time travel Jack.'"

Lisa blushed, settling into her chair. "Oh, Wakanda... we've gotten so close. We like each other so much. We're in love. It's like a floodgate opened. After all those years working together, it just... spilled over. I called him 'boyfriend,' and he called me 'girlfriend.'" She smiled down at her hands. "I feel so blessed to have him in my life right now."

"You deserve that," Wakanda said, eyes soft. "Now tell me what's going on with you two—and with this time travel business."

"Come on, let's sit in the den. I made tea and sandwiches." Lisa grabbed her phone. "Jack wants us to come over later so you can meet him. I'll text him that you're here."

She sent Jack a quick message that they'd head over in the afternoon. She spent the next hour walking Wakanda through everything—Jack's first hike, the meadow that shouldn't exist, the stopped watch, the second journey, En-tee-tee-ueh, Running Horse, the cabin, the newspaper, the poem.

Wakanda listened in absolute stillness. Goosebumps broke out along her arms, and she tucked her legs up under her. By the time Lisa finished, Wakanda was staring at her with wide, intent eyes.

"Wow," she breathed. "Lisa... this sounds like a novel or a movie, but it also feels... true. The things Jack saw—Indian camp, language, the tribe being moved—these are all pieces of history. Somehow he's stepped sideways into another layer of time that hasn't left yet. There are way too many coincidences to ignore."

"I know," Lisa said. "It's exciting and mysterious, and I feel like I'm part of it somehow. Like I'm supposed to be."

Lisa sent Jack another text: We're heading your way.

***

By the time they drove across town, the sky over North Portland had darkened again. Rain began to fall in short bursts, leaves flickering and tumbling across the streets.

"Jack lives near the University of Portland, up on the bluff," Lisa said as they turned into his neighborhood. "He's really excited to meet you."

"I can't wait to give him a big Wakanda hug," she said, laughing. "He'll either love me or hate me."

"Oh, now who's being the silly one?" Lisa nudged her. "You're the most warmhearted person I know."

"I'm just a little nervous about meeting your boyfriend," Wakanda admitted. "Don't tell him that, though."

Lisa parked in Jack's driveway. The two women hopped out and hurried through the drizzle to the porch. Jack opened the door before they could knock, a warm glow from the fireplace behind him.

Lisa and Jack shared a quick embrace and a soft kiss on the cheek.

"Jack, meet my friend Wakanda," Lisa said. "You've heard about each other for a long time."

Wakanda wrapped him in a big hug. "I am so glad to finally meet you, mystery man."

Jack laughed. "Likewise. 'Mystery man,' huh?"

"Oh, Lisa knows what I mean," Wakanda said. "She's been talking about you for two years. Always with that little smile. Always a crush."

"Wakanda!" Lisa protested, cheeks flushing.

"Don't worry, Silly One. I'm a straight shooter," Wakanda said, unbothered.

Jack stood back, grinning, hand to his chin. "So Lisa has another name—Silly One?"

"That goes way back," Wakanda said. "She's the serious one. I'm the playful one."

Lisa shook her head. "Okay, okay, save some of that for later. We haven't even had the main course."

Jack gestured toward the living room. "Come on in, sit by the fire. Can I get you something to drink?"

"I'll take water," Lisa said.

"Same for me," Wakanda added.

Jack brought two bottles of water and settled into a chair across from them. "It's really good to meet you, Wakanda. I'm guessing Lisa's already brought you up to speed?"

"She has," Wakanda said. "And Jack... that's quite a story you're walking around with."

Lisa ran her fingers through her blonde hair. "It feels like we have a lot of work ahead, figuring out what comes next."

"Hy-iu iktahs kopa tsum-klagh," Jack said quietly.

Lisa blinked. "What did you just say?"

"He said, 'many things to figure out,'" Wakanda replied automatically. "Since when do you speak Chinook?"

Jack shrugged. "I picked some up on the hike. Before you got here I printed a Chinook dictionary and went through it. Once I started reading, it felt weirdly natural. There are only about five hundred words—the whole trade language. It's actually pretty easy to learn. And it helps that you know it too."

He watched their faces—Lisa's surprise, Wakanda's intrigued focus.

"So," Wakanda said, "what's your next step?"

"That's the part that scares me," Jack admitted. "It's not just what I've seen that's sticking with me. It's... memories. On my walk this morning, things came back in flashes that weren't from this life. Not exactly. I'm sure I've lived another life, and that I was there before as Jonathan. I just don't know how it works."

Wakanda rested a hand on Lisa's arm and leaned forward. "The elders talk often about past lives. Some spirits return, some stay watching. Usually we don't remember our earlier lives unless there is a reason—unfinished work, no peace, something left undone. The Great Spirit watches over these things in ways we don't understand. This could be a blessing still unfolding... or a warning. But I'd rather keep the faith than fear it."

Jack let himself sink deeper into his chair, eyes closed for a moment, legs stretched toward the hearth. Lisa stayed quiet, unsure how to respond. Wakanda slipped her arm around Lisa and held her in a steady, loving side-hug.

After a while, Jack opened his eyes. "We need to go back," he said simply. "All three of us. Take a closer look. And this time, we should try to blend in. Clothes that look more like the 1800s and less like a hiking catalog."

"Good idea," Wakanda said. "I still have my Native dress in the car. Brought it back from the Salmon Festival in Yakima."

"That's perfect," Jack said. "Lisa, you and I can stop at that Western wear store in Troutdale on the way. I'll pick you up around eight tomorrow morning?"

"That works," Lisa said. "It's going to be... exciting. I hope."

"What was that?" Jack asked.

"Nothing," Lisa said quickly. "I am looking forward to it. Just make sure you bring your watch."

"Oh, I'm not leaving that behind," Jack said. "Speaking of leaving things behind—are you two hungry? We could go grab a bite before you head home."

"Absolutely," Lisa said. "My appetite is wide awake again."

"There's a cozy little bistro on Lombard," Jack said. "Follow me there, then you can head home from that side of town."

***

They found a booth in the corner of the bistro and ordered. Conversation drifted from the mountain to work to funny old memories. At one point, Lisa leaned in closer to Jack and lowered her voice.

"Maybe I'm being paranoid," she whispered, "but after we finish this sentence, turn around casually. Check out the guy in the corner booth. He keeps watching us, and every time I glance back, he looks down. Notice his hat."

Jack lifted his water glass and shifted slightly as if adjusting in his seat. He glanced back.

A man sat alone in the shadows of the corner. Long dark overcoat. Black western hat. When Jack's eyes found him, the man dipped his head in a small, almost formal nod, then looked away.

"Interesting," Jack murmured. "That's not a raincoat. That's a full-length duster. And that hat—definitely western."

Wakanda's eyes narrowed. "That's what outlaws, sheriffs, bounty hunters wore back in the old days."

"Oh geez," Lisa whispered. "Not a Halloween costume, then? What would someone dressed like that be doing here?"

Jack shook his head. "I come here a lot. I've never seen him before. I should go talk to him."

"No," Wakanda said sharply. "Spirits are telling me to leave him alone. It's one thing for you to step into the past. It's another if something—or someone—from the past tries to step here. Elders tell stories about such crossings. They are not usually good stories."

Jack hesitated, then nodded slowly. "Okay. We'll ignore him. If he is from the past, the last thing we should do is invite him into this mess."

They finished their meal, keeping their voices low. When they got up to leave, Jack glanced back.

The corner booth was empty.

Outside, the street was wet and quiet. No long coat. No black hat. No shadowed stranger.

"That was weird," Lisa said. "Why would someone dress like that? And why that look he gave us?"

"I'm just glad he's gone," Jack said. "Maybe our minds are playing games."

"Our minds are not playing games, Jack," Wakanda said softly, staring down the sidewalk. "I felt his presence. It was... dark. Like he wanted to know who we were, and what we were doing."

Jack stepped closer to Lisa and Wakanda. "Alright. Go home, get some rest. I'll see you both in the morning."

He kissed Lisa gently and hugged Wakanda. They said their goodbyes and headed to their cars, each of them wondering whether that stranger was just a man in a coat.—or a shadow from another time, already watching their next move.

Chapter Ten

The Crossing

"What is life? It is the flash of a firefly in the night.
It is the breath of a buffalo in the wintertime.
It is the little shadow that runs across the grassland loses itself in
the sunset."
— Blackfoot

Jack rolled into Lisa's driveway a little after eight and hopped out, the cool October air nudging him awake. Lisa opened the door before he reached the porch, throwing her arms around him.

"We're ready to time-travel with you," she said with a spark in her eyes.

Jack laughed. "Whoa. Somebody's energized. Get any sleep?"

Wakanda appeared behind Lisa, shouldering a stack of supplies. "Morning, Jack," she said with a big smile, brushing past him toward the truck.

Lisa answered as they walked out, "Actually, we slept well. Even after that creepy guy at the bistro."

Jack nodded. "Good. We'll need every ounce of strength today. I can't wait to show you both what I experienced. Just... don't be too shocked."

Lisa's expression softened. "Jack, I can't explain it, but I feel all three of us are tied to this. Somehow, it's bigger than just you."

Wakanda hollered from the sidewalk, "Come on, you two. Move it!"

Lisa pushed Jack playfully. "We better listen. You don't want to cross her."

They headed east on I-84, stopping at Bob's Western Wear in Troutdale. After some laughter, swapping outfits, and half-serious critiques, Jack and Lisa stepped out looking like they'd stepped straight from 1867.

Jack wore black trousers, a plaid shirt, tan jacket, and a black western hat. Lisa's outfit—a leather-fringed tan jacket, midnight-blue pinstripe pants, turquoise beads—caught the morning light beautifully.

Wakanda wagged her head. "Goodness. Pendleton Round-Up material right here."

"At least we'll blend in," Jack said.

"You two will," Wakanda teased. "I look like I wandered out of a powwow."

That earned a round of laughter before they hit the gorge.

Outside, a crisp autumn breeze filled the Columbia River Gorge as waterfalls glittered from recent rain. For a moment, the world felt steady. Peaceful.

At the trailhead, they packed vintage canvas knapsacks and headed to the river. Jack turned to Lisa.

"Oh—grab the keys and lock the truck?"

She dashed back, returned, and handed the keys to him.

Then Jack glanced at Wakanda in her regalia and smiled. "You look incredible."

"Thanks," she said, smoothing the beadwork. "This outfit has been years in the making."

They crossed the log, dropped into the underbrush, and entered the deep forest. Jack checked his pocket watch—still ticking.

"That's strange," he said. "The other trips, it stopped the moment I crossed the river."

Lisa whispered, "My heart's pounding so hard I can feel it in my ears."

"Mine too," Jack admitted. "But I'm certain—we're about to cross into 1867."

Sunlight began to seep through the canopy. Dust rose under their boots. They approached the clearing, and Jack slid his arm around Lisa.

"We made it."

Before them, the meadow stretched in full summer bloom. Wildflowers. Warmth. Mist drifting from the distant waterfall. A world untouched.

Lisa stood speechless.

Wakanda exhaled slowly. "We stepped from autumn into summer. Spirits above. This is real."

They made their way to the fallen log and sat, taking in the incredible valley.

***

Wakanda drifted a few yards away and froze. "Jack. Lisa. Someone's coming."

Jack climbed atop the log. "Binoculars," he said, hand outstretched.

He looked through them.

Then went still.

An army officer—bluecoat, straight from the cavalry—rode toward them. And behind him... more.

"Six soldiers," Jack murmured. "We may have trouble."

Lisa grabbed Wakanda's arm. "Jack—her outfit. They're going to think she's Watlala."

Jack swore under his breath. "Wakanda—crawl inside the hollow part of the log. Now."

She squeezed in just in time.

"Lisa," Jack said quietly, "stay calm. Let me handle the talking. I'll play the part they expect—Jonathan Butler. Get the plastic water bottles hidden."

Lisa shoved them into the packs as the soldiers approached.

The lieutenant dismounted, removed his gloves, and tipped his hat politely to Lisa.

"What are you two doing way out here?"

Jack smiled easily. "We're walking to my cabin. I'm a writer—I come up here for solitude."

"A writer? For who?"

"The Willamette World in Portland."

The lieutenant softened a little. "Ah. I read that from time to time. Writer's name?"

"Jonathan Butler," Jack replied without missing a beat. "And this is Lisa, my fiancée."

The lieutenant's gaze sharpened. "We're hunting for the Watlala tribe. You haven't seen any Indians, I presume?"

Jack kept his tone even. "Not on this trip."

One soldier circled behind the log—and shouted:

"Lieutenant! An Indian squaw inside the log!"

Lisa gasped. Jack's stomach dropped.

Wakanda emerged calmly as the lieutenant stormed forward.

Jack forced confidence into his voice. "Lieutenant, I can explain—"

"Oh, I can't wait to hear this," the lieutenant said.

Jack forged ahead. "She's Yakima. She traveled with us to visit my cabin. She hid only to avoid conflict. She is not Watlala."

The lieutenant stared hard. "How do I know that?"

"You don't," Jack admitted. "But I assure you—we mean no trouble."

The lieutenant nodded subtly.

Three soldiers seized Wakanda, tied her hands, and lifted her onto a horse.

Lisa screamed, lunging forward. Jack caught her tightly.

The lieutenant mounted up. "She'll be fine as long as she cooperates. We're not executing anyone out here. She'll be held at our fort in Hood River."

Then the soldiers turned and rode away, Wakanda shouting back:

"I'll be alright!"

Jack waved. "We'll come for you!"

***

Lisa tore from Jack's arms, running several yards as the riders disappeared.

"How could you let them take her?" she cried. "Why didn't you do something?"

Jack walked toward her slowly. "And what would you have wanted me to do against six armed soldiers? Get all of us killed?"

Lisa sobbed into his chest. "What if she never comes back? What if she's stuck here? What if—what if we changed something we can't fix?"

Jack tightened his arms around her. "We'll get her back. She's strong. Smart. She'll buy herself time."

Lisa pulled back, eyes full. "Jack... we are more than a hundred years in the past. How do we do anything?"

"We find En-tee-tee-ueh," Jack said firmly. "Running Horse knows everything. They've mingled with the soldiers before—maybe they know the layout of the camp."

Lisa wiped her eyes. "And if they've already moved? If we can't find them?"

Jack exhaled. "Then we head to Hood River. Even if it's twenty miles on foot."

A cold east wind swept across the meadow, dark clouds gathering over the mountain. The meadow felt different now—less magical, more dangerous.

Jack stared down the valley, mind racing.

He'd brought the three of them into something larger, riskier, and far more tangled with fate than he'd ever imagined.

And now Wakanda was gone.

Chapter Eleven

Night Owl

"We, the great mass of the people, think only of the love we have for our land. For we do love the land where we were brought up. We will never let our hold to this land go. To let it go will be like throwing away our mother that gave us birth."
~ Aitooweyah

Lisa steadied herself, remembering the whisper Wakanda managed to slip into her ear while Jack was speaking to the Lieutenant: "I'll be okay, Lisa. Find Jack's friend—the Chief."

Jack slung the knapsacks over his shoulder, furious with himself for everything that had happened. More than anything he feared Lisa might blame him—feared this would wedge its way between them. His heart pushed the words forward before he could overthink them.

"I'm so sorry," he said quietly. "For all of it."

Lisa stepped closer, her voice trembling but gentle. "Jack... it's not your fault. I'm sorry I reacted like that. Wakanda is my best friend and seeing them take her—" She swallowed. "It terrified me. But she did manage to whisper something."

Jack straightened. "What did she say?"

"She said she'd be okay... and for us to find the Indian chief."

Jack exhaled a shaky breath. "That sounds exactly like Wakanda. If anyone can talk her way out of trouble, it's her. She'll prove she's Yakima—she's smart enough to know how to survive this."

Lisa nodded. "Then we need to go find En-tee-tee-ueh."

Jack reached for her hand. "Lisa... before we go any farther, there's something I need to say."

She turned, eyes softening. "Yes?"

"I know this is a strange time and place to say it." He hesitated. "But I love you. I want us to be together. Always."

Lisa's breath caught. "Jack—"

"I don't want to be apart from you again," he went on. "Not after this."

She touched his cheek, tears threatening. "I love you too. More than ever."

And then Jack, without breaking her gaze, lowered himself to one knee in the soft meadow grass. Lisa gasped, pressing both hands to her lips.

"In eighteen hundred sixty-seven," he whispered, "I'm asking you to marry me. I'll love you and cherish you for the rest of my life. Will you marry me, Lisa?"

Her tears fell before the words did. "Yes, Jack. Of course I will. I want to share my life with you." She dropped to her knees, and they wrapped their arms around each other, lying back in the tall grasses, holding on as though the earth might shift beneath them.

Jack plucked a single white daisy, twisting the stem into a tiny ring and sliding it onto her finger. "It's all I can give you from this time," he said. "A proper ring will have to wait."

Lisa kissed the petal-crown gently. "It's perfect."

They walked arm in arm toward the small cabin perched on the rise above the meadow. The sun was already lowering behind Wy'east, stretching long shadows across the grass.

"This is where I spent my first night," Jack said quietly. "The old encampment is down there—where I first met En-tee-tee-ueh."

Lisa scanned the wide meadow, her expression softening. "Hard to believe the government wanted to force them off this land. They were here first."

Jack nodded. "And there's nothing we can do to change the past. But we can try to help in small ways."

They reached the cabin, the weathered boards glowing silver in the late light.

"It's exactly how I pictured it from your journal," Lisa breathed. "It feels... familiar."

"I know. It felt that way to me too," Jack admitted. "Like I've stepped back into a life I've lived before."

Inside, Jack set down the knapsacks and started a fire. Sparks rose up the stone chimney as the room warmed.

"There's only one bed," Lisa said, lifting an eyebrow.

"I'll take the floor," Jack replied. "You get the bed."

Lisa smiled. "Spending the night in your cabin, Jonathan—oh, excuse me... Jack."

"Funny," he said, laughing. "But seriously, if I was once Jonathan, then who were you back in this time?"

A small shiver traveled through her. "Let's hope we don't run into the real Jonathan. That would be awkward."

Jack agreed. "Very awkward."

They settled by the fire with their food. Lisa leaned toward the window. "I wonder what Wakanda's doing right now."

"She's smart," Jack said. "The settlers and soldiers in Hood River were civilized for the most part. They likely just want answers. She'll talk her way through this."

Lisa sighed. "I hope so."

Jack stirred the fire. "Tomorrow we find En-tee-tee-ueh. Tonight we rest."

"It's just... what if they fight back?" Lisa said softly. "What if this ends badly?"

"I don't think it will," Jack said. "But you're right—there's a lot we don't know."

The moon rose high, washing the cabin in silver light. Jack checked the old hand-pump and coaxed clear, cold water from the spout.

"You're good at that," Lisa said.

Jack frowned slightly. "It felt... familiar. Like I've done it before. I even remember installing it."

Lisa touched his arm. "If you really were Jonathan Butler, that would make sense."

Jack didn't answer, but the confusion in his eyes deepened.

Lisa climbed into the old sagging bed with a groan. "This mattress has seen better centuries."

Jack knelt beside her, brushing a strand of hair from her face. "I've been meaning to bring up a new one," he said softly. "Guess I should add it to my supply list."

She smiled. "Yes, Jonathan... don't forget."

Jack kissed her forehead and settled onto the floor by the fire.

Hours later, a noise outside snapped Lisa awake. She sat up quickly. Jack was snoring lightly on the floor, the fire glowing faintly behind him.

"Jack," she whispered. "Psst... Jack."

He jolted, groggy. "Huh? What's wrong?"

"I heard something. Outside."

Jack grabbed his knife and flashlight. "Stay in bed. Don't move."

"I promise," she whispered, disappearing beneath the blankets.

Jack opened the cabin door. The porch creaked under his weight. Moonlight silvered the clearing; wind sighed through the trees.

"Anyone there?" he called.

No answer.

He moved around the cabin, beam sweeping across the stacked wood and old rain barrels. A faint rustle made him pause.

Perched on a high branch above him, lit by moon glow, sat a great white owl. It blinked slowly, almost knowingly.

"Well, friend," Jack whispered, "you've given Lisa a scare tonight."

He lowered the flashlight and returned inside.

"It's just an owl," he said, easing onto the bed beside her for reassurance. "Nothing to worry about."

Lisa nodded, letting him fold his arms around her. She turned toward the wall, his warmth easing her nerves.

Outside, the owl gave a soft, echoing hoot... hoot.

And the mountain night held its breath.

Chapter Twelve

The Rescue Begins

"Everything on the earth has a purpose, every disease an herb to cure it, and every person a mission. This is the Indian theory of existence." — Mourning Dove (Salish)

The rays of early morning sun slipped through the flour-sack curtain and landed directly across Jack's eyelids. He blinked awake, stiff from the floorboards, then turned his head.

Lisa was right there beside him, still nestled under the thin blanket on the rickety old bed. He remembered dozing off while comforting her after the night's disturbances. For a moment he just watched her breathe.

"Hey there, Lisa," he whispered. "Time to wake up."

She stirred, rubbing her eyes. "Oh... I didn't hear the alarm. What time is it?"

Jack laughed softly and checked his pocket watch. "Ten minutes past eight — and you're late."

He grinned at the childhood phrase.

"Oh right... we have to find En-tee-tee-ueh." She sat upright. "Did you really sleep on this old bed with me?"

"Sure did," he said. "Guardian of scary nighttime noises."

Lisa grabbed her brush and began working through her hair. "What's for breakfast?"

Jack handed her a protein bar with a flourish and passed her a bottle of water. "Five-star dining. I haven't been to the store yet."

She rolled her eyes. "Very funny. Hey—look." She held up her hand. "My engagement ring survived the night... minus a few petals."

He turned toward her, his expression softening. "Once we're back in Portland, I'll take care of that for real."

***

After a quick bite to eat, they headed out, Jack limping slightly but determined. They searched for the narrow entry he'd taken before. "It's here someplace... wait—over here," Jack called.

Lisa ducked under the fir boughs behind him. "This feels like crawling into another world."

"It is," Jack said, leading them between tree trunks. "Be careful—the trail gets rocky. And that drop-off isn't forgiving."

They emerged into daylight—and immediately:

"Jonathan! You back!"

Jack startled, caught his boot on loose shale, and slid sharply off the trail.

"Jack!" Lisa screamed, frozen on the narrow ledge.

Running Horse appeared out of nowhere, swift as a shadow, and scrambled down to help Jack.

"My friend, you okay?" Running Horse lifted Jack under the arms.

Jack winced. "Hey, Running Horse... you scared the life out of me. I'm scraped up, and my ankle's shot."

"Can you stand?" Lisa called, voice trembling.

Jack tried putting weight on the foot and hissed. "Nope. Sprained, maybe worse."

Running Horse motioned for him to stay put while he sprinted back for help.

"You're going to be okay," Lisa said softly, crouching near him.

"I've been better," Jack admitted. "Terrible timing for a long walk."

Running Horse returned with two braves and a stretcher. They eased Jack onto it and began the slow return to camp while Lisa followed along the narrow trail.

***

Inside the camp, the braves carried Jack into a small hut. The old medicine woman immediately took charge, motioning for his boots and socks to come off. She prepared a thick herbal paste from a green wooden box and applied it to the raw skin on his arms.

"Ow—okay, that stings," Jack muttered.

"Medicine woman strong. You heal quick," Running Horse said.

"We have bigger problems than my ankle," Jack replied. "Where's your brother? We need him."

The braves fetched the Chief. Lisa sat beside Jack, torn between worry and frustration.

"Are you sure you're alright?" she whispered.

"I'll live. But Wakanda won't get out of that fort without help."

Running Horse sighed. "If Yakima woman shows who she is, maybe they release. Maybe not."

When the Chief entered, he greeted Jack with warmth, then turned to Lisa and wrapped her in a surprisingly tender hug.

"You speak of friend taken by soldiers?" En-tee-tee-ueh asked.

Jack nodded. "She's Yakima. They think she's one of your people. We need help, Chief."

En-tee-tee-ueh considered this carefully, then spoke in thoughtful Chinook to his brother outside the hut.

When they returned, the Chief said, "Running Horse will take white woman Lisa to Hood River with two braves. They hide. She visit friend. Running Horse stay close, unseen."

Jack tried to rise but winced, the pain flaring sharp again.

The medicine woman pressed a cup into his hands, muttered a chant, and guided it to his lips. Within a minute, his eyelids grew heavy and the pain dissolved into a warm fog.

Lisa brushed his forehead. "Jack, are you okay?"

"Mmhmm... just tired now," he murmured. "Go with them. I trust Running Horse. Bring her back."

Lisa kissed him and slipped out.

***

Running Horse and two braves waited outside. "We go now," he said. "Follow my hands. Follow my eyes."

Lisa nodded. She tightened her boots and grabbed her knapsack. "Lead the way."

They descended the meadow in long sweeping curves, hugging groves of trees for cover. Running Horse sent a scout ahead, silent as smoke.

Lisa's mind drifted between Jack—sedated, vulnerable—and Wakanda alone in the hands of frontier soldiers. But Running Horse moved with such confidence, she felt an odd comfort, as if she'd walked these lands before.

The sun dipped low. Running Horse motioned for her to continue. "Travel at night. Safer. We keep going."

Lisa swallowed hard and nodded. They pressed on into twilight, the Nichi-wana river shimmering faintly in the distance. And somewhere, far down that river valley, Wakanda waited.

Chapter Thirteen

Reunited with Lawitha

"We learned to be patient observers like the owl. We learned cleverness from the crow and courage from the jay that will attack an owl ten times its size to drive it off its territory, but above all of them ranked the chickadee because of its indomitable spirit."
— Tom Brown, Jr., The Tracker

Darkness settled over the Indian camp as Jack continued sleeping. En-tee-tee-ueh sat before the small fire, its glow flickering against the carved lines of his face. His daughter approached quietly and knelt beside him.

"Lawitha, my daughter," he said softly, taking her hand, "I did not speak while you gathered food. There were many reasons. In the medicine woman's hut you will find Jonathan. He fell from the trail. She gave him potion so he sleeps. He returned once with no memory. Now again—with friends. One taken by the white soldiers."

Tears shimmered on Lawitha's olive-toned cheeks. She embraced her father tightly.

"Klat'-a-wa ko'-pa," he whispered. "Go. Be with him."

***

With the dim light from the fire guiding her, Lawitha slipped inside the medicine woman's hut. The old healer rose, took Lawitha's hand, and gently placed her beside Jack before slipping out into the night.

Lawitha sat close, her fingers curling around Jack's. Her deep brown eyes glowed in the warm firelight as she whispered prayers of gratitude to the Great Spirit for his return. Memories — days in the cabin, walks through the meadow, evenings beside the fire — welled up inside her. Love, long buried beneath moons of uncertainty, rose fiercely to the surface.

Hours passed before Jack stirred. He blinked against the shadows, trying to focus on the shape sitting beside him.

"Lisa... is that you?" he murmured.

Lawitha said nothing, only squeezed his hand. Jack blinked again, and slowly the image sharpened: Lisa's eyes... but dark hair, soft brown skin, familiar in a way that made something ancient inside him tremble.

His breath caught. "Lawitha?"

She smiled through her tears and lowered her head to his chest. Jack wrapped his arms around her as memories came flooding back — the cabin, the tribe, the truth of who he was in this world. Yet the life he lived in Portland — Lisa, work, the present — clung to him too.

"It's complicated," he whispered. "But I do remember… and I love you so much."

She lifted her face, and they shared a long, aching kiss. The pain in his ankle seemed to dissolve beneath the heat of her closeness.

***

At dawn, Running Horse and Lisa crouched in a thicket overlooking Hood River. The first blush of daylight washed across the town and the glimmering water below.

"We wait here until full light," Running Horse said. "Then I take you to house of white friends. You tell them what happen with your Yakima friend and white soldiers."

"But how will I reach Wakanda?" Lisa asked.

"They help. Good family. Teach us white man's language. Friends to our people."

Lisa exhaled, unsettled. She thought of Jack back at the camp — injured, recovering, with the mysterious Indian woman she had sensed but never met. She pressed her back against the pine tree and waited for the sky to brighten.

***

Jack and Lawitha were still wrapped in sleep when the old medicine woman bustled in.

"Ket-op', ket-op'," she chanted. Get up, get up.

Lawitha stepped aside. Jack rubbed his eyes and managed a greeting. "Kla-how'-ya?"

The healer knelt, unwrapped his ankle, and inspected the scrapes on his arms.

"Le pee kloshe pe me-sachiepe-shuk'? Foot good or bad?"

Jack rotated his foot. The swelling was gone. "Wake pahtl. Kloshe."

The old woman nodded with approval and motioned for him to stand. As Jack rose, something in the corner of the hut caught his eye — a green wooden box etched with a sun, moon, and star.

The very box from his dream.

The box he'd found months later in the antique shop by the ocean.

The box sitting on his desk back home.

"La ca-sett'... the box," Jack whispered.

The medicine woman lifted it reverently. "Tamah-no-us la mes'-tin. Magic medicine."

Jack felt the carvings beneath his fingers. "I dreamed of this," he said to Lawitha. "An old woman gave it to me. Later

84

I found the same box at the coast. I have it at home. This is the same one."

Lawitha frowned. "How can that be? You've been to the great sea?"

"Oh yes. Many times."

"But how can you have this box there... when it is here?"

Jack shook his head. "I don't know. Everything connects in strange ways. In my dream, a young dark-haired woman ran with me at the forest edge when the old woman handed me the box. It was you."

He returned the box to the healer and stepped outside with Lawitha.

***

The morning fire crackled softly as En-tee-tee-ueh greeted them.

"Glad you are better, Jonathan."

"Thank you. Your medicine woman is incredible."

"She has gifts from the Great Spirit," the Chief said with quiet pride.

Jack met Lawitha's gaze. "I remember everything now. But with my friends here — and my life in the future — I don't know how to make sense of all this."

The Chief sighed deeply. "We ask the Great Spirit for guidance. These are troubled times. My daughter's heart is heavy. You belong in present — not future."

Jack stared into the flames. "I just need to think. Figure out why this is happening, and what I'm supposed to do."

After breakfast, Jack and Lawitha walked along a creek. They sat together on a sun-warmed rock, water murmuring at their feet.

"You have been gone many moons," she said softly. "Just before you left for Portland, I gave you the pocket watch you have now. You promised to return in fourteen days."

Jack rubbed his forehead. "I don't know why I didn't. I remember pieces — the cabin, you, the tribe — but not everything. My future and past are all tangled together. And now Lisa... and Wakanda..."

He trailed off.

Two women.

Two worlds.

Two versions of his life colliding in one moment.

Lawitha waited quietly, patient as the river.

Jack studied her closely — her raven-dark hair, the two eagle feathers near her ear, the soft deerskin dress brushing her knees. She looked so much like Lisa in spirit—strength, compassion, determination—yet belonged to another century altogether.

He touched her lips gently. "I don't want to lose either of you," he admitted. "But I have to figure out what this means. Why I was called back. And why the pocket watch lets me return."

Lawitha nodded, her fingers closing around his.

"You will tell me everything," she said. "I will trust you."

Jack looked out toward the trees where sunlight spilled through the branches.

Somewhere out there, Lisa and Running Horse moved through danger. Wakanda was held by soldiers. The tribe faced threats he did not yet fully understand.

And the pocket watch beat softly against his chest, caught between two times, two lives, and two women who each held part of his heart.

Chapter Fourteen

The Stockade

"I have seen that in any great undertaking it is not enough for a man to depend simply upon himself."
— Lone Man (Teton Sioux)

Hood River bustled with early morning life. Stagecoaches clattered down the dusty road, wagons rolled toward Portland, and farmers guided their teams toward the valley's orchards—rows of apple and pear trees sweeping up the hillside in tidy green stripes. The Watlala people still traded salmon and handmade goods, but the past five years had brought upheaval. The Federal Government planned to remove the tribal encampment east of town and force them to a reservation beyond the mountain.

Daylight strengthened as the village stirred awake. Running Horse nudged Lisa's shoulder, rousing her from a brief, uneasy sleep.

"What?" Lisa whispered.

"Time to go," he said. "People awake now—you not be noticed. We go to thicket behind blacksmith stables. From there you walk to street, turn north toward great river. Find brown house. Family name Weaver. You tell story of your friend—nothing else. They friends to Watlala tribe. Say Running Horse waits behind stables to take you and friend back."

"I will," Lisa said softly. "Thank you, Running Horse. I never would've made it here alone."

She squeezed his arms, earning a shy grin. With one last breath for courage, she slipped down the embankment, circled the stables, and stepped into the morning street.

Dust swirled as horses trotted past. Lisa straightened her hair and clothing as best she could. At the brown house Running Horse described, a warm aroma drifted through the open windows—something baked with cinnamon.

She knocked. "Is that you, Ward? The door is unlocked," called a woman from inside.

Lisa stepped into the entry. "Excuse me. Mrs. Weaver ?"

A woman with kind, intelligent eyes wiped flour from her hands and appeared in the hallway. "Yes, dear?"

"May I come in? I... I was sent by Running Horse. I need help."

The woman's expression sharpened. "Running Horse? The soldiers are hunting him. Is he safe? Hurry—close the door."

Lisa obeyed. She removed her hat, hands trembling. Mrs. Weaver gestured toward the parlor and disappeared briefly. The house was warm and simple—stone fireplace, oval green rug, a piano, shelves lined with worn books and a family Bible.

"That smells wonderful," Lisa said.

"Tea and crumpets. Sit, dear." The woman set the tray before her. "Now... what is your name?"

"Lisa."

***

After a few minutes, Mrs. Weaver—Mary—sat beside her. "Now Lisa, tell me your story."

Lisa hesitated. Running Horse had warned her: tell nothing except about Wakanda. She steadied her breath.

"My friend—Wakanda—she's Yakima. The cavalry seized her yesterday and took her to the fort. They believe she might be Watlala. Running Horse said you might be able to help."

Mary's face fell. "The soldiers built their fort on the Watlala's winter camp months ago. They rounded up several of them and intend to push the rest onto a reservation. It's all been... heartbreaking."

"Where is your husband?" Lisa asked.

"Oh, Ward is up the hill tending the orchard. He should be home soon."

She studied Lisa a moment. "How do you know Running Horse? Are you here alone?"

"Well... it's complicated." Lisa folded her hands in her lap. "I came from Portland with my fiancé to meet, um, my friend.

We didn't expect danger. We were in the meadow when the soldiers appeared."

"And your fiancé?" Mary asked gently.

Lisa swallowed. "He's at the Watlala camp. Injured. They're caring for him."

Mary nodded slowly. "You poor dear. We'll wait for Ward. He'll know how to speak to the Lieutenant."

***

Ward returned an hour later, dust on his boots, apple leaves still clinging to his shirt. He removed his hat, smiling warmly.

"Well now, hello."

Mary introduced them quickly.

Lisa stood. "My friend—Wakanda—is being held at the fort. I need help getting her released. Running Horse said you and your wife could help."

Ward's brows lowered. "They marked her as Watlala?"

"Yes."

Ward rubbed his chin. "We've had dealings with that Lieutenant. He can be... unreasonable. But we'll try. Come."

Mary grabbed her shawl. "And no long sermon this time, Ward."

Ward gave a playful smirk, bowed his head, and whispered a quick prayer. "Amen."

Mary nudged him. "Let's go."

***

They walked toward the river. The fort loomed ahead, logs stark against the windy morning. Lisa felt her stomach twist.

"State your business," the sentry barked.

Ward stepped forward. "We wish to speak with the Lieutenant about an Indian woman you are holding."

The guard vanished inside. Lisa wrung her hands, her breath trembling. The wind pushed her blonde hair across her face, carrying grit and cold.

The sentry returned. "Follow me."

He led them to a sturdy building at the southwest corner. Inside, the Lieutenant entered with an amused half-smile.

"Well now," he said. "This ought to be interesting."

***

In the adjoining room, Lisa rushed to Wakanda the moment she saw her. They embraced fiercely, both trembling with relief.

"Oh Wakanda," Lisa breathed. "I've been sick with worry."

"No worry," Wakanda whispered. "We will figure this out."

The Lieutenant cleared his throat impatiently, circling them like a hawk.

"And if it isn't Jonathan Butler's fiancée in person," he said with a sneer. "Tell me—where is Mr. Butler hiding? Off in his... cabin?"

Lisa stiffened. "Yes. Writing."

"Well," he said, "we shall see about that."

He turned his attention to Wakanda. "You speak suspiciously well for an Indian. Where did you learn such refined English?"

Wakanda held his stare. "Whitman College. I graduated with honors."

The Lieutenant choked on air. "Now that... is the finest tale I've ever heard. Whitman? Accepting an Indian squaw? Don't insult my intelligence."

Wakanda bristled. "Whitman is a Christian college. It accepts all races. And don't call me a squaw."

The Lieutenant stepped back as though she'd struck him. "Enough foolishness. You're not Watlala, but you are something. A threat, perhaps. A witch... or worse. And you—" he pointed at Lisa "—are her accomplice."

Lisa gasped. "You can't—"

"Oh, but I can." His jaw tightened. "You will both stand trial."

"Now wait," Ward interjected. "This is—"

"Soldier!" the Lieutenant barked. "Escort the Weavers off the premises."

Ward and Mary were rushed outside.

The Lieutenant faced the two women. "If you are who you claim to be, you'll have nothing to fear. I intend to send soldiers to fetch this Jonathan Butler. Misery loves company."

He nodded, and soldiers clamped irons on Lisa and Wakanda, marching them toward the stockade.

Lisa whispered, "I love you, my friend."

Wakanda touched her forehead gently. "I wish we were back at the truck right now."

Suddenly the air bent.

The walls spun.

The floor vanished beneath them.

Wind roared in their ears, a bright whirl of dizziness sweeping them into darkness.

Then—

Grass.

Cold air.

Pine needles.

Lisa blinked up at Jack's truck.

They were back in the present.

Still handcuffed.

"Oh my God," Lisa gasped. "Wakanda—we're back."

Wakanda pinched her arm. "It's real. We're home... somehow."

"But Jack." Lisa pressed her hands to her face. "He's still there. And without the watch... we can't reach him."

"So here we sit," Wakanda muttered. "Handcuffed next to a truck we can't even get into."

Lisa felt the panic clawing up her throat. "I had the keys... I swear I did."

Wakanda checked their pockets. Empty.

"They're gone," Lisa whispered. "Lost somewhere in the past."

They huddled beneath the cooling October sky, shivering as night crept in around them.

***

Back in the fort, the two soldiers lay stunned on the floor where the women had vanished. One scrambled upright.

"The prisoners are gone!" he shouted.

The Lieutenant stormed in. "What do you mean—gone?"

"They... disappeared, sir. Before our eyes."

The Lieutenant steadied himself against the table, jaw tight. "Interesting," he muttered. "Quite interesting."

He ordered the Weavers brought back. When they stood before him, he leaned forward.

"Do you know anything about this?"

Ward shook his head. "Lieutenant, we were escorted out. We know nothing."

The Lieutenant studied him long, then exhaled. "Then we forget this. All of us. Understood?"

Ward nodded. "Understood."

"And if this... bad dream returns," the Lieutenant added sharply, "you will tell me."

Ward met Mary's eyes. "Yes. We will."

They left the fort in the darkness, lanterns flickering as the gates closed behind them.

Chapter Fifteen

Two Worlds Colide

*"All things in the world are two. In our minds we are two, good
and evil. With our eyes we see two things, things that are fair
and things that are ugly— we have the right hand that strikes
and makes for evil, and we have the left hand full of kindness,
near the heart. One foot may lead us to an evil way—the other
foot may lead us to a good. So are all things two, all two."*
— *Eagle Chief, Pawnee*

Running Horse grew restless when darkness fell and Lisa had
not returned. He spoke in quick murmurs to his two braves as
they kept hidden in the thicket above the livery stables.

"This whole thing doesn't make sense," Ward said, pacing
the living room. "How could they just disappear?"

Mary folded her hands tightly. "I know when a man is lying, Ward—and the Lieutenant wasn't. Those soldiers looked
terrified. As if they'd seen... something unnatural."

"You said Running Horse was waiting behind the stables?"

"Yes. That's what Lisa told me."

Ward grabbed his hat. "I'd better go inform him. And avoid that Lieutenant. He's got a special dislike for us."

"Be careful," Mary whispered, holding the door as Ward stepped out into the night.

Ward moved through the quiet streets, lantern dimmed. The blacksmith shop was shuttered, the night air cool and still. After checking that no one followed, he climbed up behind the stables.

"Running Horse," he called softly. "It's Ward Weaver."

There was a rustle, then a whispered reply. "Weaver... come into thicket."

Ward pressed through the brush to where Running Horse and the two braves crouched.

"Glad to find you," Ward whispered. "I didn't know if you were still here."

"Why think I leave?" Running Horse asked.

"We met the woman—Lisa. She said you were waiting and needed help. But after what happened today, I wasn't sure what to believe."

"What happen? Where white woman?"

"That's the strange part. She's... gone."

Running Horse frowned. "Gone? Where?"

"I don't know. I saw her and her friend at the fort. Then they vanished. Poof. Into thin air. The Lieutenant said the same."

Running Horse relayed the story to his braves in Chinook Jargon. "Her Indian friend from Yakima—she have magic powers. Brother told me."

Ward shook his head. "If she had powers, why not use them before they got captured?"

"Maybe she know not her gift," Running Horse said quietly.

Ward exhaled. "I don't understand any of this. You should return to your camp and tell your brother. I hope those women reappear... somehow. Sad thing—her fiancé may never see her again."

Running Horse tilted his head. "Fiancée? Word mean what?"

"The man she plans to marry. The man at your camp."

Running Horse absorbed this, nodded once, and placed a hand on Ward's shoulder.

"Nesi'ka klat'-a-wa."

We go.

The three braves faded into the darkness, and Ward headed home, the night eerily still around him.

***

Lisa and Wakanda huddled beside Jack's truck, shivering in the damp cold.

Lisa jerked awake. "I have to go."

"Go where? I must follow," Wakanda groaned.

"Well—geeze—I've gotta pee."

"Then we stand. One... two... three!"

They rose awkwardly together.

"That was ridiculous," Lisa muttered. "I'd laugh if I weren't frozen numb."

They moved away from the truck through the tall grass.

Suddenly the truck alarm shrieked to life, lights flashing wildly.

"What the—?" Lisa yelped.

"You stepped on something!" Wakanda said. "Quick!"

They dropped to the ground searching through the wet grass.

"Here!" Lisa held up Jack's key fob. "Oh thank God." She stopped the alarm. "Come on—inside, before we turn into popsicles."

They shuffled to the driver's door, still handcuffed.

"Oh this is going to be fun," Wakanda sighed. "You want me to go first?"

Somehow they twisted and slid their way inside. Lisa started the engine and warm air rushed from the vents.

Wakanda reached back and grabbed a wool blanket. "Heated seats too—turn 'em all the way up!"

"At least we can get warm," Lisa said. "Clothes might be tricky, but I'm glad to have my jeans back."

"How do we change clothes with these cuffs?" Wakanda huffed.

"We'll figure it out," Lisa said. "Right now we're alive, warm... and stuck. Jack has to find us."

"We sure can't help him," Wakanda muttered. "And you're not exactly driving far with one hand."

They settled under the blanket, shivering but safe inside the truck.

***

Running Horse and his braves returned to camp at dawn. En-tee-tee-ueh met them immediately.

"Brother," Running Horse said. "Need speak."

"I know," En-tee-tee-ueh replied solemnly. "I dreamed it. Jonathan's friends gone."

Running Horse explained everything—Lisa, Wakanda, the fort, their disappearance.

"Her name gives magic," En-tee-tee-ueh said. "But she knows not how to use. Worry is... where are they?"

He went to Jack and Lawitha, who were seated by the fire.

"Jonathan—we must talk."

Jack stood quickly. "Did they return? Are Lisa and Wakanda here?"

"Friends not with Running Horse."

Jack's face drained of color. "What? Where are they? What happened?"

En-tee-tee-ueh shared the full story, ending with Wakanda's suspected powers. Lawitha held Jack as he slumped, shaken.

Jack wiped his eyes. "This is my fault. Two lives, two worlds... and now they're gone. I have to go to Hood River. I have to see for myself."

"Danger," En-tee-tee-ueh warned. "Soldiers take friend—they take you."

"I'll be careful. Lawitha... I'll come back. I promise."

Lawitha nodded. "I know your heart. You must go."

By mid-morning, Jack, Running Horse, and the braves were on the trail. They arrived behind the stables in the late evening.

Running Horse told Jack where to find the Weavers.

Jack climbed down, walked to the brown house, and knocked. No answer. After several tries, he stepped down from the porch and headed toward the center of town.

The streets were mostly empty.

A saloon glowed at the end of the block.

Jack entered.

Men drank at the bar, others played cards. He took a seat by the window.

A server approached. "Drink, sir?"

"Water, please."

Jack looked around—and froze.

In the far corner sat the Stranger.

The same man from the bistro on Lombard Street.

The same hollow eyes.

The same long duster coat.

Jack rose and crossed the room.

He sat at the Stranger's table without asking.

The Stranger lifted his gaze slowly. "Well, Jack. Took you long enough. Or should I say... Jonathan?"

"I want answers," Jack said. "Now."

The Stranger chuckled softly. "I could ask the same of you."

Jack clenched his fists. "My friends—Lisa and Wakanda—they're missing. You saw them. Who are you?"

"Better question," the Stranger said smoothly, "is who are you?"

Jack leaned forward. "Enough riddles."

"Settle down, Jack," the Stranger said. "I am merely an observer. Not a participant in your destiny."

"My destiny? I didn't choose this!"

"Yet here you are. One life unfinished. Another incomplete. Two timelines... two lovers... two futures."

"I just want them back."

"And what of Jonathan Butler's life? His promises? His people?"

"That's past," Jack snapped.

"Is it?" The Stranger's eyes glinted. "Or is it still waiting to be resolved?"

Jack sagged in frustration.

The Stranger continued, voice low and calm. "You are a writer. You know how a story ends it's always your choice. You cannot rewrite your beginning. But you can always choose your ending."

Jack swallowed, the words sinking into him.

Faith. Purpose. Destiny. Choice.

"I think... I understand," Jack whispered. "I need to finish what I started. In the past. And trust that Lisa and Wakanda are safe."

The Stranger nodded. "You will find the answers. In time."

Jack stood. "Who are you, really?"

"An interested observer," the Stranger said. "You'll know when the ending arrives."

Jack blinked.

The Stranger was gone.

Vanished.

Jack stepped outside into the night, alone with more questions than answers. At the stables, Running Horse waited in silence. Jack told him there was no sign of his friends.

Running Horse nodded, asked nothing, and led Jack and the braves back toward camp under the moonlit sky.

Chapter Sixteen

From Past to Present

"I will follow the white man's trail. I will make him my friend, but I will not bend my back to his burdens. I will be cunning as a coyote. I will ask him to help me understand his ways, and then I will prepare the way for my children. Maybe they will outrun the white man in his own shoes. There are but two ways for us. One leads to hunger and death, the other leads to where the poor white man lives. Beyond is the happy hunting ground where the white man cannot go."
— Many Horses, Oglala Sioux

Jack had to say goodbye to Lawitha again, and this time his heart swore it would not repeat the mistake of leaving her behind without returning. He loved her. The same deep, aching love he carried for Lisa. If he hoped to live with any peace, he had to finish the final chapter of his earlier life.

He entered the camp after daybreak and waited for Lawitha, his mind circling back to the Stranger's question about endings and regret.

Do you make it an ending with no regrets?

Two lives. Two stories.

In one, he stayed in Portland and lived out his days in the present with Lisa. In the other, he was Jonathan Butler, with a good life already half-written—only the ending missing.

Did he still have a chance to write it?

He let the early sun soak into his skin. This wasn't a dream. It was real—just fractured. His memory felt like a half-finished jigsaw puzzle.

"What happened after I left the first time?" he muttered. "Where did I go? Why didn't I come back?"

It was more mysterious than Atlantis at the bottom of the sea.

A quote from a writer friend surfaced in his mind:

"Today is now. Part of today is in the past, part of today is in the future. You cannot change the past, only learn from it. The future is wide open and you cannot catch it—it will come to you. Do what you want now. Be ready."

How true that felt now.

"Jonathan, you are back."

He turned. Lawitha stood there, eyes soft, relief written in every line of her face.

"Hi," Jack said, giving her a tired smile. "I missed you. But—I did come back."

"With good news?" she asked. "Did you find your friends?"

"No," he said gently, "but in my heart, I know they're safe. Back in my own time, waiting for me."

"That sounds so unreal, Jonathan." She shook her head. "I don't understand. I never met your Indian friend or this Lisa before she left for Hood River. Mystery surrounds them. Perhaps I will see them one day?"

"Yes," Jack said. "In a good way, I hope. But first, we need to talk."

They sat together. Lawitha folded her hands in her lap, bracing herself.

"I have to find out why I didn't return to you," Jack said. "Back then. Jonathan promised to come back in fourteen days. He never did. You see me as Jonathan, and I remember our life together—but there's a blank space after that. The rest just... cuts off."

He took a breath.

"An odd Stranger in Hood River opened my eyes to both halves of my life. It's hard to explain. Here, I'm Jonathan. Back in Portland, I'm Jack. Why? That's what I have to discover."

He squeezed her hands, voice thickening.

"From the bottom of my heart, I promise you—I will find out, and I will return. I don't know how time passes between here and there, or how long you'll wait. But know this: I love you, and I will come back with the answers we both need."

Lawitha lifted her gaze to the sky. Her eyes filled with tears, then she looked back at him.

"The Great Spirit brought you back to me," she said softly. "So I must believe your promise. I trust the Great Spirit, even if I do not understand how you can be in two places in time."

She dropped her gaze to the ground.

"I am confused," she whispered. "And weary of not knowing."

Jack didn't try to answer what he couldn't answer. He held her arms and let the silence breathe between them. The confusion in her heart echoed in his own.

"I'm going to wash up and rest a bit before I go," he told her quietly.

They embraced. Then Jack returned to his hut while Lawitha walked to her father's fire.

***

"Ah, my daughter," En-tee-tee-ueh said, seeing her face. "Your heart is heavy. I see it in your eyes."

Lawitha sat beside him and rested her head on his shoulder.

"I have just spoken with Jonathan," she said. "He is leaving again. Back to his place in time. I do not understand, Father. The Great Spirit gave me a wonderful man... then took him away. Now he returns only to leave again."

Her voice broke.

"I am confused by his life in the future and the two women there. This Lisa—she is his girlfriend? How can that be? How does this end, Father?"

En-tee-tee-ueh wrapped an arm around her shoulders and spoke a few quiet words skyward before answering.

"Daughter, many things the Great Spirit gives us and many things he takes away. We must trust his wisdom and timing. In my long life, I have learned there are many questions we never get answer."

He paused, staring into the fire.

"The white soldiers... I still wait for an answer to them. I seek to understand, but I am old and feeble now. Still, in my heart, I know the Great Spirit will rise like the moon and call out like the coyote. I will have my answer."

He sighed.

"Our people must follow the white man in some ways," he continued. "He has overtaken our land and outnumbered us. The path ahead is unknown. But our heritage is ours alone. The white man cannot enter that."

A moment passed in stillness.

"Did you tell Jonathan?" he asked quietly.

"No, Father," she said. "My heart is too weary. He says he struggles to understand his two lives. I will wait until he returns. If I tell him now, it may only burden him further."

En-tee-tee-ueh nodded slowly.

"You are wise," he said. "At first I believed he had fallen and hurt his head. Now I see something more. The fact that he returned—twice—means much. He will come again. My wisdom tells me he will stand before us under another moon. Next time, he must hear your words."

They sat together in front of the fire, waiting for Jonathan's return from his hut.

***

Jack dozed briefly and woke with a full-body jolt. He sat up, breath racing.

"Wow," he muttered. "What a dream."

He had dreamed of an old sailing ship thrashing through a violent storm at sea, dark waves towering over him as ropes snapped and men shouted in a language he didn't understand.

He shook off the shiver, gathered his few belongings into the knapsacks, and stepped outside.

At En-tee-tee-ueh's fire, the goodbye waited.

"Hey," Jack said quietly, setting down his gear. He sat beside Lawitha. She immediately wrapped her arms around him and rested her head on his shoulder.

"Running Horse will lead you to the meadow," En-tee-tee-ueh offered.

"I can manage," Jack said. "He's already made that trip to Hood River twice—for me. He's a good man, Chief. You must be proud he's your brother."

"Yes," En-tee-tee-ueh said. "And proud you returned seeking answers to the great mystery."

"I wish I had those answers now," Jack admitted. "But there's a gap I can't reach. Lawitha, I promise—I will come back and make this right. I don't want to place another burden on you, but I can't stay, not yet."

She clung tighter, fighting tears.

"Jonathan," she whispered, "go now, so you cross the meadow before dark. I will wait."

Jack kissed her forehead and held her in a long, quiet embrace.

She reached down and picked up a small leather pouch.

"I made this for you," she said softly, pressing it into his hand. "It will guide good dreams into your head and keep bad dreams out. Let it keep my spirit with you in your sleep, so you need not fear evil thoughts."

Jack opened the pouch and drew out a small circle of willow wrapped in sinew. Feathers and beads hung from the bottom, woven with care.

"What do you call it?" he asked.

"A dream catcher," she said. "The pieces on it are from my own life. Part of me will travel with you."

He swallowed hard, blinking back tears. Gently, he put the dream catcher back into the pouch and tucked it into his jacket pocket.

Two knapsacks over his shoulders, the third in his hand, he kissed her one last time and rose.

He didn't look back as he climbed the narrow, rocky trail. Tears burned hot down his face.

He barely remembered the short climb through the timberline forest, only that the trees gave way to the wide sweep of the meadow. To his left lay the path to his cabin. Memories flashed—writing at the table, evenings with Lawitha, laughter outside beneath the stars.

He promised himself he would stand in that doorway again.

For now, he turned downhill.

The grasses and wildflowers swayed in the late afternoon breeze as he walked. Near the log where Wakanda had been captured, he stopped to rest and took a long drink from his water bottle.

When he looked up, the bottle nearly slipped from his hand.

Riders.

Eight, maybe ten of them, horses cresting the horizon.

"Great," he whispered. "The cavalry."

He snatched up his packs and broke into a run toward the trees.

The riders saw him and urged their horses forward, hooves pounding across the meadow.

Jack reached the shadowy forest edge and plunged beneath the canopy, branches clawing at his clothes as he sprinted toward the river. The cavalry followed, but the trees slowed their approach.

He glanced back. They were gaining.

He dropped the knapsacks to lighten his load and ran harder, lungs burning.

At last, the underbrush thickened, and he crashed through the last tangle of shrubs toward the river crossing. The log stretched before him, slick and narrow above the rushing water.

No time for fear.

Jack charged across, arms out for balance, heart thundering as the river roared below. He stumbled once, caught himself, and pushed on. When he reached the far bank, he collapsed onto the rocks, gasping.

On the opposite side, the soldiers reined in at the edge of the cliff, peering down as if expecting to see a drowned body. Jack's vision wavered, the image of the cavalry going soft and shimmering, like heat above a road.

And then—slowly—they faded.

He was back. The air felt different. The light had shifted.

His watch and the riverbank agreed: he'd crossed into his own time.

Jack stayed on the rock for nearly an hour, shivering in the aftermath of fear and adrenaline. Only when his breathing settled did he climb carefully down the riverbank and start toward the trailhead.

***

"It's getting late," Lisa said, staring toward the trail. "I'm starting to worry he's not coming back."

"He'll come," Wakanda said firmly. "Those Indians are wise. They'll help him. In the meantime, we've got another problem—these handcuffs. My arms are killing me."

"How do we even get them off?" Lisa asked. "Jack doesn't keep bolt cutters in his emergency kit."

"Maybe we can use rocks," Wakanda suggested. "Or the jack handle. We pound the metal until it breaks."

Lisa snorted softly. "At least I'm getting attached to the right person."

"I'm glad your sense of humor survived," Wakanda said.

They made their way down the path to the riverbank. Wind funneled through the canyon, cold and restless, raising goosebumps on their arms.

They found a flat rock to use as an anvil and another as a hammer. Wakanda positioned the tire iron so the flat chisel edge rested against the cuff chain while Lisa braced it with her free hand.

They leaned close, faces inches apart.

Lisa whispered a quick prayer.

"Guess I don't need to say 'be careful,' do I?" she murmured.

"You better hold that bar steady," Wakanda said. "Remember—my arm is right next to yours."

Lisa squeezed her eyes shut and glanced downriver—then froze.

"Wait," she said. "Someone's coming. Down the river. Look!"

They dropped their makeshift tools and squinted into the deep shadows of the canyon.

"Jack!" Lisa shouted.

A ragged silhouette lifted its head. Then he started toward them, stumbling at first, then moving faster.

Lisa and Wakanda stepped back from the rock, lifted their joined hands, and waited, tears stinging their eyes.

Jack reached them, panting, dirt-streaked and exhausted.

"Boy," he said, grinning through his fatigue, "am I glad to see you two."

"Oh Jack," Lisa said, voice breaking. "We didn't know if you'd ever come back."

"I'd hate to disappoint," he replied.

He looked them over. "Well, are you just going to stand there, or...?"

They shared a look like two guilty kids caught in mischief, then lifted their handcuffed wrists in the air.

Jack stared for a beat, then burst into a wide grin.

"I'm at a rare loss for words," he said. "Which is unusual for a writer. What a sight. I'm not even going to ask how this happened."

"You wouldn't believe us anyway," Lisa said, smiling through tears.

Jack spotted the rocks and tire iron on the ground. "Looks like I interrupted something. Let me."

They knelt and laid the chain across the flat rock. Jack met their eyes, nodded once, then lifted the tire iron. With one solid, glancing blow, he snapped the chain.

Metal clattered against stone.

The cuffs fell apart.

Lisa launched herself into his arms, clinging to him, her half of the cuff still dangling from her wrist. Wakanda joined them, wrapping them both in a fierce three-way hug.

The last light of day drained from the sky as the three of them climbed back to the trailhead. They reached Jack's truck, started the engine, and turned the heater up.

Moonlight spilled across the windshield as they wound down off the mountain, another long, solemn drive through the dark—only this time, they were together.

Chapter Seventeen

Home at Last

"Hold on to what you believe, even if it's a tree that stands by itself. Hold on to what you must do, even if it's a long way from here. Hold on to your life, even if it's easier to let go. Hold on to my hand, even if someday I'll be gone away from you."
~A Pueblo Indian Prayer

Sometimes after a great quest there comes a moment when everything finally sinks in. The mind, body, and spirit need a chance to unwind before the stories can be spoken aloud. On the drive back to Portland, the three of them exchanged little more than fragments—soft mutters, exhausted breaths, the occasional confused laugh—as if they weren't sure whether they should cry or celebrate. Their emotions were a mixed, fragile tangle.

They passed through Troutdale when Jack finally broke the silence. "Do you want me to drop you at your place, Lisa? Or should we stay together tonight?"

Lisa glanced at Wakanda, who had already drifted asleep against the window. "We need to be together after all this," she said quietly. "Being separated through time... it's too much. Your place is good."

"Then your vote wins." Jack offered a weary smile. "We'll crash at my house and regroup in the morning."

They reached Jack's driveway a little before midnight. Once inside, the house felt still and safe, a welcome contrast to the shifting shadows of the past. They murmured their good-nights and slipped off to bed, the soft whispers of worn-out time travelers the only sound in the house.

***

Wakanda woke first, wandering into the kitchen in search of something strong enough to revive her. She rummaged through cabinets until Jack appeared in the doorway, rubbing his eyes.

"For a minute, I thought a burglar was tearing the place apart."

"A wild Indian woman on a caffeine hunt," Wakanda said with a grin.

Jack laughed and opened the refrigerator. "I'm a tea-drinker. I keep coffee for guests. Try the fridge."

"Oh, thank goodness." She set the machine to brew while Jack boiled water for tea.

"The next thing after coffee," Jack said, "is getting that handcuff off your wrist."

"That would be lovely. I feel like an escapee from a nineteenth-century jail." She held up the metal band. "Got any tools?"

"Nothing that'll cut steel."

Lisa stumbled in, hair tousled. "Morning," she mumbled.

"Wakanda's coffee could wake a corpse," Jack teased.

"We were talking about getting the cuffs off," Wakanda said.

Lisa lifted her arm. "Yes, please. Before I start clanking like Marley's ghost."

Jack thought a moment. "We need a plan that doesn't get the cops involved."

"Or one that avoids the fire department assuming we're into some kind of bondage hobby," Wakanda said, laughing. "Although—this is Portland."

Lisa groaned. "Can we remove them without witnesses? And how did handcuffs from the eighteen-hundreds travel back with us?"

"That's what I've been thinking," Jack said. "If they came back with you, then... so did something else."

Lisa pointed toward Jack's western coat. "Jack—your pocket."

He pulled out the little leather pouch and placed the dream catcher on the table. The delicate willow hoop, feathers, and colored beads caught the morning light. Wakanda examined it with reverence.

"This isn't a trinket," she said softly. "This is personal. Important."

Jack suddenly felt exposed beneath her steady gaze, but she spared him by taking a long sip of coffee instead of pressing further.

"I need to see Professor Lawson at PSU," Jack said. "There's a lot he needs to help us figure out."

Lisa raised an eyebrow. "Like what?"

Jack chose his words carefully. "Why this happened. What it means. I remember most of my past life... but something went wrong. There's a gap. I need answers."

"And I wish this whole thing was just a dream," Lisa murmured, rubbing her wrist.

Jack took a breath. "Let's talk through what happened."

Lisa recounted her journey—Running Horse guiding her, the missionary couple helping her, the Lieutenant's fury, the handcuffs, and Wakanda's impossible rescue. "She wished us back to your truck, Jack. Whatever that power was... it worked. But only in the past."

Jack nodded. "I figured something like that happened. At the fort, soldiers said you vanished."

"And what happened to you?" Wakanda asked.

"I got chased by the cavalry," Jack said. "Dropped my knapsacks, barely made it across the river. They looked like blurry ghosts across the water. Like I was watching them through time."

Wakanda exhaled slowly. "I wish I could have met your Indian chief. Lawitha too."

Lisa leaned forward. "So... did you meet her after I left?"

Jack hesitated. "Yes. And yes—they think I'm Jonathan Butler."

"You don't remember the watch she gave you?" Lisa asked.

"They said I promised to return in fourteen days and never did. I remember a lot... but not that part."

Lisa frowned as she walked down the hall to the bathroom. "There must be something important you've forgotten."

"That's why I need answers," Jack said. "I can't live two unfinished lives."

Wakanda eyed him closely. "Jack, Lisa loves you. If you're caught between two women—"

"It's not like that." He leaned forward. "I love Lisa. But something in my past was left unresolved. I need to fix it."

"And the Stranger?" Wakanda asked quietly.

Jack swallowed. "Don't tell Lisa yet. Yes, I saw him. In a saloon. And he... knew me. Knew everything. He said my past was an unfinished chapter. That I needed faith."

Wakanda stiffened. "That's no small omen. Someone from the past appearing in the present... then again in the past? That's dangerous."

"I don't think he's evil," Jack said. "Just... unsettling."

Before Wakanda could reply, Lisa returned. "Okay! Who's next?"

Wakanda stood. "Me. I'm scrubbing off a century and a half of dirt."

Jack kissed Lisa's forehead. "I'll grab a shower too."

Lisa smiled and drifted to the kitchen window, letting the morning quiet wash over her. She touched the metal cuff still on her wrist and let herself savor the memory of Jack's arms around her earlier. Whatever uncertainties swirled around his past, she set them aside—for now.

***

By late morning they piled into Jack's truck. "My locksmith friend in Vancouver will cut them off," Jack said. "No questions asked."

Brian welcomed them with a grin. "So these are the ladies you told me about?"

Jack puffed proudly. "Yep. Wakanda and my fiancée, Lisa."

Brian lifted his brows. "You didn't tell me the good news."

"Still getting used to saying it," Jack admitted.

Inside the shop, Brian snipped off the cuffs with ease. The women laughed, massaging their sore wrists, hugging each other in relief.

Brian leaned close to Jack. "These are old. Really old. Where'd you get them?"

Jack smiled faintly. "It's... a long story."

Lisa hugged Jack. "Feels like being set free."

"No more cuffs," Wakanda agreed. "Let's never repeat that experience."

They thanked Brian, promised lunch soon, then headed for the Dairy Queen up the street, where burgers and laughter took the edge off everything they'd been through.

After lunch, Jack dropped the women at Lisa's house. Wakanda stretched, still tired. "Well, Lisa... the wild west sure wasn't as fun as the movies."

"No," Lisa said softly. "It was harsher. Sadder."

Wakanda nodded. "Living it is different than reading about it."

Jack helped them carry their things. "Call me if you need anything. Wakanda—safe travels to Yakima."

She hugged him tight, whispering, "Take care of Lisa. She loves you. Don't mess this up."

"I won't," Jack promised.

He hugged Lisa, kissed her cheek, and drove away. Wakanda watched him go, then yawned.

"Lisa," she said, heading inside with her, "this is one for the memory books. And maybe the psychology books too."

Lisa laughed softly. "Yeah... but we made it."

And together, they closed the door behind them.

Chapter Eighteen

What are you Asking?

"Ask questions from your heart and you will be answered from the heart."
~ Omaha

Jack tossed his western clothes into the wash and reached for a mug of tea. At the kitchen table he held the dream catcher Lawitha had given him, turning it gently so the feathers and beads swayed. It brought back images of the two of them at the cabin, wandering the meadows, sharing laughter in a world that, somehow, was both his past and not-past. Good dreams, good memories.

Before bed, he hung the dream catcher above his headboard and switched off the light. Sleep took him quickly.

"Jonathan, is that you?"

"How did you guess?"

"I can tell from those soft white hands you have."

"I had you blinded there for a moment."

"Yes, you shouldn't sneak up on an Indian maiden and cover her eyes. Did you just get here?"

"Yes. I haven't been to the cabin yet."

Lawitha rose, smiled, and wrapped her arms around him. The young Englishman and the Indian maiden walked arm in arm across the meadow toward his cabin, the grass whispering at their feet.

Jack jerked awake. "That was so vivid," he whispered. "I was right there."

He fell back asleep and dreamed of her the rest of the night. No nightmares—only Lawitha, and the sense of being known.

***

Bleary-eyed, Jack shuffled into the kitchen the next morning and put the kettle on. While the water heated, he thumbed out a text to his friend, Professor George Lawson, asking to meet. He was halfway through his tea and toast when the reply came: no classes this afternoon—how about lunch?

Jack agreed, then stared out the window, replaying the night's dreams. They hadn't felt like imagination. They'd felt like memory.

He called Lisa.

"Hey, good morning. How'd you sleep?" he asked.

"I slept great. You?"

"Same. Surprised, actually."

"I figured I'd have nightmares after all that, but I didn't," Lisa said. "How about you? Any bad dreams?"

Jack glanced toward the bedroom and smiled. "Nope. Guess the dream catcher did its job."

"Oh yeah, I forgot about that. I wouldn't put too much stock in that trinket. Superstition anyway, despite what Wakanda says. I mean, how can an object bring only happy dreams?"

Jack let a few seconds pass. "Hey, I'm meeting with the professor later today."

"Nice. I'm curious about what he'll say. Think he'll believe you?"

"We'll find out. What's your plan today?"

"I'm going into work to look at the stack on my desk. I haven't been away this long in years," she said.

"Got it. I'll call you after my meeting. Let's do dinner."

"Sounds great."

"I know a nice cozy bistro…"

"Not the one on Lombard Street," she warned.

Jack laughed. "But their lamb kabobs are hard to beat."

"Okay, but if that dark stranger is there, I'm leaving."

"Deal. Talk later. Love you."

"Love you too. Bye."

***

Jack showered and dressed, then grabbed the dream catcher, the broken handcuffs, and his laptop, stowing them in his backpack. Driving toward the small bar and grill near Lloyd Center, he wondered how he would even begin. Charts and equations weren't going to cover the ache in his chest; he'd have to speak from the heart.

Inside the restaurant, he spotted George in the lobby.

"Hey, George. How are you?" They shook hands and did the quick back-pat ritual old friends fall into.

"Haven't seen you in a long time," George said. "Written that novel yet?"

"I wish. Too busy writing copy. The book's still simmering on the back burner. How are things with you?"

"Classes, research, more classes. Never ends."

"Let's get a table," Jack said. "I've got a lot to tell you."

They ordered lunch. Jack stirred his iced tea, then looked up. "George, what do you think of time travel? Is it possible?"

George chuckled. "Time travel? Where do you want to go?"

"I'm serious. You've studied this stuff. I need real answers."

"What answers? Theories, math, Einstein on a whiteboard? We can go back to campus."

"I've already traveled to the past," Jack said quietly. "For real."

George set his coffee cup down and narrowed his eyes. "You've got to be kidding."

"Do I look like I'm kidding? I've gone three times. And I took two other people with me."

George exhaled. "Okay. Start from the beginning."

Jack told him everything: the dream and the box, the pocket watch, the first hike, the portal at the river, the meadow, the tribe, Lawitha, Running Horse, En-tee-tee-ueh, the fort, the cavalry, Lisa and Wakanda, the Stranger in the bistro and again at the saloon. He shared as much as he dared of his divided heart.

Two hours later, George ran his hands through his graying hair. "I've studied time travel for years," he said, "but I've never heard a case like this. The laws of physics don't allow easy answers. Time is space, space is time. A time machine is fiction—but portals, wormholes, distortions? Those show up in the math."

He lifted Jack's pocket watch, turning it under the light. "You said this existed in 1867. Now it's here, aged, worn, still functional. It didn't 'teleport.' It moved through time because you did."

He leaned forward. "Einstein's relativity makes time flexible. Motion changes how we experience it. But what you're describing—going back to a period before your own birth—is a paradox. Born in 1975, living in 1867 as someone else. If you'd met your other self, things could have unraveled even more."

He studied Jack. "Maybe that's the key: you might already have been in 1867 as Jonathan Butler, discovered the portal, and came forward. Reincarnation, parallel timelines, overlapping identities—that's the territory we're in now."

Jack listened, absorbing every word.

"In the parallel universe models," George continued, "every major change spins off a new branch of reality. If you alter something in the past, you risk landing in a different branch entirely. That's why you have to be careful. You might not be able to get back to the version of the present you're living in now."

Jack swallowed hard. "So what have I done already?"

"The good news is that, so far, the world hasn't collapsed," George said dryly. "But we can't assume there haven't been ripples. The main issue in traveling to the past is causality. If an effect shows up before its cause, you get paradox. The classic time-travel headache."

He frowned thoughtfully. "The watch seems to act like a key. When everything froze and only started moving again after you crossed back to the river—that's not random. That's a mechanism."

Jack nodded. "I get that the box and watch existed back then and aged. They're antiques now. But there's more."

He set the dream catcher and the sawed-through handcuff on the table. "These came back too. The cuffs are stamped U.S. Army. Lisa and Wakanda were wearing them when they snapped into the present. The dream catcher—Lawitha gave it to me just before I ran for the portal. I had it in my pocket."

George picked up the handcuff piece, then the dream catcher. "In theory, objects native to one timeline shouldn't move into another intact. The handcuffs should have... vanished, for lack of a better term. As for magical powers, I'm a scientist. I don't believe in magic—just forces we don't understand yet."

He turned the dream catcher slowly. "And yet, here we are."

Jack cleared his throat. "I hung this above my bed last night. No nightmares. I dreamed about Lawitha all night. It was like she was with me—talking, laughing. I know I loved her. That hasn't gone away. And I love Lisa. It's like they're... connected somehow. Or I am."

George set the dream catcher down. "Then part of Lawitha may have come back with you. A piece of her spirit, or your connection to her, anchored to this object. I have no idea what that does to the past—or to you. But I can't argue with evidence sitting on the table in front of me."

He looked squarely at Jack. "What exactly are you asking me to do?"

Jack's voice softened. "I'm asking from my heart, because my head's a mess. I need to know what happened back then. Why Jonathan left and never returned. How I ended up here with only a partial memory of that life. I can't keep living in two stories with one of them unfinished. I need closure. I need to know if I'm supposed to go back and, if so, how to do it without destroying everything."

George sat quietly for a moment. "So you want me to help you find the missing piece in your past—through an open portal—with as little damage as possible."

"Yes."

"I've already warned you about the risks," George said. "You've been lucky so far. The idea that a woman is still waiting for you over a hundred fifty years ago... it's staggering. Time stopped for her in one sense, while you've moved on in another."

He drew a slow breath. "I'm a scientist. This is the kind of opportunity people dream of in abstract equations. I can't ignore it. Yes, I'll help you. But we're not rushing in. We map this out. We plan every step. And we assume there's a chance we don't come back."

"What do you mean?" Jack asked.

"I mean we'd be leaving the present, where you're alive as Jack Bellard, and dropping into a time where you were also alive as Jonathan Butler," George said. "We might miscalculate and get stranded. Or land in a slightly altered branch of reality."

Jack thought of Lisa. Of Lawitha. Of En-tee-tee-ueh, waiting for an answer from the Great Spirit. "It didn't feel that dangerous before," he said quietly. "Not until the last time, when the cavalry almost caught me."

"The soldiers are the least of your worries," George replied. "The dark stranger you met? Whoever or whatever he is, he's tied into this. Encouraging or not, he's a variable we don't understand."

He leaned back. "Winter's coming to the mountain. The weather alone makes it a bad idea to go up there now. If that portal holds, we aim for spring. That gives us time to study, map, calculate."

Jack frowned. "Spring feels a long way off. How long will the portal stay open?"

"I don't know," George admitted. "But everything about this suggests at least one more crossing. Maybe only one. When we go, we go with our eyes open. It'll be an expedition. We'll know far more than you did on your first three trips."

"Will Lisa go with us?" Jack asked.

"Absolutely not," George said firmly. "She already felt too much—like she'd lived there before. That's risky territory. Don't mention the next trip to her. Start making your wedding plans. Keep this on the side. Enjoy your life while I work on the science."

He slid the dream catcher back across the table. "Lawitha's world doesn't seem to be moving as fast as yours, from what you've told me. Time there may be stretched differently. She'll still be waiting."

George finished his coffee and stood. "Email me everything you can. Dates. Names. Locations. Journal entries. I'll start building a model. For now, give your mind a rest. Live in the present. We'll get to the bottom of it."

They walked out together, trading a few lighter comments at the door. Jack thanked him, then headed for his truck, thoughts buzzing.

So much so that he forgot, entirely, about dinner plans until his phone rang.

"Hey there," he answered. "I just left lunch with George. Sorry—we got wrapped up. Where are you?"

"It's okay," Lisa said. "I dropped by the office and caught up on what I missed. I'm thinking about heading out now."

"Still up for dinner?"

"Of course. You're not getting out of spending time with me. I'm downtown—want me to meet you at your place?"

"Yeah, that works. You'll be right behind me. See you in a few."

"On my way. Love you."

"Love you too."

Jack pulled into his driveway, grabbed the mail, and stepped inside. He left the front door cracked and was just turning up the heat when Lisa's car pulled to the curb. She came up the walk and into his arms, and he kissed her like someone who'd been gone much longer than a few days.

"Man, it's starting to pour again," she said. "I don't think there's a leaf left on the trees now."

"Let me bump up the heat so the house is cozy when we get back. Then we'll grab dinner and I'll fill you in."

"Perfect. I'm starving. And I'm craving a glass of red wine."

Jack grinned. "Then off we go, my lady."

He drove them through the rain-slick streets toward the bistro. "I'm having the lamb shish kebab tonight," he said. "Spanakopita, basmati rice pilaf, the works."

"Do they serve eggplant there?"

He scanned the menu. "Yep. Eggplant moussaka. Layered with seasoned ground beef, topped with béchamel and Asiago, baked in the oven."

Lisa's eyes lit. "Yum. With that red wine."

"You got it. Tonight we celebrate being home and together."

The wine arrived, rich and dark. They clinked glasses.

"So," Lisa asked, "what did George say? Did he think we're crazy?"

Jack laughed. "He thought it was fascinating. He's studied time travel for years but never had a real case until now. He can't wait to dig in. He says it's complex and it's going to take a lot of research, but that's his happy place—equations."

"So... where does that leave us?" Lisa asked.

"He wants me to send him everything: my journal entries, notes, dates, names. All of it. He'll build a picture from there."

"And going back?" she asked quietly.

"He says we wait," Jack replied. "Winter's starting on the mountain. The portal isn't going anywhere in the short term. He wants us to rest, live our lives, make plans. When he's ready—and when conditions are safer—we might try one more trip. In the spring."

"That's a long way off," Lisa said, relaxing a little. "So we move forward in time for a change."

"I'll drink to that." Jack lifted his glass. "There is one more thing, though. To give him solid information, he thinks it'd help to take a drive up to Hood River. Just the town—not the mountain."

"Why?"

"Landscape, history, context," Jack said. "We can visit the museum, dig into the Native American history, see what's documented about the Watlala. The old village site is on the opposite bank of the river. Take Friday afternoon off, and we'll make a small adventure of it. I'll even buy you a burger at the Charburger."

Lisa smiled. "Okay. But this is the last trip up there for a while, right?"

"Right," Jack said. "Just one more look. From this side of time."

"Then I'm in," she said. "The museum sounds interesting."

They talked about Saturday, about ring shopping, about colors and settings. Jack raised his glass again, relieved to be sitting in the warm light of the bistro with no dark stranger in the corner. Tonight, the only spirits near them came from the bottle on the table, wrapping the two of them in a gentler, simpler kind of magic.

Chapter Nineteen

Mouth of the Hood River

"There is a road in the hearts of all of us, hidden and seldom traveled, that leads to an unknown, secret place."
~ Chief Luther Standing Bear, Oglala Sioux

The week passed quickly, the weekend always hovering just ahead. Jack picked Lisa up after her morning hours at work and they headed east toward Hood River. A clear October afternoon greeted them, sunlight pouring into the Columbia River Gorge. Long shadows reached deep into the canyon walls, touching pockets of flame-colored maples and oaks tucked between the dark vertical curtain of evergreens.

"How was work, Lisa?" Jack asked.

"I have no idea," she said, laughing. "I spent the whole morning thinking about today—our outing to Hood River—and tomorrow's shopping expedition."

Jack smiled and took the exit for the Charburger.

After parking, they walked toward the restaurant, passing a front porch full of relics and characters that looked like they'd stepped out of another century—Ma and Pa Kettle lookalikes, rusted farm implements, and weathered tools leaning against the walls. Inside, they ordered the famous Charburger and found a table near a window. While they waited, they wandered along the walls, reading old newspaper clippings and studying black-and-white photographs that had yellowed in place over decades.

"This is good," Lisa said around a bite of burger a few minutes later. "Great idea to eat here. I've never stopped in before."

"You didn't know what you were missing," Jack said. "I always swing by after hiking or skiing on the mountain. The food's solid and the history's everywhere. Newer places in town cater to the wind surfers, but this place... it feels like stepping back in time."

Lisa set down her hamburger and grabbed another napkin. "Was that a pun?"

Jack dipped a French fry in ketchup and smirked. "Didn't even realize I said it until it came out. But yeah—back in time. Guess that's my theme these days."

***

After lunch they took the marina exit and turned into the museum parking lot. Out on the river, a few wetsuited wind surfers were still braving the October breeze, neon sails bouncing across the choppy water. As they walked toward the entrance, Jack pointed to the footbridge spanning the Hood River.

"That's the exact spot of the old Watlala camp," he said quietly. "And where the fort stood, back in our last... adventure. We'll walk over after we're done in the museum."

Lisa stared at the bridge with an empty, thoughtful look, then nodded.

They paid the small admission fee and began winding their way through the exhibits. The first room focused on the early inhabitants: mid-Columbia Chinook tribes, maps and stories of Lewis and Clark, and the evolution of the river's name. The explorers had called it Labeasche River, after Francis Labiche. Later, in the days when starving travelers resorted to eating dogs to survive, it became Dog River. Eventually, in 1856, the name changed to Hood River after the mountain where its waters began.

Jack's pace slowed as he read every word on the interpretive panels. Lisa drifted ahead, drawn to the photographs.

Near the far wall, she stopped short, then turned sharply. "Jack. Come here. You need to see this."

"I will in a minute," he said. "I'm finishing this article."

"No," she insisted, her voice tight. "Now."

Jack crossed the room. "Which photo?"

"This one. Read the caption."

He stepped closer and felt his throat tighten.

"Missionaries Ward and Mary Weaver with seventeen members of the Watlala tribe who assisted in the building of their house—the two missionaries befriended and taught local natives the English language and ways of the white man."

They both stepped back. Jack pointed to one of the men in the photograph.

"Isn't that Running Horse?"

"It sure looks like him," Lisa whispered. "And those are the Weavers. I was inside that house."

In disbelief, they sank onto a nearby bench and sat in silence, fingers laced together.

The museum curator approached them, concern in her eyes. "Is everything all right? You look like you've seen a ghost. Can I get you a cup of water?"

"Sure," Jack said. "Water would be great."

"We're just... overwhelmed by some of the photos," he added.

She nodded and stepped away.

"Imagine if we hadn't time traveled," Lisa murmured. "We'd just walk through like anyone else and say, 'Oh look—old pictures.'"

Jack exhaled slowly. "I'd bet there's more in here we've brushed past without recognizing."

The curator returned with two paper cups. "Here you go. Feeling better?"

"Yes, thanks," Jack said. "We got a little lost in the history for a minute."

"It can be powerful," she said with a smile. "You can't truly go back in time, of course—but in a museum, you can get close."

Jack and Lisa managed polite smiles and sipped their water.

When the curator moved on, Lisa leaned closer. "I wanted to tell her everything. But yeah... no. She'd have us escorted out."

Curiosity tugged at Jack. He walked up to the front desk. "Excuse me. The photos and artifacts here are incredible. Do you have archived records for deeper research?"

"Why yes," the curator said. "On the mezzanine we have a computer with historical databases and file cabinets full of documents. We also stock several local history and Native American books in the gift shop. Are you interested in something specific?"

Jack glanced at Lisa, then back. "Not yet. I just wanted to know what's available in case I come back. I'm especially interested in the tribes that lived here."

She removed her glasses and smiled. "We do have quite a bit on that. Next time you're in town, plan for a longer visit."

"Will do," Jack said. "Thanks for all your help."

He rejoined Lisa at the door.

"That was surreal," Lisa said as they stepped outside. "Felt like we wandered into our own melodrama."

"I'm afraid to dig any deeper right now," Jack admitted. "We've seen enough for the moment. When I send everything to George, I'll suggest he come up here and comb through the archives himself."

Lisa nodded. "Good idea."

"The footbridge is over this way," Jack said. "C'mon."

They walked across the bridge and stopped midway to look down. Meltwater from Mount Hood roared beneath them, white and fast, racing toward the Columbia only a short distance away.

"Beautiful," Lisa said. "Hard to believe this is the same river from back then—and that we were... there."

Jack rested his arms on the railing. "Glacier runoff below us, the Columbia just ahead, and all those wind surfers trying to tame it."

He lifted his head, watching the colorful sails dart and lean on the distant swells. "They're relentless. Always out there, no matter the season."

They finished crossing and followed a dusty path into a vacant field on the far bank. Weeds and gravel stretched toward the water. Jack walked ahead, scuffing at the dirt with his shoe.

"What do you think?" he asked.

Lisa looked around. "Honestly? It just feels like an empty lot. What am I supposed to be seeing? The village is long gone."

Jack turned in a slow circle. "Don't you think it's strange? A prime strip of riverfront—right at the mouth of Hood River, with freeway access and views. Everything else nearby is developed. And this piece? Nothing. No buildings. No plaque. No marker. Just... vacancy."

Lisa threw up her hands. "What are you getting at, Jack?"

"I'm not sure yet," he said. "Just seems odd the old Watlala village site is the only untouched spot. It's almost like this patch of ground refuses to hold anything else."

Lisa folded her arms, shivering a little. "To tell you the truth, it creeps me out. They destroyed the village and built a fort here. I was held captive on this soil a few days ago—or a hundred and fifty years ago, depending on how you count. This land belonged to the Watlala. It should be sacred. But as for why it's empty now, I don't know if it matters."

Jack snapped his fingers. "Exactly. That's what's been bugging me. Sacred ground. That's why nothing stays here."

"You stopped pacing," Lisa said, "but now you're talking in circles."

He walked to the edge of the bank. The sunset burned low in the west, light pouring gold across the river. Lisa joined him, cheeks flushed pink in the cold autumn wind.

"There'll never be anything here," Jack said quietly. "Not for long, anyway. It's protected. The Great Spirit guarding it, maybe. We respect this place because of the people who lived here—and what happened to them. Our hearts led us right back to it."

Lisa's eyes shimmered. "You're probably right. For everyone else, this is just dead ground they drive past without noticing. But for the Watlala, this was everything. And now cars rush by at sixty-five miles per hour only yards away, and wind surfers play at the mouth of the river... all around a piece of land nobody sees."

Jack checked his watch. "It's almost five. Let's head back to the truck. I've got one more question for the curator before they close."

Lisa opted to stay in the car and get the heater going. Jack jogged back across the bridge and slipped inside the museum a few minutes before closing.

"Excuse me," he said.

The curator looked up from the paperwork on the counter and removed her glasses. "Back so soon?"

"We took a walk across the footbridge," Jack said. "We were just looking at the vacant property on the other side and I was curious—who owns that land?"

"The Port of Hood River," she replied. "Why do you ask?"

Jack leaned lightly on the counter. "It just struck me as odd that it's the only undeveloped piece of riverfront around here. Seems like prime real estate."

She tilted her head, intrigued. "Vacant, yes. But not for lack of trying. Private ownership has not been... successful."

"In what way?" Jack asked.

"The first development was a motel, built about fifty years ago," she said. "The night before its grand opening, the river flooded and swept the entire building into the Columbia. Years later, there were two more attempts. One was a self-storage facility, the other a tire shop. Both burned to the ground shortly after completion. After that, the Port took ownership and left it alone."

Jack let out a low whistle. "That's... something."

He hesitated, then asked, "Why isn't there any kind of historical marker on the property?"

She walked to the glass door and flipped the sign to CLOSED, then joined him again at the counter. "A marker?

We'd need documented significance to justify one. As far as the records indicate, it's just a location with a string of unfortunate business failures. The deeper historical importance of that particular plot... is unknown."

Jack shook his head. "None? Nothing at all?"

She studied him. "Mr....?"

"Bellard. Jack Bellard."

"Mr. Bellard," she said, "I've spent my life studying this stretch of the Gorge. I've never found anything concrete that would elevate that parcel to historical-site status. Just odd luck for the owners, I'm afraid."

Jack held the door for her as she switched off the lobby lights. "Well, thank you for the information. I still find it unusual that nothing has survived there. Business mishaps, maybe. But it feels like more than that. I left my card on the counter—if you ever do uncover anything about that piece of land, I'd love to hear it."

She locked the door behind him and watched through the glass as he crossed the lot and climbed into his truck.

"What did she say?" Lisa asked as he started the engine.

"She said the Port owns it. Three businesses tried to build there—a motel, a storage place, and a tire shop. One washed away in a flood. The other two burned to the ground right after they opened. After that, nobody touched it again. And as far as she knows, there's no official history on why the land matters."

Lisa shivered. "So the village is gone, the fort is gone, and nothing else is allowed to stay."

"Pretty much," Jack said, merging onto the freeway. "Sacred ground, even if nobody's written it down."

Darkness settled around them as they drove west toward Portland, the Gorge closing in like a familiar shadow. Home was ahead, lights waiting. Behind them, on a forgotten strip of riverbank, the wind moved through the grass of an empty field—refusing, even now, to forget.

Chapter Twenty

The Promise Ring

"Now you will feel no rain, for each of you will be the shelter for the other..."~Apache Wedding Blessing

Saturday couldn't come fast enough for Lisa. She was practically glowing, eager to slip a ring onto her finger from the man she had admired for years.

She pulled into Jack's driveway early that morning. Sunshine poured across the neighborhood—crisp, bright, one of those perfect November days when autumn clings to the trees by a few stubborn leaves. Thanksgiving was only weeks away.

Jack burst out the front door, a steaming cup of tea in hand. He slid into the passenger seat, leaned across, and kissed her.

"Okay," he grinned, "let's be off!"

Lisa laughed. "Let's get this show on the road."

"I barely slept last night," she admitted as she pulled away from the house.

"I'm sorry," Jack said, "but I bet you'll sleep tonight."

"Oh, absolutely—having you all to myself," she teased.

They merged onto the freeway.

"Any thoughts on a wedding date?" Jack asked.

"Well," she said, "lying awake last night, I kept thinking about it. I dreamed of an outdoor June wedding. But it's only November now—and that's a long stretch to wait before becoming Mrs. Jack Bellard."

"June sounds perfect," Jack said. "Weather might be iffy, but that's what event canopies are for." He chuckled. "Either way, we'll be together. And we've got a lot to figure out—two houses, one life to merge…"

"Exactly," Lisa smiled. "Two of us becoming one story. You can keep me warm on those cold nights. I'll expect plenty of cuddling."

Jack pointed ahead. "Take the next exit. Left on Everett, then left on Twelfth. Parking should be right there."

They pulled to the curb outside the jewelry store.

"Do you think we'll find anything here?" Lisa asked. "The big mall stores have more choices."

"Oh, trust me—we'll find something. These folks repaired my pocket watch. They've got amazing pieces."

Inside, the shop was quiet and smelled faintly of old wood polish and metal. Dozens of rings sparkled under warm yellow lights.

"What's your style—white gold or yellow?" Jack asked.

"I'm not sure," Lisa said. "Something old-fashioned, not flashy."

Just then, the jeweler emerged from the back. His face brightened.

"Well now—haven't I seen you before?"

Jack smiled and shook his hand. "Yes sir. You repaired my old pocket watch."

"How's it running?"

"Perfect, as long as I wind it."

The jeweler chuckled. "Fine piece from the eighteen hundreds. I imagine it's traveled many places."

Lisa nudged Jack, reminding him not to engage too deeply in that line of conversation.

"We're looking for wedding rings," Jack said quickly. "We'll browse a bit."

They moved slowly down the cases, studying row after row of glimmering bands.

"So many," Lisa murmured. "But not the one. I can't imagine going to multiple stores—I'd be dazzled blind."

An hour passed.

The jeweler returned. "No luck yet?"

Lisa shook her head. "Beautiful pieces, but not quite what I picture."

He studied her for a moment, then lowered his voice. "I do have another collection. Old. Antique pieces—new and used—kept in the back. Shall I bring it out?"

Lisa and Jack exchanged a glance.

"Yes, please," Lisa said.

The old man disappeared through a back door.

Lisa whispered, "Jack... does something feel strange about this place?"

"Maybe a little," Jack said. "But not in a bad way."

He was still speaking when the jeweler returned. He carried a heavy oak display case and a small leather-bound journal.

The box looked older than the shop—older than anything in the bright modern display cases.

He set it near the front window, wiped away a layer of dust, and began unlocking the brass clasp with a worn, old-fashioned key. With a soft creak, the lid lifted.

Jack and Lisa both inhaled sharply.

Rows of antique ring sets lay nestled on velvet. Each pair had a tiny handwritten tag tied to it.

"These," the jeweler said, "are pieces you don't see anymore. Some nearly as old as the city itself."

Lisa leaned in—and froze.

"Jack... that one." She pointed to a set labeled 17.

The jeweler removed the rings and placed them gently on a small velvet pad.

Lisa barely breathed as she lifted the bride's ring. She slid it onto her finger.

It fit. Perfectly.

Jack reached for the men's band. It slid onto his finger with the same impossible perfection.

"Uncanny," the jeweler murmured. "No adjustments needed at all."

The old-mine–cut diamond caught a streak of sunlight from the window. Light fractured upward, shimmering across the shop ceiling like a handful of tiny stars. The petal-shaped gold setting gave the stone a soft, vintage elegance; the band itself gleamed smooth and warm.

Jack studied the two rings, a strange flicker of recognition tugging at him. He couldn't place it. Maybe he didn't want to place it.

"Nice, huh?" he said, hugging her gently.

"More than nice—I love it."

The jeweler leaned back with a quiet grunt, pressing a hand beneath his chin.

He opened the old journal, thumbing through delicate pages.

"Handmade in Georgia," he read aloud. "Eighteen-karat rose gold. One-carat old mine–cut diamond. Color nearly colorless, clarity described as extremely bright and lively. According to this... on a clear mountain day, it would sparkle for miles."

Jack and Lisa exchanged a look—one full of the unspoken.

He cleared his throat. "Anything else we should know about them?"

"Well," the jeweler murmured, "interesting note here. The set was purchased at Alexander's Jewelry on Northwest Front Street. Fully paid for. But never picked up. Sat for decades before coming to my father, probably in an estate auction. Quite old, I'm afraid—likely as old as your pocket watch."

Lisa stared at the ring, captivated.

Jack asked softly, "Does it list the customer?"

"Name's too faded to read." The jeweler squinted at the page. "Ink from that era doesn't hold well."

Jack held out his hand. "May I?"

The jeweler passed the journal. Jack studied the entries. The date... smudged, but unmistakable enough to raise the hairs on his arms, 1867.

He closed the book and handed it back without a word to Lisa.

Meanwhile, Lisa was searching the velvet-lined case. "Isn't there a band for the bride? Shouldn't there be a wedding ring and an engagement ring?"

The jeweler shook his head.

"Not back then. A woman often wore just the wedding ring. Sometimes, before the ceremony, the man would give her a birthstone ring—a sort of promise ring—worn on the opposite hand."

Jack met Lisa's eyes. He knew exactly where this was going.

"How about we follow the old tradition?" he said softly. "A birthstone ring until the wedding."

She smiled. "Why not? And yes... it can double as a promise ring. You do promise, don't you, Jack?"

He wrapped his arms around her. "Always."

The jeweler chuckled approvingly.

A moment later he cleared his throat. "Let's choose that birthstone, then. This way." He guided them to another case. "Now, remind me—your name was Lisa, correct?"

"Yes sir."

"And your birth month?"

"October."

"Ah! Then an opal. Do you own one yet?"

"No, but I've always wanted one."

"Well then—have a look. Something in here might tickle your fancy." He grinned and ambled back to the wedding set. "And while you browse... shall I box up the rings?"

"Oh yes, please," Jack said.

They removed the bands from their fingers reluctantly and handed them over.

"How much do I owe you for them?" Jack asked.

The jeweler sighed almost wistfully.

"Well... they were paid for once already. But I suppose I must charge you again." He flipped a few more pages in the journal. "Let me see if the pricing is noted. I'll be right back."

As he vanished into the back room, Lisa exhaled.

"This is the strangest day since we returned," she whispered. "Those rings... Jack, it feels like the past is somehow alive in this place. Same era as your watch. It's like everything is coming full circle."

Jack nodded. "Maybe too full."

"I wish I could wear the ring now," she said softly. "But waiting until June—maybe that will make the moment special. Don't you think so?"

"Yeah," he said. "I do."

She nudged him playfully. "You know... I think you missed my birthday."

Jack froze. "Oh no... when was it?"

"Don't worry about it—we were a little busy at the time." She smirked. "Wakanda and I were locked up at the fort, remember?"

Jack grimaced. "Still... I should've known."

"You couldn't have. There's still a lot we don't know about each other. But that'll be the fun part leading up to the wedding. Besides..." She tapped his shoulder. "Your birthday is in April."

His head whipped toward her. "How'd you know that?"

"A little bird."

"Silly One suits you perfectly," Jack said. "I'll come up with a name for you too. Beware."

She raised an eyebrow. "Whatever you say, Jack."

He nodded toward the case. "Any ring catch your eye yet?"

"Yes." She lifted a delicate opal ring, slipped it onto her finger, and walked toward the window. The sunlight scattered inside the stone—greens, blues, amber flecks dancing like a tiny storm. "Jack," she whispered, "it's perfect."

She twirled once, admiring the opal's soft fire. "You still need to propose here in the present, don't you?"

"I figured," Jack said with a grin. "But you've got to admit—that proposal in the meadow was hard to beat."

Lisa's smile softened. "I'll remember lying beside you out there forever. How do I ever tell anyone I was proposed to in 1867?"

The jeweler returned with the boxed rings and offered Lisa a gentle smile. She slipped off the opal and handed it back to him.

"A lovely choice," he said. "A beautiful placeholder for the real one."

Lisa brushed a finger across the ring. "This isn't from the nineteenth century, is it?"

He chuckled. "Oh heavens, no. The opal itself may be ancient, but the setting is modern—probably only a few months in the shop. No worries there."

Jack settled the bill and thanked the jeweler, extending a grateful handshake. Together, he and Lisa walked toward the door—only to hear the old man following behind them.

"Jack and Lisa?"

They turned.

"Do come see me again, will you?"

Jack smiled. "We sure will."

Lisa nodded warmly. "Of course."

"Well then." The jeweler clasped his hands. "May the two of you enjoy every blessing the world has to offer. And may your days be long upon the earth."

Lisa glanced back as they crossed the street. In her rearview mirror, the jeweler still stood outside his shop, waving to them like a sentinel from another time.

Jack reached across the seat and took her hand. They shared a quiet smile as the Willamette River came into view.

"Hey," Jack said softly, "I'm starving. You?"

"Yes—after everything that just happened, I'm famished," said Lisa.

"Then how about—?"

"Don't tell me," she cut in, laughing. "The bistro?"

"Well... we'll be driving right past it."

Lisa pulled to the curb outside the Bistro on Lombard. Jack opened her door, escorting her inside the warm little restaurant where they claimed a window table. He ordered his usual lunch, and Lisa—still floating a little—decided to match him.

When the plates arrived, Lisa lowered her voice. "So... we have the rings. How do we want to do this?"

Jack shrugged playfully. "I can surprise you with a proposal and the promise ring... or we can do it right here and now."

"Jack," she said, laughing softly, "you proposed a long time ago. A ring now is perfectly fitting. Besides... you're not topping that meadow."

"Fair enough."

He slid the opal ring from his pocket, took her hand, and spoke with a sincerity that quieted the room around them.

"Lisa... I promise to always love and cherish you. I want you beside me for the rest of our lives."

He slipped the ring onto her finger.

Her eyes shimmered. "I accept. And my dream finally came true. Took us long enough."

Jack leaned back, absorbing her happiness. "So, outdoor wedding in June. What day?"

"Well, that depends on the location," Lisa said. "That decides everything."

Jack considered this. "You want to get married on the mountain?"

"I thought of that too. But with all our... adventures there, and your past life—would it be distracting? We still don't have closure."

"I know," Jack said. "But maybe that's the point. Maybe marrying there gives us the closure."

"Or we could do it at the coast," Lisa countered. "You know how much I love the beach."

"True. But the weather..."

"Fog," Lisa added. "And wind."

Jack nodded. "On the mountain, we're above the low clouds. I once went to a wedding at Timberline Lodge—it was gorgeous. Trail ceremony, the peak of Mount Hood glowing behind them."

Lisa's eyes brightened. "That sounds incredible. Let's do that."

He smiled. "I can picture it already."

They lingered over their meal, chatting about guest lists, colors, vows, what to wear—filling in all the quiet spaces of two lives becoming one. Both were foster kids. Both grew up without family. Yet here they were, planning something that felt like a beginning neither ever expected.

By the time they stood, the sky had turned dark beyond the window. The return drive carried a peaceful hush between them, the kind reserved for two people who feel the future settling in.

At Jack's place, they curled up on the couch in front of the fireplace with a steaming mug of hot chocolate—leaning into the warmth crackling before them.

"We have so much to be thankful for," Lisa murmured, resting her head on his shoulder.

"We sure do," Jack agreed. "Hard to believe a couple of months ago I was just talking about needing time away. And now..."

"It was meant to be," Lisa said.

Jack suddenly stood. "Oh—I forgot something."

"What?" she asked.

He fetched the small curio box from his office. "I'm putting the wedding rings where they belong until June."

"Why in that box?"

Jack smiled gently. "Because without that dream... without that box... we might never have come together."

"There," he said, closing the lid. "Waiting for June. Mysterious... but perfect too."

Lisa slipped her arms around him, and together they looked at the box that had carried so much of their journey.

Weeks slipped by. For Thanksgiving, Jack took Lisa to Sunriver, Oregon. They feasted in the Great Hall, watched the resort glow with Christmas lights, skied through whispering snowfall, and rode a horse-drawn sleigh across fields blanketed in white.

Christmas came and went. New Year's followed. They celebrated with friends from Lisa's office, sharing smiles that held something deeper, steadier, permanent.

The past began to fade a little. Not forgotten—never forgotten—but softened. They rarely spoke of it. And each night, Jack still whispered a quiet goodnight to Lawitha as he glanced at the dream catcher hanging in his bedroom.

But winter stayed silent. No visions. No callings. No footsteps from long ago. Just peace—for now.

Chapter Twenty-One

My Shadow

"We did not think of the great open plains, the beautiful rolling hills and the winding streams with tangled growth, as 'wild.' Only to the white man was nature a 'wilderness,' and only to him was the land 'infested' with 'wild' animals and 'savage' people. To us it was home. Earth was beautiful and we were surrounded with the blessings of the Great Mystery."
— *Chief Standing River, Lakota*

Jack was settling in with a cup of tea when his cellphone buzzed.

"Jack, do you have a minute?" came the familiar voice on the other end.

Jack lifted the phone to his ear. "Sure—what's up? I haven't heard from you for a while."

"Well, that's by design," said George Lawson, chuckling softly. "You weren't supposed to think about any of this for months. How's the wedding planning going?"

"Oh, great. Outdoor wedding in late June is the current idea."

"Outdoors? Near Mount Hood?" George teased.

"Don't laugh," Jack replied. "We've tossed around a few spots—the coast, Timberline Lodge, central Oregon. Still deciding. So what's the real reason you called?"

George cleared his throat. "I hate to interrupt domestic bliss, but I've finished most of my research. To complete the final calculations, I need to go through the portal immediately. I have to take samples on-site. It can't wait for spring."

Jack leaned back, watching gentle snow drift down outside his window. "George... have you looked outside?"

"I know, I know—it's mid-January. Heavy snow, tough travel. But it has to be done."

Jack sighed. "I'll go if you think it's necessary. These past months... honestly, they've been tough. I've tried putting all of this out of my head."

"I understand," said George softly. "Can you get away tomorrow?"

"Sure. Anything to get closer to answers."

"Good. Bring your watch. I'll be ready at seven-thirty—pick me up at the university."

"See you then," Jack said.

"Take care, Jack. We're making progress."

***

He went to bed early but forced himself to do one more thing—call Lisa. She didn't answer, and he didn't want to leave a detailed message. He simply said he was turning in early, then climbed under the covers.

Sleep swept him away quickly. As always, the dream catcher hung above his headboard. And as always, his dreams drifted to Lawitha—soft, warm, and bittersweet. Even with a wedding on the horizon, part of him still lived a split life, still carried two loves, two pasts, two versions of himself. The only way forward was closure, whatever shape that might take.

His phone rang at dawn. He jolted awake. Lisa.

"Thanks for calling me back," he said.

"You bet. Why all the early calls? What's going on?" she asked.

Jack hesitated. "Let me explain it the best I can. I'm... going back to the portal tomorrow. Just briefly. Maybe an hour."

Lisa's breath caught. "What? Why now?"

"George needs to take measurements to finish his equations. We won't go far—just to the forest edge and the meadow."

"What kind of measurements?"

"I didn't ask."

"Jack, it's snowing. Roads could be dangerous."

"I know. But I've got four-wheel drive and studs on all four tires."

"That's not what I'm worried about," said Lisa. "What about the portal? What if something changed? What if you can't get back? We're getting married in a few months, Jack. I can't lose you."

"Nothing's going to happen. George wouldn't go if he thought there was risk. He's careful. And he's brilliant."

"I want to go with you."

"No way. You stay home."

"So it's safe for you but not for me?"

"Lisa..." His voice gentled. "We both need answers. You know that."

She sighed. "The last two months have been peaceful. I almost forgot how much this weighed on us. But if he says it's necessary..."

"It'll be fine. I'll call the moment we're back at the truck."

"I love you," she whispered.

"I love you too. Sleep well."

Before drifting off, he whispered toward the dream catcher, "Good night, Lawitha."

***

Snow fell all night—light but steady—leaving six inches by morning. Jack arrived at PSU to find George standing outside under an awning with two bulging bags at his feet.

"Good morning!" George called cheerfully. "Nice day for a trip to the sunny past, don't you think?"

"I just hope everything hasn't changed over there," Jack muttered, helping load the gear.

George climbed in. "Everything will go smoothly. I can feel it."

"How?"

"Oh, I believe in optimism and leaps of faith."

As they headed east on I-84, snow whipped across the freeway in swirling white sheets. George reviewed his notes while Jack focused on the road.

"So what exactly are you measuring?" Jack asked.

"Air samples, soil samples, solar angle readings—and something special." George tapped a compact device in his lap. "I modified a Swiss chronometer. It should give us the exact date and time once we're through."

"How without satellites?"

George smiled. "My own invention. If it works, it'll be a breakthrough."

Jack laughed. "Mad scientist."

George smirked. "Writers live in their own worlds too, you know."

The deeper they drove into the gorge, the worse visibility became. But the truck held steady. When they finally turned toward the trailhead, Jack spotted the fresh tracks of a recent plow.

"Lucky us," he said. "If this lot hadn't been cleared, we'd be stuck."

Five feet of snow blanketed the forest, though it thinned under the towering evergreens. They shouldered their packs and started down the trail.

"Careful along the riverbank," Jack said. "Snow can hide an icy edge. You slip in that water, you're done."

"I'll follow your lead," said George, brushing snow from his hat.

They trudged through swirling powder, occasionally showered by clumps of snow shaken loose from Douglas fir branches. When they reached the rock outcropping holding the fallen log bridge, George stared upward.

"It looks... challenging."

Jack smirked. "It is. Let me tie off the rope first."

He climbed carefully, brushed snow from the log, secured the rope, and hauled the packs up. Then he belly-crawled across the frozen log, signaling for George to follow.

Minutes later, both stood on the opposite bank, breath steaming in the warming air beneath the ancient canopy.

Soon the snow thinned. Ferns unfurled beneath their boots.

"It's getting warmer," Jack said, unzipping his parka.

George nearly glowed with excitement. "Wow. After all these years of theory... to actually step into the past—this is incredible."

They shed their heavy layers, leaving them in a pile, and continued toward the forest edge.

When the sunlight broke through, George inhaled sharply. "Spectacular."

Jack led him to the fallen log in the meadow—his familiar resting place. "This looks safe," he said. "Nobody around."

George unpacked instruments like a field surgeon preparing tools. "Ready to pinpoint our date?"

Jack grinned. "I'm guessing eighteen-sixty-seven."

The modified chronometer spun, clicked, and stopped.

"One thirty in the afternoon," George announced, "July sixteenth, eighteen hundred sixty-seven."

Jack pulled out his ancient pocket watch. "Matches perfectly."

"Remarkable," George said. "Now for time-flow measurements."

While he worked, Jack wandered a few steps away, thinking of Running Horse, the tribe, the fort, the chase—everything he'd lived through here.

"Jack," George called. "Come look at this."

"What's up?"

"Your pocket watch keeps perfect time back home, right?"

"Like a charm."

George gave him a strange look. "Then this makes no sense. According to these readings, time is barely moving here. A sixty-to-one ratio. For every sixty seconds of our time, only one second passes here. So how is your watch synchronized?"

Jack had no answer.

George scribbled furiously, took photos, recorded measurements of sun angle and humidity, and stepped back to take in a long, thoughtful breath.

"This place..." he whispered. "It's calling you, Jack. Waiting for you. A wilderness and a mystery."

Jack swallowed hard. "What now?"

"We'll analyze everything. My colleague and I will run simulations. Then we'll decide our next steps—carefully."

Jack nodded.

Then George froze.

He slowly lifted his gaze, eyes widening. He took out a handkerchief, wiped his brow, and stared at the ground in front of him.

"Jack," he said quietly, "come here."

Jack walked over, puzzled. "What is it?"

George pointed at the snow-dappled grass. "Look. What do you see?"

Jack squinted. "Your shadow."

"Right," George said. "Now look in front of you."

Jack turned. The sunlight stretched across the meadow—bright, warm, clear.

But the ground in front of him was empty.

No silhouette. No outline. Nothing.

Jack blinked, stepped sideways, then forward, then back again, searching for any trace of himself.

His voice cracked. "George... where's my shadow?"

"That," George whispered, "is exactly what I'm asking."

Jack's face went pale. He looked down, then at George, then down again. "How is this possible?"

George didn't answer immediately. Instead, he lifted his camera, snapped a photo of Jack, and checked the display. "Here—see for yourself."

Jack stared at the image. George's shadow fell across the meadow behind him, long and dark.

Jack's side of the picture was untouched by darkness. As if the light refused to acknowledge he existed.

"I don't... I don't understand," Jack murmured.

George took another photo—this time of himself—then handed the camera to Jack. "My shadow is there. Yours isn't."

Jack swallowed hard. "Does this mean something's wrong with me? Am I... fading? Am I running out of time?"

George shook his head slowly. "No. I don't think this is the end of anything."

He placed a reassuring hand on Jack's shoulder.

"I think," he said gently, "this is the beginning."

Interlude - Lisa's Refection

Lisa stood at her bedroom window, the opal ring still warm on her finger. Evening had settled softly over the neighborhood, the winter sky washed in violet and fading gold. She lifted her hand again, letting the ring catch the last scraps of light. The tiny fire-colored flashes inside the stone seemed alive—breathing almost. Like the heart of some distant ember.

She exhaled, smiling to herself.

Mrs. Jack Bellard.

She had imagined those words for years, quietly, privately—dreams she told no one, not even Wakanda. But now they were real. Real enough that her heart felt too full for her ribcage.

And yet... something else tugged at her.

A faint note of unease she couldn't name.

Lisa walked away from the window and sat on the edge of her bed. The house hummed with its familiar stillness, but she couldn't shake the sensation that she wasn't entirely alone. Not in a frightening way—more like someone was thinking of her from far away, brushing against her thoughts the way wind brushes a field of tall grass. Gentle. Searching. Sad.

She pressed her palm to her forehead.

"This is silly," she whispered.

But the feeling didn't fade.

It had been that way since Jack first told her about the strange events up on Mount Hood. Since he showed her the dream catcher. Since she learned he carried pieces of a life that wasn't wholly his... and yet was. She tried not to dwell on the other woman from that other time. It didn't feel like jealousy. More like standing near the shadow of a story too big to fully understand.

She rose, opened her nightstand drawer, and took out the old photo of Jack she'd kept tucked away for years—long before they were ever together. He looked younger, wind-tousled, wearing a half-smile like he didn't know whether life was about to bruise him or bless him.

"You came back to me," she murmured.

Her fingers brushed the dream catcher Jack had once let her borrow when she couldn't sleep. She'd returned it the next morning, unsettled by dreams she couldn't recall but could still feel—sun-warm grasses, echoing drumbeats, a voice calling a name she didn't recognize.

She closed the drawer, though the memory clung to her like a faint fragrance.

"I won't lose you," she said softly.

Her phone buzzed—a simple goodnight text from Jack. She smiled, touching the screen as gently as if she could reach through it.

Lisa slipped under the covers but lay awake, watching the opal glint faintly in the dark.

Whatever storm Jack had been through, whatever strange world he had once walked in...she would walk beside him now.

Through the mystery.

Through the fear.

Through whatever tomorrow asked of them.

And if the past tried to tug him away again?

She would tug back.

Hard.

She placed her hand over the opal ring and whispered into the dark—not to Jack, but to the unseen presence she had sensed all evening:

"You had him once.

But he's mine now.

And I will fight for him."

The room fell still.

Outside, the wind sighed against the glass—almost, it seemed, in acknowledgment.

Interlude — Jack's Reflection

Jack sat alone in his living room, the fire burned down to a bed of soft orange embers. The house was quiet, but his mind wouldn't settle. He held the old pocket watch in his palm, feeling the faint, ticking pulse beneath the brass casing—steady, ancient, familiar. Almost like a heartbeat that didn't belong to him.

He turned it over again, tracing the engraving with his thumb.

It still felt strange sometimes... how one small object could anchor him to two completely different lives.

Two loves.

Two futures.

He closed his eyes and leaned back, letting the crackling hush of the fire settle around him.

Lisa.

The thought of her brought a warmth that spread through his chest. The opal ring he had slipped onto her finger glowed in his memory like a lantern in fog. He had loved her for so long in quiet ways—admired her strength, her humor, her gentleness. And now, finally, they were building a life together. A wedding to plan. A future to shape.

But another name tugged at him still.

Lawitha.

Not in a romantic way anymore—at least he told himself so—but in the way one sometimes misses a dream long after waking. A life lived in a world he never should have touched. A heart he once held in a time that was never truly his.

He let out a long breath.

"Why can't it ever be simple?" he whispered.

He set the pocket watch on the table and rubbed the bridge of his nose. That strange sense of being pulled—forward and backward at the same time—wouldn't leave him. And tomorrow he'd step through the portal again. Not for long, George had said. Just a few readings. A quick trip.

Jack didn't believe in "quick" when it came to the past anymore.

He rose from the couch and wandered to the window. Outside, snow drifted down in slow, silvery spirals. He rested his hand on the cold glass.

What am I still afraid of?

He knew the answer immediately.

Not the portal.

Not the strange time-warping meadow.

Not even the risk of getting stuck there.

He was afraid of the part of himself that still lingered in that other world. The part that felt unfinished. Untethered. The part that whispered in his dreams.

The part that had once whispered Lawitha's name.

Jack closed his eyes, letting the memory fade.

"Lisa," he murmured. Saying her name grounded him, like stepping onto solid earth after drifting too long at sea.

She was his home now.

He turned from the window, walked toward the bedroom, and paused beneath the dream catcher hanging above his headboard. The feathers stirred faintly in the warm air rising from the fireplace vents—almost as though acknowledging him.

He touched the woven ring gently.

"I will come back," he whispered. "To her. To the life I chose."

He lay down, pulling the covers up to his chest, and let sleep begin to soften the edges of the room. As he drifted, one last thought rose clear in his mind—quiet, steady, resolute:

Whatever happens tomorrow, whatever strange answers they uncover, his future was already chosen.

Lisa.

Always Lisa.

And if the past still had one last grip on him... he would find a way to let it go. For her. For them.

Interlude — George's Reflection

The university lab was quiet at this hour—just the low hum of ventilation and the soft tick of instruments settling as the building cooled for the night. George Lawson stood alone in the pale glow of a desk lamp, sleeves rolled up, glasses perched low on his nose as he traced a line of numbers across the page for the third time.

He stopped.

Stared.

Rechecked the variables.

"No... that can't be right."

But the equations didn't change.

He leaned back in his chair, the old wood squeaking under his weight. Outside the windows, snow drifted in gentle spirals under the campus floodlights, a calm contrast to the knot tightening in his chest.

He lifted the chronometer prototype from the table—the same one he would take through the portal tomorrow. Its gears clicked faintly, a precise, mechanical heartbeat.

Sixty-to-one.

He whispered the ratio under his breath again. The chalkboard behind him was already filled with arcs, time dilation curves, and a scattering of gravitational symbols that even his brightest grad students had trouble following. He always told them that time was elastic, playful, unpredictable. But this...

This was something else.

A tear in the fabric.

A hinge.

A doorway.

A place where time didn't just bend—it waited.

George rubbed his face with both hands. "Jack... what have you been walking into?"

He wasn't afraid for himself—not really. He was a scientist; he had lived his whole life hunting phenomena that shouldn't exist. But Jack? Jack had already been changed by whatever lay on the other side of that forest.

And the shadow.

That missing shadow kept gnawing at him.

A sign of... what?

A thinning?

A fading?

A divergence?

He shoved the thought aside, but it crept back immediately.

He opened Jack's file drawer and removed the few items he'd collected—soil samples, sketches, map notes scribbled over and over until the original lines had vanished beneath corrections.

At the bottom was Jack's first written description of the meadow:

Familiar but distorted... like remembering a dream I'm still inside of.

George exhaled long and slow.

He had promised Jack they were "making progress."

That wasn't a lie.

But it wasn't the truth he was worried about.

The truth was sitting on the desk in front of him—cold, mathematical, unavoidable.

If time ran differently there...

If Jack's shadow didn't behave like a body tied fully to this world...

If the portal aligned more with Jack's presence than with any fixed spatial coordinate...

Then it wasn't just Jack visiting the past.

The past might be pulling him.

George clicked off the desk lamp, leaving only the luminescent green glow of the chronometer dial in the dark.

"Tomorrow," he whispered, "we find out what you really are, Jack Bellard... and what that place wants from you."

Outside, a gust of wind rattled the window.

The chronometer ticked once, sharp and metallic.

And the lab settled back into silence—waiting, like the meadow.

Epilogue — From Jack's Journal

January 17th

I'm writing this by lamplight, long after Lisa has gone to bed. The house is quiet—too quiet, almost. The kind of quiet that makes you aware of your own heartbeat.

Today was... unsettling.

I can still feel the warmth of the meadow sun on my face, and yet my boots are drying by the fire from the snow I slogged through only hours ago. Two worlds clinging to me at once.

Two timelines.

Two lives.

George tried to hide it, but I saw the fear behind his calculations. I'm not sure what frightened him more—the numbers, or the way I didn't cast a shadow.

I didn't tell Lisa. How could I? She worries enough. I can't add another weight to her heart when she's been nothing but joy and light to mine. The opal on her finger glowed like a tiny sunrise tonight. She deserves full mornings. Not half-truths.

Still... something is shifting. Something is changing in me. I feel stretched thin, as if part of me lingers in that meadow long after my body has returned home. Maybe George is right. Maybe time over there doesn't run—it waits.

Sometimes, when I close my eyes, I hear drums.

Sometimes I hear my name, but not the one Lisa speaks.

Sometimes I feel warmth on my left side, like someone standing close, just out of sight.

Lisa felt something tonight too—I could tell by her voice. There's no hiding between two worlds forever. Not without hurting someone I love.

I don't know what the next step is.

Maybe George will find an answer in his equations.

Maybe the past will call again.

Maybe I'll find a way to silence it.

Or maybe a man can love two different lives without losing himself.

I hope so. Because I don't want to lose either world.

—J.B.

The ink dries slowly on the page, curling slightly at the edges—as though even the paper knows something is beginning.

PART II Back in the Day

Chapter Twenty-Two

Jolly Old England

"All men were made brothers. The earth is the mother of all people, and all people should have equal rights upon it... You might as well expect the rivers to run backward as that any man who was born free should be content when penned up and denied liberty to go where he pleases."— Chief Joseph

Dense fog pressed low over London, cloaking rooftops and cobblestones in a damp gray shroud. A steady drizzle tapped the darkened streets, carrying with it the reek of soot from a thousand chimney pots and the tidal stench rising off the Thames. The gas lamps, choked by the murk, cast only faint halos of light—weak little islands in a sea of shadow.

But far from the crowded lanes of lower London, the home of Oliver Butler glowed warm and bright. Rain traced delicate patterns on the clear windowpanes, revealing a spacious den wrapped in amber firelight. Floor-to-ceiling cherrywood shelves lined the walls, gas sconces brushing the spines of books with a soft golden sheen. A teapot steamed beside fine china cups.

Oliver checked his pocket watch yet again. Jonathan was ten minutes late. Not surprising, he thought, pacing before the fire. He'll come breezing in at any moment, excuses in hand.

A knock sounded behind him.

Without turning, Oliver said, "Come in, Jonathan."

A young, broad-shouldered man stepped through the door.

"Hello, Father."

Oliver gestured sharply toward the chair opposite his own.

"Late. Yes, indeed—late."

Jonathan sank into the seat. "My writing group was having a discussion and—"

"The writing group," Oliver scoffed. "Can you not keep your commitments? Must everything wait upon your whims?"

"Why must I always schedule an appointment to see you?" Jonathan countered. "You're my father."

"And you," Oliver said, "are a son who is rarely present."

Jonathan sighed. "We've been over this. Let's just get to why you asked me here."

Oliver pressed his fingers together. "Several months since Cambridge. You know my offer. Have you reached a decision?"

Jonathan ran a hand through his wavy brown hair. He dreaded this moment.

"You want me in the company, but you also know what I want—"

Oliver cut him off. "Why you majored in literature, I shall never know. What practical use is that? Philosophy would have been better than this... scribbling."

Jonathan's frustration boiled. "Father, I loved my studies. You gave me the opportunity to learn, and I'm grateful. But it is my life. I want to write—share ideas, stories, reflections. I want to contribute."

Oliver stood, hands shoved deep in his pockets, staring down at him.

"Share with the world? And what, exactly, does that mean?"

Jonathan steadied himself. "It means I'm going to America."

Oliver choked. "America? In heaven's name—for what purpose?"

"I told you. To write. To experience the West and send stories home."

"Rubbish!" Oliver barked. "Who wishes to read about Americans and their lawless frontier? Corruption and savagery."

"You hear only rumors," Jonathan said sharply. "Do you remember Richard Shively?"

"That scoundrel?" Oliver snapped. "How is he involved?"

"He encouraged me to pursue writing. He wants to represent my work. He lives in Portland, in the Oregon Territory."

As the tension slowly rose like heat from the fireplace, Mrs. Adeline Butler swept into the room.

"What is all this noise? My goodness, it sounds like a boxing match in here."

"Adeline," Oliver said, "do you know what our son intends? He wants to run off to America with that Shively fellow and get into God-knows-what!"

Adeline crossed her arms. "Although I would rather he stay in England, would you deny any man his liberty to travel? It is the mid-eighteenth century, Ollie, not the dark ages. It could be a marvelous opportunity."

"A marvelous opportunity for disaster," Oliver muttered. "Wild tribes behind every tree."

Jonathan shook his head. "Father, didn't you take risks when you founded your trading company? Exploration is no different for me. Beyond any city gate lies discovery—and risk, yes, but also meaning."

Oliver loosened his collar, breathing hard. Adeline quickly poured him a brandy.

"You'll cause your heart to burst," she warned. "Let him go."

Silence hung for a moment as Oliver regained his composure.

"So," he said, "when do you intend to start this grand adventure? And how, pray tell, do you plan to cross the ocean?"

"Next month," Jonathan said. "I'll book passage on one of the ships leaving up north."

Oliver slapped the arm of his chair. "One of those rat-infested, scurvy-breeding vessels for transmigrants? Absolutely not. If you insist on this folly, you will go properly. I know the captain of the Atlantic Sailing Line. I'll speak with him. Can you endure two months at sea? The weather is ruthless."

"Father, I could endure twice that. Thank you."

"Don't thank me," Oliver muttered. "Your mother would never forgive me otherwise. And truth be told—I was much like you once."

Adeline smiled, poured a second brandy, and raised her glass.

But Oliver lowered his, his expression changing. "Jonathan, before this goes any further... have you spoken to Emily?"

Jonathan's heart faltered. "Not yet. I needed to speak to her father first."

Oliver sighed. "It will be a difficult task. She will be heartbroken."

Jonathan nodded slowly. "One of two people in this world I truly love... and one I now must disappoint."

Adeline touched her husband's shoulders, blinking back tears.

"I will visit her in the morning," Jonathan said. "I pray the right words come to me."

Later, the rain pattered softly against the windowpanes while Oliver and Adeline sat quietly before the fire.

***

Jonathan barely slept. Thoughts of Emily tangled through his dreams—her smile, her voice, the life he could have had if he stayed.

When he entered the dining room, his mother looked up. "How did you sleep?"

"As poorly as expected. Where's Father?"

"He left early to meet the ship captain." She set down her teacup. "What will you say to Emily?"

"That's the trouble, Mother. I know what I must say, not how to say it kindly."

She reached across the table, grasping his hand.

"Speak from the heart. Dickens said, 'A loving heart is the truest wisdom.' Let that guide you."

Jonathan pressed her hand gratefully. "My heart speaks of America. But when I picture my departure, I do not see Emily at the city gates."

***

The family carriage rolled through Crestshire, sunlight breaking through the trees after weeks of fog. A servant opened the door at the grand estate, and Emily met him at the entrance, radiant as ever.

"Oh, Jonathan—it is so nice to see you this fine day."

He hugged her, guiding her inside. "You look enchanting."

They sat together on a red velvet loveseat as a servant brought tea and crumpets.

"It feels wonderful to see sunshine again," Emily said.

"Yes," Jonathan replied. "It lifted my spirits as I rode here."

"So," she asked gently, "what are you writing these days?"

He hesitated.

Then took her hands in his.

"Dearest Emily... I don't know how to tell you—"

She pressed her fingers lightly to his lips.

"Say no more. I've seen it in your eyes for months. You wish to go to America."

Jonathan's breath caught. "How did you—?"

"I know you," she said softly. "You love me deeply. But you also yearn to write, to explore. I will not hold you back."

He stared at her in astonishment.

She opened a basket near the hearth and lifted several folded papers.

"I saved everything you ever wrote to me."

"May I read them to you?" she asked.

Jonathan nodded.

Emily unfolded the first page, her voice trembling slightly as she read:

You Are Calling Me
Looking into your eyes I see the rising and setting of the sun...
Your heartbeat swings into my chest and speaks to my being.
Yeah, you called to me,
Yeah, I came to you, and yeah—we are here.

She set it aside gently.

"Your words," she whispered, "have always been a gift."

Another sheet rustled softly.

My Calling

I look to the sea calling me...
My spirit drifts over the aqua waters...
This world where I dwell has so many stories to tell...
Let the earth feel your stature.

"I close my eyes every time I read this," she murmured.

The final letter fluttered open.

My Dear Emily

The cones on the bough were laden with dew...
The fog floating just above the earth reminds me of our enchant-
ment...
As night gives way to a new day,
I give you these thoughts from my pen.
Most fondly awaiting our time together.

Emily wiped tears from her cheeks. Jonathan memorized the curves of her smile, knowing he would carry the image across the sea.

"I will return one day," he said softly. "I promise. I'll write you words meant to be read by candlelight."

Emily leaned against him as the brass pendulum of the grandfather clock swung gently behind them—time moving, time slipping, time urging Jonathan toward a future he could no longer resist.

Chapter Twenty-Three

Anchors Aweigh

"A very great vision is needed, and the man who has it must follow it as the eagle seeks the deepest blue of the sky." — Crazy Horse, Sioux Chief

Jonathan had barely stepped inside his parents' house when a familiar voice drifted from the long hallway.

"Is that you, Jonathan?"

He hung his jacket and hat on the rack and walked softly toward the study. "Yes, Father."

Oliver appeared in the doorway. "Come in, son. I have great news for you."

Jonathan followed him inside and settled into the well-worn brown leather chair he'd occupied since childhood.

"Are you ready to begin your voyage?" Oliver asked.

"Yes. I visited Emily today. We said our goodbyes. She's excited for me... and excited to read my writings from America."

"That's good. And I'm glad you made proper arrangements with her. Did you speak to her father?"

"No. He wasn't home. Emily said she'll tell him everything when he returns. But truly, all is well."

Oliver lit his pipe, paced toward the fireplace, then turned back. "Well then... your ship leaves tomorrow."

"Tomorrow?"

"Yes. I visited Captain Revelstoke today. His ship sails in the morning. If you're going to chase a crazy vision, you might as well start without delay."

Jonathan knew better than to challenge his father's decisiveness. And truthfully, excitement was rising in him like a tide. "Then I should make haste, Father."

"Your mother and I placed two trunks in your bedroom. Charles is waiting to help you pack."

Jonathan shook his father's hand, then surprised them both by embracing him. Oliver stiffened, then smiled and nudged him toward the stairs.

He stood in his room, momentarily unsure where to begin. Books seemed the safest start. As he crouched at his desk, carefully arranging reference volumes in the bottom of the trunk, anticipation warmed his chest. A new beginning. Blank pages waiting to be filled. A life unfolding like a novel yet unwritten.

"Master Jon?"

He turned to see Charles in the doorway — the family's faithful servant, white-haired and stiff-backed, with a soft soul wrapped in formality.

"Come in, Charles. I could use your insight."

Charles stepped inside, eyes falling to the half-packed books. "May I suggest layering your jackets over the top, sir? It protects the bindings."

Jonathan grinned. "Excellent idea."

They fell into an easy rhythm. Charles laid jackets on the bed while Jonathan packed his writing materials and tablets. The old man had known Jonathan since he was a towheaded toddler crawling under tables. Over the years they'd spoken of life, dreams, and the quiet courage needed to follow one's own path — conversations Jonathan treasured far more than anything he learned at Cambridge.

As they finished, Jonathan walked over and embraced Charles. "I will miss you. More than you know."

Charles held still a moment, then his lanky arms rose, hesitant but sincere. "Though our souls will be a world apart, Master Jon... I will linger with you in the peripheral shadows."

"And I am grateful. You have been more than a servant — you've been a mentor. A friend."

They continued packing and talking until the late hours, the room warm with lamplight and memory.

***

Dawn glowed pale at the window when Jonathan awoke still dressed. Hunger tugged at him as he descended to the kitchen.

His mother appeared as he reached for a scone.

"I was just about to prepare your breakfast."

"Oh, Mother, don't trouble yourself. A scone and tea will do. I'm both hungry and not. Too excited, I think."

Adeline hugged him tightly, tears rising. "I'm going to miss you, Jonathan. Promise you'll write."

"I will. Always."

While she prepared tea, Oliver strode in. "Carriage is ready. Charles is loading your trunks. I'll ride with you to the docks."

Jonathan nodded. His mother handed tea to his father and stood in the doorway as the men stepped outside.

Charles and Adeline waved from the cobblestone circle drive as the carriage pulled away. Jonathan kept his eyes on them until the bend in the road swallowed both from view.

"We'll miss you, son," Oliver said, voice quieter than usual. "I was against this idea at first. But then I remembered my own youth, and the visions that drove me." He paused. "My father thought me foolish too."

Jonathan swallowed. "We haven't always agreed. But you've given me more than I can ever repay. Thank you."

Both men turned toward their windows, pretending the moisture in their eyes came from the sea breeze creeping into the carriage.

***

The docks erupted with noise — crates slamming, sailors shouting, gulls wheeling overhead. Then a voice boomed above the chaos.

"Oliver!"

Captain Revelstoke approached, uniform immaculate, stride brisk.

The men shook hands. "Captain," Oliver said proudly, "my son Jonathan."

Jonathan nodded. "Honored to meet you, sir."

"Adventure-bound for America, eh?" The Captain grinned. "Your father has told me of your writings. You'll have a stateroom near my quarters. We sail with a full passenger list."

"I'm grateful for the passage, Captain."

"What do you write? Poetry? Essays?"

"Short stories, prose... whatever inspires me."

"Good. Perhaps tonight at dinner you'll read a bit?"

Jonathan smiled politely. "Of course."

The Captain gestured toward the gangplank. "Best say your goodbyes. We depart soon."

Jonathan hugged his father one last time. "I'll make you proud."

"You already have. Write your mother often."

With a final nod, Jonathan walked up the gangplank into a world of ropes, sails, and roaring steam. The Livingston towered above him — a hybrid steamer and three-masted vessel, barely a year into service and capable of crossing the Atlantic in six weeks or less.

His stateroom overlooked the bustling city. When the porter left, Jonathan paused at the mirror, straightened his suit, and steadied himself. This was real. No turning back.

On deck, ropes were being drawn in. Crowds waved from the pier. The Captain beckoned him to the bridge, where the giant steam engine rumbled below deck and salt wind pressed against his face.

"Ever been at sea?" the Captain asked.

"Never."

"Then take the wheel for a moment."

Jonathan blinked. "Truly?"

The helmsman stepped aside. Jonathan gripped the wheel, feeling the weight of the rudder beneath the surface.

"Steady now," the Captain said. "Let the ship meet you. She runs through your veins."

Jonathan closed his eyes briefly — and saw Charles' soft smile, heard his whispered encouragement. "Captain... it's as if the ship speaks."

The Captain clapped his shoulder. "You'll do well."

***

Dinner that evening was formal, stiff, and far too social for Jonathan's liking. Candlelight glinted on silverware and china. Conversations felt rehearsed, as though each guest performed more than conversed.

Introductions circled the table until the Captain called on him. Jonathan stood, offered a modest explanation of his westward journey, and endured the murmurs of astonishment. A gentleman from India toasted him with kind words about courage and vision.

Jonathan smiled, nodded politely — then fled to the deck as soon as courtesy allowed.

The air outside was cooler, honest.

That's when he heard it — a sudden loud thud from below.

An old man emerged from the shadows. Thin, ragged, limping.

Jonathan rushed to him. "Sir! Are you all right? You're not thinking of jumping—"

"Let me be!" the man rasped. His accent was rough, his eyes hollow.

"I'm no officer," Jonathan said gently. "Just a passenger. And who are you?"

The man bowed his head. "A slave, more like. Locked in the belly of this ship. No daylight for weeks. Paid near nothing."

Jonathan's heart clenched. "How many of you?"

"Too many. Drinking took me there. Now labor keeps me."

He learned the man's name — Milo — and listened as sorrow poured out: the wife and daughter long gone, a granddaughter left behind, no one expecting him home.

Jonathan crouched beside him. "You must endure for her sake. Life can begin again, even after ruin."

The man wept. Jonathan tore a page from his journal, scribbled a message, and handed it to him. "When you return to London, go to this address. Ask for Charles. He will help you."

Milo pressed the paper to his chest, nodded, and shuffled back below deck.

Jonathan watched him go, troubled. Should he tell the Captain? He wasn't sure. Not yet.

***

The Atlantic crossing tested them all. Storms threw the Livingston side to side. At times he couldn't leave his cabin. Dinners with the Captain ended after the first week; even the crew grew restless.

But through it all, Jonathan wrote. He filled his first journal completely — observations, fears, hopes, and the shifting landscape of the sea that seemed endless and alive.

It was only the beginning. His journey to the Pacific—and to whatever awaited him there—had only just begun.

Chapter Twenty-Four

Overland Journey

"If the vision was true and mighty, as I know it is, it is true and mighty yet; for such things are of the spirit, and it is in the darkness of their eyes that men get lost."
— *Black Elk, Sioux Medicine Man*

Weeks went by. One morning, as Jonathan woke, he heard cheering outside his cabin. He sat up quickly and peered out the window. Clear skies. Bright sun. Passengers stood along the gangway.

He hurried into his trousers, opened his door, and joined the small crowd.

"What's the commotion?" he asked.

"Land ho on the starboard side, mate!" one of the crew shouted.

Jonathan moved to a clear vantage point. There, far off on the horizon, lay a faint strip of land.

He could hardly believe his eyes. After all those days and nights at sea, he was this close to the country he'd dreamed about. The journey had begun in the last week of February, and now, on April fourteenth, he would set foot on American soil.

"How long before we arrive?" Jonathan asked.

The seaman, squinting through his spyglass, replied, "Oh, high noon, I'd say. The Captain'll raise steam and we'll be harbor-bound before you know it."

Jonathan made haste back to his cabin. He washed, dressed carefully, and began packing his few belongings. Before closing his trunk, he sat on the bed and opened his journal.

This morning we woke to America on the western horizon. After seven long weeks confined to a man-made hunk of flotsam, we will enter New York Harbor. From there, I embark on the next leg of my journey toward the west coast of America. At sea, I have been at the mercy of the deep. On land, I will be at the mercy of its inhabitants.

The morning hours crawled. He perched on the top deck, watching the harbor grow closer and closer. Gulls wheeled overhead, their endless cries cutting through the creak of timbers as sails were lowered. Men hurried about, preparing the ship for docking.

New York Harbor soon lay fully in view. Throngs of people lined the piers. Ships crowded the docks, masts jutting into the sky like bare winter trees. This would be one arrival where no one was waiting for him. His only friend in the New World, Richard Shively, was still three thousand miles away in Oregon.

The Livingston eased alongside the dock to the cheers of a few hundred people. Ropes were thrown and secured. The gangplank lowered with a groan.

Jonathan walked down with his bags while a porter trundled his two trunks behind him. The Captain stood near the gangplank, offering a final farewell to his passengers.

When Jonathan approached, the Captain tipped his hat. "Well, son, have a safe journey to the West Coast."

Part of Jonathan despised the man, knowing what went on below decks, but he kept his tone polite.

"Thank you, Captain. It was a... memorable voyage. You have quite a ship here, yes indeed." Jonathan held his gaze a heartbeat longer than necessary, then moved on.

He made his way through the bustle to a waiting taxi and told the driver to take him to a hotel near the train station. The ride was short but slow, mired in a tangle of carriages, wagons, and pedestrians. New Yorkers seemed to be in a constant hurry to get somewhere, though where, he could not guess.

At the hotel, he checked in, left his trunks in the room, and walked to the train station. There he purchased a ticket to Independence, Missouri, on a train leaving the very next morning.

That evening he ate supper in the hotel dining room, sorting through pamphlets about western travel and wagon trains. Five days on the rails to the beginning of the Oregon Trail; then another fifteen hundred miles or so to reach the Willamette Valley and Portland. First by sea, then by land.

Somewhere along the way he had chosen to turn his back on the safety of England—on the chance to write among his country's most esteemed literary minds. He had given up Emily, too, or at least risked losing her. Yet Shively had urged him to come, and the vision lodged deep in his heart to discover a new land and write of it had carried him this far.

Later, he opened his journal again.

New York is a large city with buildings climbing everywhere and construction on every corner. A busy town with thousands of people who, unlike London, appear to be in a hurry to reach some unknown destination. Irish and Scottish immigrants are plentiful here. Beggars and peddlers roam freely in the streets. In the alleys, shenanigans occur—cockfights, boxing matches, and children rolling pennies against the walls of buildings. Shively warned me of pickpockets and thugs. I leave on the morning train, heading west, not knowing how or with whom I shall travel on the long wagon-train journey over the Oregon Trail. Great perils remain, and likely encounters with the native Indians. I must keep my vision true and strong and my eyes always on the western horizon.

His hand cramped. Satisfied, he closed the journal and, for the first time in six weeks, slept on land.

***

Just after sunrise came a knock at the door.

"Mr. Butler, are you awake?"

He wiped the sleep from his eyes and sat up. "Yes?"

"Your wake-up call, as requested, sir."

"Thank you. I am awake."

Silence returned. He fumbled for his pocket watch. Six o'clock.

"Two hours until the train leaves. Mustn't dally," he muttered.

He splashed water from the washbowl onto his face, dressed quickly, buttoned his jacket, and headed downstairs. In the lobby, he snatched a slice of toast and a cup of tea.

At the front desk he asked the clerk to fetch a coach and have his luggage brought down. Outside, the city was already gathering speed—carriages rattling past, men carrying crates to unknown destinations, voices rising.

When the carriage pulled up to the curb, the porter loaded his trunks.

"To the train station, please. I'm in a hurry," Jonathan said.

The driver smirked. "Everyone in this city's in a hurry. Where you headed?"

"Independence."

"Taking a wagon train west, are ye?"

"Yes. Traveling to the Oregon Territory."

"Well, hope you're ready for a rough, dusty journey, my friend. I hear them savages play no pity with white settlers along the Oregon Trail. You got a firearm, I presume?"

"No, sir, I do not. I haven't planned that far ahead."

"You best be prepared, son, or you may not see the light of day in the Oregon Territory. My advice: hire a guide. Someone experienced who can watch your back. You're an Englishman—from London, eh?"

"You have a good ear in that regard, sir. Yes," Jonathan replied.

"I thought so. Your dialect gives you away. Spent a spell in London myself, before I finished my journey from Ireland. Brought the whole family over. Struggled all the way, but it's a great country. Free men, one and all—if they can keep it." He glanced at Jonathan. "You planning on becoming a citizen, then?"

Jonathan considered. "That is yet to be determined. I'll see how my stay goes."

"Fair enough. It'll come to ya." He flicked the reins. "All right, here we are. Let's see to your luggage."

Jonathan pointed out the gate number. "Gate four, if you please."

"Best of luck to ya, laddie. Be safe."

Jonathan paid the man, retrieved his trunks, and pushed his way through the crush of travelers. He handed his ticket to the conductor, who waved him aboard.

Inside the railcar, he found a window seat. Steam rose in clouds outside, curling past the glass. People streamed in every direction along the platform. Americans, he decided, were a different breed entirely—faster, louder, less inclined to dawdle over a cup of tea.

"All aboard!" cried the conductor.

The car lurched. The train inched forward, then gathered speed. The second leg of his journey had begun.

Jonathan opened his journal again and recorded more observations while the New York buildings slipped away and the countryside opened. Houses and farms punctuated the rolling land. The steady clickety-clack of the wheels on the rails filled the car.

He glanced at his ticket, punched by the conductor: New York and Erie Railroad Company printed across the top.

"Excuse me, is this seat taken?"

He looked up, startled out of his thoughts. A young lady stood in the aisle, dressed in the height of fashion.

"Uh, no—no, not at all. Please, have the seat," Jonathan said, rising.

"Thank you. It was getting far too stuffy back in the parlor car, if you get my drift."

Not entirely sure what she meant, he tipped his hat and sat.

She straightened her blue flowered silk blouse and jacket. "My name is Louise. I'm traveling to Saint Louis. Where are you headed, kind sir?"

Jonathan cleared his throat and removed his hat again. "I'm going to the end of the line."

"Don't tell me—you're heading west from there?" she asked, eyes bright.

"Yes. On to the Oregon Territory."

"I thought as much. Most folks go to the end of the line to seek their independence." She giggled.

Jonathan smiled. "That was a good one. I was wondering about the town's name. It makes good sense."

"You're British, aren't you?" she said.

He laughed. "My speech gives me away, does it not?"

Louise grinned. "Yeah, I know you bloody Englishmen. Have to watch out for you." She blushed slightly. "But I certainly enjoy your accent—and your gentlemanly ways. Are you planning on wearing those clothes on your western journey?"

"I hadn't given it much thought. That's a pity," Jonathan admitted, glancing at his suit.

"You'd best have proper attire and not stand out too much. Save that look for the city," she said.

He nodded, suddenly aware of how polished he must seem.

"And what are you carrying to protect yourself?" she asked.

"Why, I... ah..."

"You know—a firearm. You'll need one on the Oregon Trail with the savages."

"You are the second person to mention that," Jonathan said.

Louise opened her purse. "This is my protection. Not big and flashy, but it does the job up close."

She held up a small silver Derringer.

Jonathan stared. "Could you really use that on someone?"

"Mr. Butler, with due respect, you're young and do not realize the dangers here in America—especially where you're going. Into the Wild West." Her voice softened, but her eyes were firm. "I have no reservations about using my weapon in self-defense."

"I cannot imagine taking a life..."

"Better theirs than yours, don't you think?" she said plainly. "It happens before you know it. You must be in the right frame of mind. I recommend you protect yourself,

Jonathan. You've traveled a very long way. Don't you want to live long enough to fulfill your dreams?"

He paused, thoughtful. "Did you say why you're traveling to Saint Louis?"

"You're changing the subject," she teased. "But since you asked: yes. I'm a fashion designer. I've opened a dress boutique. I bring the latest fashions from New York and Paris."

Jonathan shifted in his seat, looking out at the blurred countryside. "I suppose you are correct, Louise. I'll soon come to grips with reality at the end of the tracks."

"I say, if nothing else, secure a small handgun and a knife. Strap them to your lower calf under your trousers. You can still present yourself as a gentleman and still be ready for thugs and shysters," Louise advised.

The landscape rolled by, and the steady rhythm of the rails lulled them. Jonathan leaned against the window, turning her words over. Before long, the clickety-clack carried both of them to sleep.

***

"Hello there, Miss Pretty!"

Jonathan woke with a start. Leaning over Louise was a scruffy man, flanked by two others. The sour smell of alcohol and tobacco clung to them.

Startled, Louise sat up straight. Jonathan blinked himself fully awake.

"I told you earlier to leave me alone," Louise said, her voice steady and sharp.

"Oh, come now," the man drawled. "We were just gettin' to know one another. Come have a drink. Let's get better acquainted." He reached for her arm.

Louise jerked back and reached for her purse. "I think you gentlemen have had quite enough to drink."

She pulled out the Derringer and leveled it at them. "And as I told you in the parlor car, I do not wish to know any of you. Now get out of this railcar and leave me alone, or you'll be crawling out of here."

Passengers gasped and leaned away from the aisle.

The man rocked back, glancing at his companions. Turning toward Louise again, he raised his eyebrows and forced a chuckle. "We didn't mean no harm. Just havin' a bit of fun. Thought you could use some company."

Jonathan had risen halfway from his seat, jaw clenched, eyes fixed on the man.

Louise's voice cut through the car. "I will give you to the count of three to make haste."

The drunken intruder muttered something under his breath and lunged toward her.

Bam!

The little pistol roared, the shot tearing into the floorboards just beside his boot. He jumped back, wide-eyed.

"The next bullet goes right between your eyes," Louise said. Her grip never wavered. "Je ne vais pas me répéter."

The three men stared, then slowly backed down the aisle. They fumbled with the door to the next car, then disappeared through it.

The tension in the railcar released in a collective breath. Jonathan reached for Louise's arm.

"That will teach them," she said. "Now you see what I meant about having a weapon?"

"I suppose I have lived a sheltered life. That was... terribly ungentlemanly," Jonathan said.

"They are not gentlemen in any fashion. They're the very thugs and shysters I warned you about. Don't get me wrong—there are good people, too. Some really good. But as foreigners, we will always find those ready to take advantage."

"I see." Jonathan frowned. "You spoke in French. What did you say? I'm curious—did they leave because you threatened to shoot him between the eyes, or because you spoke French?"

Louise smoothed her blouse, then chuckled, her composure returning. "Probably a bit of both. I added the French to give them a touch of uncertainty. Je ne vais pas me répéter means 'I will not repeat myself.' Speaking in a foreign tongue often sharpens your warning in English. Between the pistol, my promise, and a language they didn't understand, he decided not to test me."

The train began to slow as the conductor walked through, calling out their arrival in Saint Louis.

"Well, Mr. Butler, this is where I get off." Louise reached into her bag and handed him a small card. "It has been a pleasure. I wish you the best in your endeavors—and please, heed my advice. Here is my business card and address in Saint Louis. Keep in touch when you reach Oregon."

"Thank you, Louise. You are a most remarkable person. I truly hope your business venture goes exceedingly well."

"Yes, we both begin our adventures," she said, smiling. "Take good care."

"Oh, I shall." Jonathan gave her a brief hug.

Louise left the car. Jonathan sat back down and watched her through the window as she walked along the platform. Before disappearing into the crowd, she turned and waved. He lifted his hand in reply.

***

A couple of hours later, the train jerked to another stop. Jonathan woke with a start.

The end of the line.

He gathered his things and followed the other passengers down to the platform. After retrieving his luggage, he stood among the swirling crowd. Friends and relatives claimed travelers. Trail guides and opportunists shouted offers and prices. In moments, the platform emptied.

Jonathan, in his well-cut British suit with fine leather luggage, suddenly seemed the only one left—sitting on one of his trunks amid the fading bustle.

Beyond the wooden train depot, Independence boiled with activity. Covered wagons clustered in groups. Livery stables and vendors hawked supplies. White canvas tents stretched in every direction.

"You waitin' for someone, young man?" asked a voice.

Jonathan turned. Behind the glass of the ticket window sat an old man with white hair and small wire-rimmed spectacles. He rubbed his wiry mustache and studied Jonathan with mild amusement.

"Oh, no one in particular," Jonathan replied. "But could you kindly point me toward a wagon train? I am in need of travel to Oregon."

The old man raised his eyebrows and chuckled. "There's a whole sea of activity out there and several trains of wagons gettin' ready to head west. Don't rightly know what to tell you, 'cept be wary of shysters. They'll see you comin' a mile away, take all you have, and leave you stranded here penniless. Happens all the time. There's little law and order in these parts. If you like, I can offer you a return ticket back East." His eyes twinkled.

"Oh no, I can't do that. I must get to Oregon." Jonathan dropped his head into his hands for a moment.

"You go to Oregon? I take you."

Jonathan lifted his head. In the far corner of the depot, sitting in the shadows on a bench, was a middle-aged Indian. He wore jeans, a plaid shirt, a leather vest, and a derby hat. A rifle rested against his leg. A long, dry stem of grass dangled from the corner of his mouth.

Jonathan stood and walked over. "Who are you? Are you a guide?"

The Indian kept chewing, then looked up.

"I am Omache," he said. "I take you to Oregon. Get you there safe."

Jonathan studied him. With no other clear options, he weighed the offer. Louise's warnings about shysters echoed in his mind, but something about Omache did not ring false.

"What would be your required compensation for accompanying me to Portland?" Jonathan asked.

"One hundred dollars," Omache replied. "You pay for wagon and supplies. I drive wagon, cook food, take care of horses. You no complain about my cooking; I no complain about your... inept character." A faint glimmer of amusement touched his eyes. "We go now. Must get wagon and supplies. Leave in morning."

Before Jonathan could fully answer, Omache rose, hoisted the trunks onto a cart, and started toward the door.

"I lead. You follow, Englishman."

Jonathan blinked, then set his hat on his head, gathered his remaining bags, and followed. Whether he had chosen a guide, or a guide of strange character had chosen him, he wasn't entirely sure.

Behind them, the old ticket master stepped out of his booth, lifted his hat, and wiped his brow. Smiling, he nodded in quiet approval as the unlikely pair disappeared into the flurry of people.

Chapter Twenty-Five

Oregon or Bust

*"Great Spirit, help me never to judge another until I have
walked in his moccasins."*
— *American Indian Proverb*

Life could be excruciating, especially in times of great stress
and unknowns. This was one of those times for Jonathan.
Following in the wake of an American Indian he knew nothing
about did not quite fit with his traditional, esteemed British
upbringing. Yet in this daunting moment, unbeknownst to
Jonathan, his destiny was unfolding. It would carry him far
beyond the miles of plains, deserts, and mountains on the final
leg of his journey to Oregon.

Omache pushed the cart with Jonathan's luggage
through the silt-laden street, away from the throngs of settlers,
toward an obscure alley. Jonathan was about to ask where they
were going when the Indian spoke without looking back.

"Follow me, Englishman."

They moved down the dead-end alley toward a large,
weathered barn built into a small rise. Omache set the cart

down, walked to the door, and pulled it open. Jonathan peered inside.

"What is this?" he asked.

"Our wagon and horses to Oregon," Omache replied.

"I thought we still had to seek and purchase a wagon and horses."

"This is my wagon and horses. You rent."

Jonathan watched him lift the trunks into the wagon and toss in the remaining bags. Two horses stood in their stalls, one white and brown, the other white and orange.

"These are beautiful horses," Jonathan said. "I've never seen colors like these. Our horses in England are mostly black or dark brown."

"These are Indian horses," said Omache. "Strong. Not afraid of journey. Quiet in darkness and steadfast in day. You ride horse?"

"Oh yes—in polo and fox hunts."

"What is this polo?"

"A game played on horseback. I hold a long-handled mallet, and we hit a wooden ball across a field toward the opponent's goal."

"Oh. Like horse race?"

"Well, sort of. You must be fast and keep the ball away from the other team."

"Sound like waste of time," Omache said. "Why you hunt fox?"

"In England it is a sport. We follow the dogs, chase the fox, corner him, and kill him."

"Not understand your games. You must have dumb foxes in England. Here you must be clever to catch fox. Smart animal—best let him run and be free." He picked up the cart handles again. "We go now and get supplies."

***

The late-afternoon sun beat down on the restless crowd anxious to hit the trail. Farmers, prospectors, merchants, would-be miners bound for California—pioneers all—swarmed the streets in search of their own promised lands.

Omache slipped through the chaos like a man in his own element. He was keen-eyed and efficient, practiced in the art of buying and bartering. He had done this many times before.

At his urging, Jonathan acquired a set of trail clothes, reluctantly shedding the last threads of his English tailoring. While Omache continued to gather supplies, Jonathan wandered through the maze of vendors and found himself in front of a gunsmith's stall.

"Excuse me, sir," Jonathan said, clearing his throat. "Do you have one of those small pistols?"

The gunsmith—a well-groomed man in a white shirt with a neatly curled mustache—reached into a display case and set a small silver pistol on the counter.

"No, I mean one of the really small pistols," Jonathan clarified.

"Ah," the man said, his mustache twitching. "You mean a Derringer. Popular with the ladies, if you take my meaning."

Jonathan felt his cheeks warm. "Yes. That is what I'm looking for."

"No problem. It's a relatively new firearm but in high demand with all the fashionable women arriving lately." He laid out several Derringers, in silver and bronze.

"I'll take the bronze pistol—and a supply of bullets."

He paid, thanked the gunsmith, and turned to go.

"Give my regards to your lady," the man called, chuckling.

Jonathan lifted a hand in vague acknowledgment and walked briskly into the crowd.

He found Omache again, the Indian pushing a cart stacked high with sacks, crates, and tools.

"Boy—that looks like a ton of supplies," Jonathan said.

Expressionless, Omache continued toward the alley, muttering something under his breath in a language Jonathan could not decipher. Jonathan followed alongside, burdened with bags of clothing.

Back at the barn, they loaded the wagon. Omache filled two weathered oak barrels attached to the wagon with water from a hand pump out back. Jonathan sat on a bale of hay and opened his journal. The setting sun cast long shadows from the hill beside the barn, and the dimming light slipped through gaps in the old boards.

As he wrote, Jonathan let his thoughts roam ahead to the long journey across the continent. What encounters awaited him on the road to the Oregon Territory? He felt surprisingly safe with Omache. So intent was he on his writing that he did not notice when daylight faded entirely and the only light was from a lantern the Indian had lit more than an hour earlier.

The smell of something cooking finally drew him from the page. He slipped his journal into his pack and tossed it into the wagon. The horses shifted in their stalls, snorting softly.

Outside, Omache crouched near a small campfire, smoke curling into the twilight. He held out a tin plate as Jonathan approached.

"Here," he said.

Jonathan sat on a blanket and accepted the plate. "This smells wonderful." He took a bite of the golden-brown meat, chewed, and swallowed. "Delicious. Absolutely delicious. Best chicken I've had in America."

The Indian nodded, a half-smile on his face. "That is rabbit, not chicken."

Jonathan swallowed his second bite and washed it down with a cup of water. "Well, then it is the best rabbit I've had in America. If this is what I can expect on our journey, I am ready to go."

"Not have rabbit every night," Omache said, laughing and showing a row of straight white teeth, one gleaming gold. "Might be snake. We eat what we find on trail. Variety blessed by Great One."

Jonathan hesitated, then voiced a lingering concern. "I've been thinking... what are the chances we encounter hostile Indian tribes along the way?"

After they finished eating, Omache doused the fire. "Not much," he said. "I might be most hostile Indian on journey if you complain." His eyes glinted. "We see other tribes along the way but no worry. Most friendly. Leave us alone. You hear stories of massacres—not true. Mostly battles with U.S. soldiers, not settlers. We respect them; they respect us. We take only what we need from land." He studied Jonathan. "You be honest in your writings."

"I will," Jonathan said quietly.

"Good. Now we sleep. Leave at first light." Omache handed him a bedroll. "Find soft place in hay. Last night on soft ground for long time."

Jonathan found a spot behind the wagon and spread his bedroll. Omache fed the horses and wrapped a blanket around his shoulders, settling near the stalls. A bright full moon climbed the sky and spilled silver light across barn and field.

Tomorrow would be here in the blink of an eye.

***

A thin layer of ground fog simmered like steam from a kettle as the sun climbed. Half-asleep, Jonathan heard the horses snorting and shifting. The barn doors squealed open, flooding the dim interior with light.

He blinked awake to see the wagon already moving. Omache, reins in hand, was guiding the horses out into the morning.

Yawning, Jonathan rolled up his bedroll and hurried outside.

"Up front," Omache called.

Jonathan climbed onto the rickety wooden seat. The Indian handed him a tin cup and a hunk of bread.

"Bread and milk for breakfast?" Jonathan asked.

Omache flicked the reins. "You got up too late for bacon and eggs. Bread and goat's milk will suffice."

"Goat's milk?" Jonathan echoed, then stopped himself from saying more. He downed the contents of the cup, nodded, and managed a smile when Omache glanced his way.

Still groggy from the early start, he did not at first notice that they were traveling alone. The town was already a smudge on the horizon behind them.

After a couple of hours, he woke from a doze and looked back through the wagon. Empty trail. No wagons. No others.

He lurched forward on the bench, heart thudding. "Omache, where is the wagon train?"

The Indian kept his gaze straight ahead. Only after a long moment did he answer, voice calm.

"Probably still gathering back in Independence. We go alone. Much faster."

Jonathan stared at him. "But I thought we were to be in a wagon train. What about our safety?"

Omache allowed himself a small grin. "Never said we be in wagon train. Said I have wagon, take you to Oregon. No complaints." He faced forward again. After a few quiet minutes, he added, "No worry about safe travel. Been on trail many times. Still here, doing it again. I protect you from trail hazards." He glanced sideways. "You protect yourself from yourself."

Jonathan fell silent, letting the words sink in. His arrival in Missouri had already felt beyond conventional understanding; now he was crossing a vast continent with a guide he had met only hours before. He already felt lost, and the journey had barely begun.

Would he ever feel at home in this strange land? The journey in his mind seemed to stretch even farther than the one beneath the wagon wheels. He missed England—his friends, the libraries, even the predictable conversations of social gatherings. Yet he had chosen this. He had seen this journey in his dreams long before he set foot on the ship. Perhaps it was more than a dream. Perhaps it was his calling.

The land around them lay flat and unbroken, stretching to the farthest edge of sight. The trail, a pair of deep ruts pressed into hard-baked clay, ran ahead like a brown ribbon. Omache sat straight-backed and steady, eyes always on the distance, hands sure on the reins.

He tried to write, but the jolting wagon turned his script into a series of crooked lines. Eventually he snapped the journal shut with a sigh. Evening by the campfire, he decided, would be best for his words.

As the light faded, Omache guided the horses toward a small stand of trees and drew the wagon to a halt. He tethered and watered the horses, then built a fire in quick, practiced motions.

Jonathan stood awkwardly by, feeling as uncertain as a university freshman on his first day.

"You get hang of it soon," Omache said. "You green around collar. I think word is 'greenhorn.' Grab blanket and bedroll. Put by fire."

Jonathan stumbled through the motions, feeling every bit the newcomer. There was nowhere to hide from his own inexperience. This was it: the real thing. Time to be a man and grow up. No lecture hall or textbook could have prepared him for this.

He thought of Charles and the quiet wisdom the old servant had shared over the years. How Jonathan wished he were here now, showing him how to do the simplest camp tasks. As he stared into the dancing flames, he looked across at Omache through the wavering heat and, for a moment, saw the faintest likeness of Charles in the set of the man's shoulders, the calm in his gaze.

A wise man like Omache. Perhaps, in some mysterious way, Charles was here with him after all—walking beside him in spirit, wearing moccasins instead of polished shoes.

Chapter Twenty-Six

Rain in Distance Hills

"Although I am far from the lands of my people, I hear their voices in the wind."
— *Old Indian Saying*

Day by day, the routine became the same. Up early, a quick bite to eat, then back on the trail with relentless hours of dusty, bone-jarring travel across barren land. Dust devils rose and twirled in the penetrating sun. Jonathan often walked beside the wagon simply to escape the constant rattling and shaking of the bench seat. He could not comprehend how Omache endured such punishment.

In one entry of his journal he wrote: The vastness of the American land is beyond comprehension. I can see for days ahead. One evening, when we stopped to make camp, I could see the landmark where we had slept the night before. It is wild and untamed — and we have not yet arrived at the Wild West. On a good day we manage twenty miles. My guide, Omache, may not take the most direct path, but he follows the land where water can be found. The horses relish such sacred

227

waterholes. He seems to care more for them than for us. He has an uncanny way of foraging for food...

Jonathan often joined him in the hunt. Many times he fetched a rabbit or small game while Omache kept the wagon rolling. When the Indian spotted his quarry, he would raise his firearm, rest it on his other arm, and fire — no small task while holding reins and compensating for the rickety wagon's jolts. One night around the campfire, Jonathan asked about his guide's name.

"Omache means good medicine," the Indian said.

Good medicine indeed. Day after day, the two quietly grew into a strange but sturdy companionship. Jonathan's young character matured — slowly, like a sapling hardening into a tree. He took naturally to the daily routine: preparing breakfast, hitching the horses, tending the fire, finding water where none seemed to exist. His skin bronzed under the sun, his feet toughened from miles of walking, his eyes sharpened to the subtleties of the land.

Occasionally, Omache taught him to fire the rifle. Jonathan's first successful shot — a rabbit — brought a surprising surge of pride and independence. He watched as Omache skinned the animal and prepared the hide for drying. Nothing harvested ever went to waste.

The trail was not entirely uninhabited. Homesteads dotted the plains the nearer they drew to the Rockies. Immigrants who, for one reason or another, had abandoned their original plans chose to settle there instead. Signs of hardship and despair littered the roadside: broken furniture, discarded belongings left behind to lighten the load, makeshift graves —

many of children — reminders of the cruelty and fragility of the journey.

The dream of the Oregon Territory was not for the faint of heart. Like salmon struggling upstream to their birthplace, not all travelers reached home.

Yet many were kind. Omache often traded trinkets for supplies and food, and travelers offered them warm meals and stories. Jonathan would share his tales of England, and soon laughter and fellowship replaced the loneliness of the open prairie.

A month into the journey, Jonathan was slightly disappointed. Not one encounter with an Indian — other than Omache — had crossed his path.

That would soon change in a way he never expected.

***

With the jagged silhouette of the Rocky Mountains rising before them, Jonathan felt a surge of excitement.

"How much longer to Oregon?" he asked.

As he hitched the horses for the day's travel, Omache replied, "About forty days — maybe less. Depends on weather. Easy part behind us. Many challenges come now. Rivers to cross, mountains to climb. But more water ahead."

Jonathan took comfort in that, ignoring the grim warnings tucked within the answer. He was getting close. This was the final leg of a six-month journey since leaving England.

The sunrise that morning bled an eerie red across the sky. As they ventured into the pine forests of the eastern foothills, Omache cast his eyes upward with a look Jonathan had come to recognize: caution.

Behind them, the sagebrush plains disappeared. Ahead, the wagon trail twisted through thickening forests of juniper and pine.

Late that afternoon, dark clouds roiled above the craggy peaks. Jonathan, walking beside the wagon, heard Omache call:

"On wagon! We move fast."

The horses broke into a quick trot. Soon a wide, shallow river glimmered ahead — the first true water in days. Thunder rumbled in the distance, lightning flashing across the western sky.

"Secure all loose things," Omache instructed.

Jonathan obeyed, his eyes widening as he studied the hundred-yard stretch of swift-moving water.

Taima — "Thunder," Omache's lead pony — stepped into the cold stream. The wagon followed, sinking into loose river rock and dragging heavily. They were almost halfway across when disaster appeared.

A wall of muddy water and debris, nearly three feet high, surged around a bend and thundered toward them.

A flash flood.

Omache jerked the reins hard and yelled at the top of his lungs. Jonathan held on as the wave struck the wagon broadside, shoving it yards downstream.

The horses strained desperately, water rising nearly to their necks. Sticks and branches slammed against the canvas cover, forcing the wagon into a crooked angle. Another inch of water would swamp them entirely.

Jonathan prayed — for his life, his family, Emily... anyone who might hear.

Then, through the chaos, came shouts from the riverbank.

A hunting party of Arapaho Indians had arrived.

Several braves leaped from their horses and plunged into the river, ropes tied around their waists. Their leader barked orders. Two men waded to the wagon, securing ropes to the horses and the wagon bed.

"Klat'-a-wa, klat'-a-wa!" Omache yelled — Go, go!

The combined strength of horses and men slowly tugged the wagon toward the shore. Water splashed high, hooves churned the riverbed, and finally — miraculously — the wagon climbed onto solid ground.

Jonathan and Omache collapsed, dripping and exhausted, as the Arapaho unhitched their horses.

The Arapaho Chief rode forward. Jonathan looked up, breathless, and saw a tall, bare-chested warrior with braided black hair and a stern expression. After a brief exchange with Omache, the Chief looked down at Jonathan and allowed the faintest grin.

"Lucky," he said.

Jonathan tried to steady his shaking voice. "Where are we?"

Omache placed a hand on his shoulder. "Not in Indian Heaven, if that what you think." He pointed across the river. "We on other side. Safe. My mistake. Should cross before floodwaters."

"But it didn't rain," Jonathan protested. "Where did that come from?"

"You see dark clouds over mountain?"

"Well... yes. But we had sunshine."

"No matter. Storm on peak. Rain falls fast. Water runs down like fire. We watch for flash floods now."

That evening they sat with the Arapaho around a glowing fire. Jonathan couldn't understand the conversation, but laughter and gestures told their own stories. He smiled, wrote a few lines in his journal, and marveled that these supposed "savages" were far kinder than many white men he had met.

Stars glittered through the pines. Crickets and owls sang into the night. As Jonathan drifted toward sleep, he thought he saw Charles — his loyal servant — lingering in the shadows, watching over him still.

Chapter Twenty-Seven

River of Snakes

"A very great vision is needed and the man who has it must follow it as the eagle seeks the deepest blue of the sky."
— Crazy Horse, Oglala Lakota Sioux

After an early breakfast, Jonathan and Omache gave their thanks and farewells to the Arapaho and resumed their journey westward. The towering mountain peaks of the Rockies closed around them as the trail followed a narrow river valley through steep, craggy walls. Meadows appeared frequently now, green and wet with life — a welcome contrast to the dry prairies behind them.

Ten days later they reached Fort Hall, Idaho. Here pioneers had the choice to continue on the Oregon Trail or turn south toward California.

Jonathan gazed at the massive timber walls of the fort, the largest settlement he'd seen since Independence. Wagons clustered everywhere. Traders hawked goods. Horses grazed freely in the meadows.

He and Omache were greeted by friendly traders. Soon a small mountain of supplies lay beside their wagon. The horses grazed peacefully while Jonathan paid twenty-five cents at the fort for a hot bath, shave, and haircut. Feeling reborn, he added a new derby hat for good measure.

The fort impressed him — its enormous timbers, its wide open space, and the few cavalrymen wandering about. It was owned and operated by the Hudson's Bay Company, which explained its efficiency.

Meanwhile, Omache bathed in the creek, washed down the horses, and began loading the wagon for the final stretch.

Jonathan joined him for supper. "I feel like a new man, Omache!"

The Indian released a faint grin.

"I heard in the fort that Oregon was only three miles away," Jonathan said.

"Yep. Not far."

"When do you figure we'll reach Portland?"

The Indian swatted mosquitoes away from his face. "Should not take bath. Dust keep mosquitoes away." He smirked.

Jonathan chuckled, accustomed by now to Omache's roundabout answers.

A few minutes passed before Omache added more wood to the fire. "No weather trouble, you be in Portland less than one new moon. Maybe less."

Jonathan leapt to his feet and danced a little Irish jig around the flames. Omache watched, amused.

"Three weeks!" Jonathan exclaimed. "Then we shall be there before October first. I can hardly wait to see my dear friend Richard Shively."

Omache lit his pipe and sent three blue rings of smoke drifting into the dark. "I imagine he like to see you too," he said.

Jonathan watched the rings rise and fade among the stars.

"The men at the fort told me we have to cross a river tomorrow," Jonathan said. "A big one. Full of snakes."

Omache nearly choked on his pipe from laughing. He rolled in the grass, tears forming.

"Are you all right?" Jonathan asked, startled.

It took several moments for Omache to regain control. "Always on each journey there is one thing worth a hundred Indian ponies. I think this is it."

"What's so funny?"

"You not listen to everything you hear. They fool with you." Then he shrugged. "Maybe one snake. Harmless."

"They were teasing me, then? A bit of raillery?"

Omache wiped his eyes. "Do not know your words, but yes. They make fun of you. Pull wool over eyes."

"Well," Jonathan said, "no harm done except my pride. But I say cheerio to that." He paused, then added, "No snakes then? Maybe one?"

"Great river called Snake River — not from snakes that bite. River slither like snake from mountains to Nichi-Wana. In morning we cross. No biting snakes. Maybe water snake. Harmless."

Jonathan felt relief. "Not like that other river where we nearly drowned?"

Omache chuckled. "Water slow at Three Island Crossing. Oregon other side. Like crossing little pieces of river. No floodwaters."

That night, with only a few miles left before Oregon, Jonathan wrote in his journal and drifted to sleep.

***

The next morning they rose early. Omache wanted to cross the Snake River before the wagon train behind them caught up.

The river gleamed in the early sun, patches of fog twisting through the reeds. The Indian ponies stepped into the knee-deep water. They climbed onto the first island, crossed a deeper channel to the second, and then approached the last gap.

Far behind them, the wagon train crested the hill.

Jonathan held his breath as the wagon wheels disappeared into the third channel. Water splashed high, rushing just below the spokes. But under Omache's steady hands, the horses crossed cleanly.

They climbed onto dry land — Oregon.

The instant the wagon halted, Jonathan jumped down, raised his arms, and shouted, "I'm in Oregon! I'm in Oregon!"

Omache, expressionless, looked back at the crossing wagon train.

"We go now."

Jonathan scrambled back into the seat, still beaming.

The trail ahead unfolded like a book nearing its final chapters. The high, barren plateau seemed endless. Scarred by erosion and scorched by sun, it offered little comfort. Still, progress was steady.

That evening, under a blistering sunset of orange and red, Omache caught a prairie jack rabbit and simmered a savory stew. Jonathan marveled at how the Indian could turn the thinnest supplies into a feast.

They spoke little. Jonathan leaned against the wagon wheel, watching embers drift into the sky. His thoughts wandered to England — his parents, and especially Emily. He pictured her by the fireplace, curled on the soft velvet chesterfield, reading his stories aloud.

Under the solemn, star-studded heavens, Omache wrapped himself in his braided blanket and watched Jonathan drift toward sleep. A faint, quiet smile softened the deep lines of his face.

Then he, too, closed his eyes and surrendered to the deep night.

Chapter Twenty-Eight

River or Mountain?

"May the stars carry your sadness away. May the flowers fill your heart with beauty.
May hope forever wipe away your tears, and above all, may silence make you strong."
— *Chief Dan George*

The next ten days along the Oregon Trail were among the most grueling Jonathan had endured. Many times he and Omache were forced to climb down from the wagon and push from behind, helping the Indian ponies struggle over steep ruts, rocks, and cruel obstructions. The Blue Mountains and the harrowing slope known as Deadman's Pass tested both man and beast.

Eventually the land evened out. They reached the dry sagebrush plains and stopped at Wells Spring to refill their water vessels. Two modest springs fed the emigrants: one for drinking, another for the horses.

Under the early September sun, Jonathan rinsed thick gritty dust from his mouth. They camped for the night, then continued west the next morning. Along the way they crossed paths with several Indians—mostly friendly—who offered hardtack or dried meat. But sometimes mischief won out. One brave, eyeing Jonathan's derby hat, simply rode up, snatched it clean off his head, and galloped away in a cloud of dust. Jonathan stood stunned, but Omache shook his head ever so slightly: do not react. Jonathan mustered a reluctant smile as the thief disappeared down the trail.

Exhaustion from the long trek had nearly lulled him into sleep when the wagon lurched to a sudden halt. Jonathan shot upright.

"What in the bloody hell—are we under attack?"

Omache didn't answer. He slid off the wagon and moved deliberately toward a dense thicket of willows ahead. Jonathan scrambled to his senses, glancing around. The wagon trail had vanished entirely. And now his guide had disappeared into the brush.

A ripple of unease crept up Jonathan's spine. He reached for his small cavalry pistol strapped to his calf, steadying himself in a defensive stance. The wind moved through the willows, creating soft eerie whispers that seemed almost like voices. Jonathan held his breath, straining to decipher them.

He didn't hear Omache return.

"Glad you awake," Omache said dryly from behind him, "and protect wagon from outlaws."

"Outlaws? What...?" Jonathan lowered the pistol, a wince forming.

Omache climbed back onto the wagon. Only then did Jonathan notice the Indian's trousers soaked up to the waist.

"Put your gun away," Omache said. "Raise netting across back to secure belongings. We cross river now."

Jonathan's face drained of color. "River? Not again. How many more—?"

The Indian ignored the question.

"River is swift but peaceful," he explained. "Better place to cross than wagon trail ford. Here we see bottom. Horses keep eyes on other side. Safe."

Under low-hanging willow branches, Jonathan could hear the river whispering ahead. His breath thinned as they rolled onto a flat rocky bank.

"Which river is this?" he asked shakily. "The Deschutes?"

"John Day," said Omache. "Deschutes after that. Then big river, Nichi-Wana."

Jonathan shivered despite the warm morning. The memory of the earlier flood—the wall of mud roaring downstream—was still very much alive in his bones. He reached up to secure his derby before remembering he no longer had it. Another loss along the way.

But Omache guided the ponies confidently into the sunlit river. Unlike the last crossing, this section had a bed of smooth solid stone. The water hissed softly around the hooves. Jonathan clutched the wagon rail, knuckles white, heartbeat thudding louder than the river itself.

***

They camped on the far side of the John Day River that night, then climbed back up to the Columbia Plateau the next day. Three days later, as they descended the last ridge toward Biggs Junction, the landscape opened before them like a painted canvas.

There it was—the great river Nichi-Wana.

The Columbia shimmered under a crimson sunset, wide and mighty, swallowing the western sky in a wash of red. Jonathan stared silently, breath caught in his throat.

Tomorrow they would cross the Deschutes and make a final decision: take the dangerous, costly route by raft down the Columbia to Portland... or brave the new Barlow Trail around Wy'East—Mount Hood—toward Oregon City.

Neither choice was easy. Most migrants regretted whichever one they chose.

At the confluence of the Deschutes and the Columbia, the river ran deep and swift. Omache secured the wagon, walked to the water's edge, studied the river-scape for several long minutes, then returned to Jonathan.

"We cross here," he said.

Jonathan sputtered into a string of frantic, exhausted objections, but Omache merely placed a wrinkled hand on his arm and gave a small nod.

He braced for death as the ponies stepped into the Deschutes. But Omache's instincts were uncanny. He guided them upstream first, then angled across a series of sandbars, using the shallows to avoid the deeper channels. Only twice did the water reach worrisome depths, but the ponies pushed through.

Moments later the wagon rolled up the western bank of the Deschutes.

Jonathan was speechless. How did he do that?

Providence? Skill? Something older?

He knew then it was no accident they had traveled together.

***

A mile from the river crossing stood the bustling settlement of The Dalles and Fort Dalles: a cavalry post, a mission, a trading hub, and a thriving frontier town. It was also a place where white settlers had pushed many native people from their homelands, and where several violent battles had left scars on both sides.

Just east of the fort, a small village remained—survivors of the Cayuse, Wasco, and others—holding on to what was left of their traditions.

Omache pulled the wagon to the village. He sat with elders in long conversation while Jonathan tended the horses.

A group of native children ran circles around him, laughing. Yet beneath the play he sensed sorrow—something old, heavy, lingering in the people.

He felt like an intruder on someone else's sacred soil. He realized he was witnessing the very edge of a disappearing world, swept aside by the westward tide he was now part of.

Later, around the campfire, the villagers offered a generous meal. Jonathan bowed his head slightly to each one he made eye contact with, trying to convey respect and gratitude. The fire crackled, blending with chants, laughter, and the soft cadence of their language. Something in him shifted—quietly, but deeply.

He slept that night with a fuller heart.

***

The next morning, only ninety miles remained in their two thousand-mile journey. The last little stretch—yet it would feel like the longest.

Jonathan fed and watered the horses and hitched them to the wagon. Omache climbed into his seat but wore a troubled look, his thick eyebrows knit tightly together.

Jonathan didn't notice. He was thinking of the night before—the stories of massacres, loss, betrayal.

"If I were a sleuth," he murmured, "I'd take this to Scotland Yard. Investigate the whole damn thing."

He stopped, realizing Omache was staring at him.

"Sorry," Jonathan said. "I was deep in thought. I'm... troubled."

"What trouble you?" Omache asked, removing Jonathan's derby from his own head and brushing his grayish hair back. He set the rifle down with his other hand.

"It's the massacres," Jonathan said quietly. "The way whites treated them. Taking what isn't theirs. Taking land without even attempting fairness. It isn't right."

"Oh, they get deal from Great White Father in Washington," Omache said bitterly. "Take Indian land. Move Indian to reservation—poor land, no water. Like corralling horses. Take freedom. Many tribes be no more. No respect. No remorse. White man rule all land someday. Many dark moons to come." He pointed toward the Columbia. "One day maybe white man take water too. Everything wild will be harnessed."

"Gosh, Omache..." Jonathan whispered. "We do feel alike. But I don't know what I can do."

"You writer," Omache said simply. "When you in Portland, maybe you write words white man understand. Share Indian feelings. Maybe too late... but maybe not."

A few tears slipped down his weathered face.

"Indian have troubles. Me and you have troubles too."

"What troubles?" Jonathan asked.

"We decide end of journey." Omache sighed. "Before, I take people down river on log raft. Indians help. But now white man run Indian off river. Charge big money. Not safe. Many rapids. Many die."

Jonathan swallowed. "Then what do we do? I can pay."

"We not go down river," Omache said. "We go over mountain."

Jonathan nearly choked. "What mountain?"

Omache pointed toward a snow-tipped peak rising like a giant sentinel in the morning light.

"Wy'East," he said. "White man call Mount Hood."

"You mean we cross over it?"

"White men make road—Barlow Road. Trail around mountain. My brothers say dangerous. Maybe as dangerous as river. I never go over Wy'East. Not want anger Tyee Sahalie."

"Who is Tyee Sahalie?" Jonathan asked.

"Great Spirit," said Omache. "Indian legend say mountains were chiefs once. Wy'East and Klickitat fight for beautiful woman Loowit. Great Spirit punish. Turn all to mountains of fire forever."

"Volcanoes," Jonathan whispered. "But there's no fire now, only snow."

"Yes," Omache said. "But danger still there."

Jonathan took a deep breath. "Well, if the road exists, then I say we press on."

Omache hesitated but finally snapped the reins. The wagon turned south toward Mount Hood.

The first stretch of the Barlow Road seemed tame enough. But neither man knew the trials that awaited them beyond the next ridge.

Jonathan gazed toward the towering mountain and thought of the future. Someday, he believed, there would be a safe passage carved along the cliffs of the river—a road to

Portland. Someday, the wilderness would change again. But for now, they would take the mountain.

Chapter Twenty-Nine

The Canyons Below

"Everything on Earth has a purpose, every disease an herb to cure it and every person has a mission. This is the Indian theory of existence."
— *Mourning Dove, Salish (Christal Quintasket)*

The roadway, its deep ruts filled with a fine flour-like dust, rose into the air with every turn of the wagon wheels and every step of the horses. The dust sifted through the wagon, making it nearly impossible not only to see the road ahead but even to draw a clean breath. Both Jonathan and Omache wore bandannas across their faces.

The September sun climbed high in the sky, pouring its fierce heat down upon the travelers. Sweat mixed with the sticky dust, forming a muddy mask on their exposed skin. Even the horses were whining and snorting.

Forever southward they seemed to journey, crossing several small creeks until at last the road turned sharply west toward the back side of Wy'East. The brown, wrinkled, barren earth gave way to sagebrush and scrubby juniper. A warm, resinous scent filled the air from the sun-baked vegetation. In the distance, the first line of pine trees appeared along the eastern slopes of the mountain.

Following the northern rim of the White River Canyon, climbing slowly in elevation, the air cooled and the dust settled. The relief was welcome—though the drop-offs at the canyon's edge were nothing short of terrifying. The Indian ponies seemed to sense the depth just a few feet away; they trotted with their heads fixed straight ahead. No blinders required.

The wagon swayed and jolted over the rocky trail before finally entering the thick green forest. Eventually they reached the tollgate, where Jonathan paid five dollars for passage on the Barlow Road. From there it was less road and more rugged trail.

The toll keeper took Jonathan's money, then studied the pair—the Englishman and the Indian wearing the derby hat. He shook his egg-shaped head, stroked his chin, and lifted the peeled-log gate.

As the wagon passed through, he leaned on the gate and called out, "Got plenty of rope, do ya?"

Jonathan frowned. "Rope? Whatever for?"

"Well now," the man said, "trail gets mighty steep in places. Too steep for them ponies to go down with the wagon without toppin' over. You'll want several hundred feet of rope to lower that wagon first and have the ponies hold the slack. Yep. I'm thinking so."

Jonathan glanced at Omache. The Indian grunted that they had rope. Jonathan, uneasy, asked if it would be enough.

Omache stopped the wagon and thought over the man's words. "Maybe not. Always can use rope."

"Do you have any for sale?" Jonathan asked.

The gatekeeper nodded and disappeared into a small shack beside the road. He emerged carrying two large coils of braided hemp rope.

"That'll be twenty dollars," he said.

"Twenty dollars?" Jonathan gasped. "That, sir, is four times the road toll."

"Yep, I suppose it is. But you'll thank me when you're lowerin' down those steep canyons ahead."

Jonathan looked at Omache. The Indian's jaw tightened; his expression made his frustration clear. But Jonathan was too close to the end of the journey to risk a foolish economy. He paid the man.

"You'll think kindly on that decision in due time, young fella," the toll keeper said. "Good luck to you—and the Indian."

Annoyed, Omache raised the derby in a half-sarcastic gesture and led the horses through. Jonathan glanced back. The gatekeeper waved and nodded, the very picture of satisfaction.

Did I just get swindled? Jonathan wondered, recalling Louise's warning on the train: beware those who would take advantage of you. He found himself suddenly wondering how she was faring with her dress boutique in Saint Louis.

The forest beyond the gate was dense and shadowy. The thick canopy of fir and pine almost swallowed the daylight. Hours later they reached an empty campground and made camp for the night. While Jonathan tended the horses, Omache started a fire, then took his rifle and disappeared into the woods in search of supper. Jonathan settled by the wagon wheel, opened his journal, and began to write.

***

Onward they traveled through the close, nearly impenetrable forest until at last it opened into a wide, sunlit meadow. Jonathan let out a long breath he hadn't realized he was holding. After miles of dark, suffocating woods, the open space felt like a benediction.

They followed the edge of the forest along the boggy green meadow, spirits raised. Only Omache remained quiet, a shadow in his eyes. He had never traveled this route and still harbored deep doubts about what lay ahead.

They stopped to water the horses. The ponies grazed in the lush grass while Jonathan and Omache sat on a fallen log, gazing up at the close, towering presence of Wy'East. The mountain seemed so near Jonathan felt as though he could reach out and brush the snow from its shoulders. He tried to capture the scene in his journal, but words felt clumsy against such beauty.

With plenty of daylight left, they moved on.

Before long the trail brought them to the lip of a steep canyon. The two men stood several hundred feet above a narrow stream, the road plunging down one side and clawing its way back up the other. Jonathan immediately thought of the gatekeeper and his rope.

"We camp here," said Omache. "Cross canyon in morning."

Jonathan scratched his head, staring at the incline. "We have extra rope, yes. But how do we get the wagon and horses to the bottom?"

Omache pointed to a pair of sturdy fir trees near the rim. "We wrap rope 'round tree, tie to wagon. Horses hold slack—slowly lower wagon down. Good thing we have plenty rope."

That night a full moon rose over the meadow. Stars shimmered like scattered embers across the sky while frogs and crickets sang in layered chorus. An owl hooted from the forest, its deep notes weaving into the song of the night. Jonathan slipped quickly into a deep, exhausted sleep.

Omache remained awake for some time, lying on his bedroll, staring into the heavens.

***

The shift from bright moonlight to pale dawn roused him. He rose quietly, started breakfast, then walked to the ponies and stroked each one, whispering in his native tongue. He prayed softly to the Great Spirit for safe passage across the canyon.

After securing everything in the wagon, they wrapped the rope around one of the fir trees and tied it to the rear axle. With the ponies positioned downhill from the tree, rope taut, they were ready to descend.

"Slow," Omache said, signaling the horses to back up.

Step by step, inch by inch, the wagon eased down the slope. Bark peeled from the tree as the rope scraped against it. Jonathan watched the wagon while Omache led the team.

The wagon settled into deep, worn ruts made by earlier travelers and continued downward. Then, about thirty-five feet from the bottom, it jerked to a stop.

Jonathan peered over the edge. "Looks like a rock wedged behind the rear wheel," he called.

The horses snorted as Omache commanded them to hold steady. He glanced at the distance between them and the tree.

"Not much rope left," he muttered. "Maybe wagon not make bottom. Good thing for rock."

He removed his derby, ran his hand through his hair, and then said, "You stand by horses. Hold them tight. I go down and fix rock."

Jonathan took the reins while Omache found a stout stick and sidestepped down the steep road. Reaching the wagon, he saw a gray rock jammed against the right rear wheel. He climbed into the wagon, retrieved a small shovel, and began to dig it out.

When he was ready, he called up to Jonathan to keep the rope tight, then pried the rock loose. It rolled, then tumbled the remaining distance to the creek below. The wagon lurched as the pressure shifted, and the team surged forward to take up the slack.

Omache lay still in the hard-packed red dirt for a heartbeat, then rose and walked to the edge, measuring the remaining distance to the canyon floor.

He had already paced out the rope between the tree and the horses. Now he knew for certain: they were short. The wagon would not reach the bottom safely on rope alone.

Once more he ran his hand through his hair, then climbed back to the top.

"We short on rope," he said, "but no worry. I have fix."

"How?" Jonathan asked.

"I go back down, make choke. Slow wagon."

"Is that safe?" Jonathan asked, but Omache was already on his way down again. After five months on the trail, Jonathan knew better than to press for reassurances.

The Indian searched the canyon floor for large limbs, dragging several to a spot below the wagon. He fetched a hatchet and some short pieces of rope and rawhide from the wagon and set to work.

He lashed two long poles together with a crosspiece, forming a kind of drag. He tied this to the rear axle so that the poles and crosspiece lay behind the wagon on the ground—a makeshift brake to dig into the dirt as the wagon slid.

At the front he drew his long knife and began to cut the rope. As the last strands stretched to breaking, he shouted for Jonathan to move the horses forward.

The rope snapped free. The wagon lurched, the drag biting into the slope. It bumped and slid down the remaining thirty-five feet, slowing just enough to reach the flat ground beside the creek without overturning.

Once it came to rest, Omache gathered the severed length of rope and called up to Jonathan, telling him to lead the horses forward. Holding the rope, he climbed back up the slope to meet him.

After a short rest, they led the team down the canyon road and hitched them to the wagon again, this time facing uphill on the opposite side. With the rope and tree arranged much as before—only in reverse—they slowly pulled the wagon up the far slope.

It was no small feat. Not all pioneers were that skilled—or that fortunate. And they would have to repeat this entire process two more times before they cleared the worst of the mountain road and reached more forgiving ground to the west.

**

As they rolled toward the end of the Oregon Trail at Oregon City, they met more and more white settlers along the way. It was as if they had crossed an unseen border into another world—the promised land of the westward dreamers.

Jonathan's spirits lifted. At one trading post he purchased another derby hat.

Omache just shook his head and muttered something in his own language that Jonathan chose to interpret as affectionate disapproval.

They bathed, changed into clean garments, and brushed the dust from their hair and coats. Even the Indian ponies seemed to sense the journey's approaching end.

Oregon City lay only a few miles ahead. From there, it would be a short journey to downtown Portland, where the two travelers would part ways.

At least, that was what Jonathan had always imagined.

Chapter Thirty

End of the Trail

"Don't let yesterday use up too much of today."
— Cherokee proverb

Oregon City greeted them with a quiet indifference. Their arrival barely stirred notice amid the bustle of one of the territory's fastest-growing communities. Jonathan, however, was captivated. The mix of rough-hewn buildings, busy storefronts, and sawdust-lined streets hinted at a town rising quickly from wilderness.

Omache stopped at the livery to arrange boarding for the wagon and the ponies. Jonathan's trunks and belongings were transferred to the stagecoach for the short ride to Portland.

The two men walked to the stagecoach terminal and waited on the wooden platform for departure.

"Wow, Omache," Jonathan said, shaking his head in disbelief. "I can't believe I finally made it here. It feels like years since I left England. Everything I've learned on this journey... I'd say it equals a university education. I have stacks of journals to go through—more material than I could ever dream of. I never would've made it without your help."

Omache exhaled softly. "Yes. Long journey. Many moons. My pleasure to travel with you. Never knew Englishman before. I learn much from you too." He tried to hide the heaviness gathering in his eyes.

"What will you do now, Omache?"

The Indian thought for a moment, weighing his words. "I think this was my last trip on Oregon Trail. Maybe settle down somewhere. Find home for my ponies. Maybe go up the Nichi-Wana, help my brothers there. Maybe return to Okanogan. But first I go with you to Portland. Meet... what you call him?"

"Mr. Shively," Jonathan said, grinning. "Yes—please do. He will absolutely want to meet the man who guided me all the way here."

The coach arrived, luggage loaded, and the two climbed inside—perhaps the most unusual pair in town, both wearing derby hats. Soon they were rumbling toward downtown Portland.

***

As the coach descended toward the waterfront, they saw boats on the Willamette, a lumber mill churning out planks, and construction stretching along the riverbanks in every direction.

"Big change," Omache muttered. "Last time I here, little village. Now... too much noise. Rather ride outside wagon than in this iron box."

They rolled down Main Street until the driver pulled up in front of the Willamette World newspaper building.

"I unload baggage. You go find Mr. Shively," said Omache.

Jonathan nodded, stepped inside, removed his derby, and approached a young red-haired woman at the counter.

"Good afternoon. I'm Jonathan Butler, from England. I'm here to see Mr. Shively. Is he in?"

She lowered her spectacles and set aside a stack of papers. "You don't have to be so formal, Mr. Butler. Are you the writer he's been going on about?"

Jonathan blinked. "Um—yes. It has been a rather long journey."

"Well, he's arranged a reporter position for you. You'll find your desk back near the wall—yes, that corner with all the old newspapers piled up."

Jonathan glanced uncertainly at the disheveled corner. "Right... I suppose I'll get started soon. I'll need a place to stay as well, so I do need a word with Mr. Shively. Do you know where he is?"

"My name is Daisy. Daisy McClay. Do you prefer Butler or Jonathan?"

"Jonathan suits me just fine," he said with a small laugh.

"Well then," Daisy replied, amused, "you'll likely find Mr. Shively down the street at the saloon. Let's see... yes, it's half-past three. He'll be there. Probably Mr. Block, the editor, with him."

"Thank you, Daisy. I'll return after I've found him and, ah... prepared my desk."

He tipped his hat and turned toward the door.

"Jonathan," Daisy called after him.

He paused. "Yes, Miss Daisy?"

"Where on earth did you get that hat?"

"The derby? Well—my Indian friend has one, and I thought it rather fashionable, so I picked mine up in Oregon City."

"You don't see many of those out here."

"They're new, really. In England we call them bowler hats. First saw one at university three years ago. I was shocked to see Omache wearing one when I first stepped off the train in Independence—being an Indian and all—but it's rather becoming on him. Makes him a jolly old soul."

Daisy smiled. "You have many stories in you, Mr. Butler. People here could use some lighter reading."

Jonathan nodded and stepped outside.

"I can see this will be a challenging position, Omache."

The Indian shrugged. "I find white man's words amusing. Wonder if they know what they say half the time. Where is your friend Shively?"

"At the saloon down the street. Do you know what a saloon is?"

"White man call it watering hole. Drink spirits. Get drunk."

"Oh—a pub."

"Don't know pub. Know saloon."

"In England we call it a public house."

"Me sure saloon here different from your public house. We go."

***

The two derby-hatted travelers walked along the board-walk toward the saloon. Jonathan pushed open the double swinging doors, and they stepped inside. Before he could survey the room, a booming voice rang out.

"Jonathan, my boy!"

He spun around to see Shively grinning widely at the bar. Jonathan rushed to him, and the two embraced.

"It is so good to see you," Jonathan said. "I can't believe I'm finally here."

"Look at you!" Shively laughed. "I see you've made it across in fine fashion."

"Couldn't have done it without my guide—and now dear friend—Omache."

Shively clasped both of the Indian's arms and thanked him warmly for bringing Jonathan safely across the trail.

"Keep!" Shively shouted to the barkeep. "Food and drink for my friends!"

He introduced Jonathan to Editor Talbot "Tally" Block, and they all gathered at a table.

"So tell me," Shively said, "how was the journey across the sea and the wagon road?"

Jonathan drew a deep breath. "Richard, there is so much to tell. My entire journey is written in my journals—every hardship, every wonder. I feel I aged five years in six months. But I hope to share it all with the readers back home."

"Jolly good," Shively said. "Block here has some ideas for you."

Block leaned in. "Young man, Shively's told me a fair bit about your skill with a pen. This paper needs more than news—it needs stories readers feel. Something fresh. Something human. I want to attract new eyes, new advertisers. I've been looking for someone who sees the world differently. An outsider's voice. Perhaps our new feature editor."

Jonathan blinked. "Why... that is most flattering, Mr. Block. I have no experience as a reporter, mind you. I've only just arrived in America—"

"Exactly," Block said with a grin. "Fresh eyes. New words. That's what we need. You'll do just fine."

"Of course he will," Shively added. "This place is full of strange happenings and opportunity. Not a day goes by that doesn't make a good story. After supper we'll get you settled. I've secured a room for you at Ma Griffith's boarding house—a few blocks away. Fine place with hot baths and a lovely view of the Willamette."

Block nodded. "Yes, yes—go get your room arranged, then be at the paper first thing tomorrow. We'll go over the basics. Oh, and call me Tally. Talbot is far too formal."

After a hearty meal and a long chat, the men parted ways. Shively escorted Jonathan to Ma Griffith's boarding house, while Omache decided to camp along the riverbank.

One journey had ended and another was just beginning.

Chapter Thirty-One

Of Ink and Press

"Only to the white man was nature a wilderness and only him was the land 'infested' with 'wild' animals and 'savage' people. To us it was tame, Earth was bountiful and we were surrounded with the blessings of the Great Mystery." ~Black Elk, Oglaha Lakota Sioux

It seemed like forever, the journey from far away England to Portland. Jonathan settled deep into the mattress as the early morning sun peaked through the curtains covering the white wooden window panes. Gazing at the ceiling he figured he better get up and make his way to the newspaper office.

Downstairs in the boarding house Ma Griffith had breakfast ready for the boarders. Jonathan grabbed a muffin nodded at the folks seated at the table and dashed out the door. Omache was waiting for him at the sidewalk.

"Good morning my dear friend."

Omache released a rare smile and hugged Jonathan. "I go now, head up the Nichi-Wana visit tribe at Hood River."

Jonathan shrugged his shoulders and with watering eyes, placed his arm on the old Indian, "Go in peace my brother, you were sent from Heaven to guide me into the unknown. I will forever be grateful and part of you will remain in my soul. I do look forward to seeing you again as I venture and explore this region. Maybe I write story about you."

The Indian with frowning wrinkles draping down his weathered cheeks replied. "You one great fellow. Always my white brother. I part now, not good with good-byes."

Jonathan stepped back and Omache began his walk along the riverbank. Jonathan stood there probably longer than he should have until the old Indian had disappeared into the distance.

He wiped his face with his handkerchief and walked to the Willamette World office. It was a bittersweet day, a new beginning on the coattails of an old departing adventure.

"Good morning Jonathan," shouted Daisy as he walked into the office. He grinned and waved as he made his way to his desk. Standing there over his desk in deep thought, Daisy added, "Good luck with that."

Turning to her he replied, "Anywhere to box up and store these papers?"

"There are some empty boxes over there in the corner, you can take them upstairs and stash them wherever you can in the storage room. There's plenty more up there."

He removed his jacket and rolled up his sleeves. After an hour or so he had the dusty pile of papers upstairs. Dusting and sweeping his work area complete he sat at his desk. He organized the files and acquired paper and pen and a box of wooden pencils.

He removed several photos from his bag of his parents, Emily and one of their faithful and wise servant, Charles. While he was excited beginning his new career, he had yet to feel the deep absence of his family and friends.

Approaching Jonathan, Daisy suddenly broke his solitude, "There is coffee on the wood stove and alongside fresh bagels from Donald's Bakery."

Looking up at her he replied, "Why thank you. Is there a bit of tea as well?"

Smiling almost interrupting him, "Some how I knew you were going to ask that. Silly me, of course, the English like their tea, don't they?"

"That is one thing I really missed on the trail was tea. Had to stomach the taste of coffee a few times. Is there . . ."

"General store up one block and then one block toward the river," she quickly replied.

"Okay then, I will be back directly. By the way, who's desk is that next to mine?

"Our news reporter Daniel, you can call him Danny. He'll be in sooner or later, doesn't keep steadfast hours but when he is in writing, he is a whirlwind of activity."

"Very well see you shortly." Jonathan walked toward the general store for hopefully, some English tea.

Back at his desk and sipping on some hot tea he reviewed his travel journals, thinking of stories to write and questions about the Portland area to ponder and discover.

"Hold the presses! Hold the presses!" shouted an ambitious young man running through the door with a handful of papers wearing a plaid checkered jacket and bowtie.

"Am I too late Daisy? I've got a hot one." Before she could answer he dashed out the back door to the pressroom.

"See what did I tell you?' Daisy took another sip of her coffee. Jonathan looking rather astonished, smiled.

"Are they printing the paper today?" asked Jonathan.

"Yep, every Thursday and it is out on the street Friday morning. I haven't taken you back to the pressroom, have I?"

They walked to the back of the newsroom and through a set of double doors. There were several platen printing presses and drawers and drawers of type along one wall. Bundles of newsprint were in the rear by the doors to the loading dock. Several men with black ink smudges on their hands and face were busy running the presses. Danny was shouting to one of the printers about to run the front page.

"They look like they are in a heated conversation are they not?

Daisy chuckled and raised her voice to Jonathan over the noise of the activity, "Nothing new, he dashes in all the time with a hot story."

"I'll introduce you later to the rest of the staff after the rush is over. Everyone is a bit in a frenzy at the moment as you can see."

"Very well," replied Jonathan as they returned to the newsroom.

"We have other stringers who gather and write news stories and bring them in daily. Also, a man who works closely with Block soliciting advertisements for the paper. We also print other documents for individuals and businesses. You will always see plenty of action as the days go by."

Jonathan, more accustomed to structure and the hallowed halls of Cambridge could see he would have to adjust to the new world and occupation he had entered.

Block arrived a short while later and called Jonathan in his office. "Did you get settled in? I hope you didn't find this place overwhelming?"

"Well . . ." He was interrupted quickly.

"No worry now, you'll get the hang of it. Just pick that pen up and start writing some words. Introduce yourself to the readers, tell about your travels. What's going on back east. How is England fairing these days and so forth?"

"Great, there will be no shortage of things to write about." Jonathan trying to hold back his look of bewilderment.

"Alright then, I'm always here if you need something or advice. Daisy can fill you in with the deadlines, schedules and other protocols.

"Thank you, Mr. Block, for this opportunity I won't let you down." Jonathan smiled and left his office.

Danny returned to his desk from the pressroom and he and Jonathan chatted a while. "What was all the excitement when you rushed in this morning?" asked Jonathan.

"They found a body floating in the river early this morning."

"Really?"

"Yep and it wasn't the first either. Seen several here this past year."

Jonathan raised his eyebrows a bit, frowned and replied, "Have they all been identified? How did they get in the river?"

"Drowned. This one looked like he was strangled. No idea what his name is and probably won't be able to identify the body."

"Why not?" asked Jonathan.

"He was Chinese. Probably from Chinatown. Perhaps they were caught up in a shanghai."

Jonathan thought of the old man below deck of the ship that was forced to work the sailing from London. "Does that really happen here?"

"All kinds of shady things go on down at the waterfront where the ships dock. I hear things, can't prove it; the police won't talk about it. People come and go in Portland, who knows?"

"Why don't the police look in to that kind of stuff? A good detective could most likely figure that out. In London we have Scotland Yard, difficult to pull the wool over their eyes."

Danny chuckled. "We have two kinds of police here. The East Precinct on the other side of the river, the police are much more cooperative and honest. Here on the west side, not so much."

After Jonathan settled back at his desk he thought of his recent journey across the prairies and mountains of the United States. Before his journey from England, he had heard of savages and wild beasts lurking in the shadows and life and death perils.

The savages were Indians and for the most part were quite friendly and wanted their rights to the territory which they inhabited for centuries. The beasts were the natural wildlife found in the countryside as he traveled. They were more afraid of man than anything and tended to avoid humans. Confronted yes, the wild instincts took over. Omache knew how to avoid and confront them in peace. Only killing an animal for survival and no part of an animal went to waste to the Indians.

Jonathan could now see how the Indians felt about the influx of white settlers. Could they be the savages and beasts? One land and two different types of peoples.

Could they live in peace with one another? The white man had difficulties living with others of any breed it seemed to Jonathan. He had plenty to learn in this new frontier of the west. Not that England didn't have a dark side as well.

Chapter Thirty-Two

Portland's Dark Secret

"It is easy to be brave from a distance." ~Omaha Proverb

The winter rains had settled over Portland in a long, steady curtain, softening the outlines of the wooden buildings and turning the unpaved streets into thick ribbons of mud. Gray clouds hung low above the Willamette, and every roof—from shingled boarding houses to the riverfront saloons—echoed with the slow, persistent tapping of the season.

Jonathan, now several months into his new life in the city, had grown accustomed to the chill dampness that seeped into one's coat and bones. Yet with each passing storm he felt a deeper stirring, a sense that the true work of his journey was only beginning.

***

Block, notoriously sparing with praise, pointed to Jonathan's latest feature story one afternoon. "You've got a manner of seeing things," he grunted. "Makes folks read past the first paragraph." Coming from Block, this was essentially a medal of honor.

Even Shively, who had known Jonathan long before the trail, shook his head in pleasant astonishment. "You bring a gentle feeling to your words," he told him. "People sense that. They trust you."

Jonathan accepted their compliments with modesty, though privately their words warmed him. His journals back in England had been whispers to himself. Now his words belonged to a city—one growing by the day.

But beneath his progress, another feeling gathered like fog on the Willamette.

Portland brimmed with stories, but some of them felt wrong—like threads deliberately tucked out of sight. Down by the waterfront he heard whispers: a missing deckhand, a frightened Chinese boy who'd seen "men in the fog," a sailor who'd been beaten and warned to keep silent about the shanghai trade.

Jonathan kept these details tucked in his pocket like sharp stones. He wasn't ready to write about them. Not yet. But he would.

A journalist worth anything must walk toward shadows, not away from them.

***

Jonathan had found his footing at the Willamette World. He wrote steadily—small features, human-interest pieces, reflections on life in the West—yet something in the deeper undercurrent of Portland was beginning to tug at him. A feeling. A whisper. A knowing that the surface bustle of the town concealed a darker mechanism at work.

It didn't take long before Danny confirmed it.

Jonathan was halfway through revising a column on river commerce when Danny dropped into the chair beside him, smelling faintly of ink, wet wool, and urgency.

"You've heard about the third floater this month, haven't you?" Danny asked quietly.

He put his pencil down. "Only that a fisherman found him tangled in the pilings. No identification, I suppose?"

Danny shook his head grimly. "Chinese. Same as the last two. Marks around the wrists. Throat bruised. Shirt torn. And no one's asking questions."

Jonathan frowned. "But that's absurd. Surely the police—"

Danny raised an eyebrow. "Which police? East Side or West?"

Jonathan blinked. "There's a difference?"

"A world of one." Danny leaned closer. "East Side constables do their jobs. Here on the west bank? Money changes hands faster than a poker deck. Captains, saloon owners, the law—half of them are in each other's pockets. You want answers, don't go asking them."

His pulse ticked upward. "Are you saying these men were... taken?"

Danny didn't blink. "Shanghai'd."

Jonathan sat back slowly. "Like sailors carried off in London...?"

"Worse," Danny said. "We're the shanghai capital of the West Coast. Some won't admit it, but men vanish here. Free whiskey, drugged drinks, trapdoors, tunnels under half these saloons. Wake up on a ship halfway to Honolulu."

A soft knock on the desk made both men jolt. Daisy stood beside them holding a stack of envelopes, her auburn hair a bit wind-tossed, her eyes alive with their usual spark.

"You two look like a pair of undertakers planning a sale," she teased lightly. "Should I be worried?"

Jonathan forced a small smile. "Only discussing Portland's... peculiarities."

Daisy's expression softened. "Then let me add one thing: if you go snooping down by the docks, don't go alone."

Jonathan's chest warmed unexpectedly. "You're concerned for my safety?"

Her lips curved just enough to make him question what she meant. "I'm concerned we'll lose a perfectly good writer before he's learned where we keep the spare pencils."

But when she turned away, he caught the faintest flicker of genuine caring in her eyes.

***

That evening the rain had eased into a fine mist as Jonathan walked toward the riverfront. Curiosity had always been part of him—sometimes a blessing, sometimes a trouble. Tonight it felt like both.

The Willamette rolled dark and wide beneath the lantern lights. Saloons glowed amber through their windows. Steamships honked downriver. The city breathed an uneasy rhythm. Then he saw it.

A red lantern—dim, weathered—hanging above a door with no sign and no window. A saloon, but one with secrets. A dull thud sounded beneath the floorboards. Then another. And a low groan that seemed to vibrate through the wet planks.

Jonathan stepped back.

A man in a dark coat leaned against the building's corner, pretending to smoke but watching the door too intently. Jonathan turned away and walked down a narrow side street sloping toward the river. Fog clung low to the ground. The silence behind him felt weighted.

Halfway down the alley he noticed a grate—small, iron, half-hidden beneath ivy. Warm air drifted through it. And behind that... voices.

Shouts. Chains. Men calling out in fear.

Jonathan's breath stilled. He crouched to listen and saw a flicker of lantern light dancing in the dark hollow below.

Before he could think what to do, footsteps approached. Heavy. Purposeful.

Jonathan slipped into the shadow of a recessed doorway as two men trudged past carrying a limp figure between them—arms dragging, boots scraping. They turned behind the red-lantern saloon and disappeared into an alley thick with darkness.

He felt the truth settle like ice in his bones.

Danny was right.

Daisy was right.

This was no rumor.

He had stumbled upon the hidden machinery of Portland's underworld, and he was far too close.

***

The next morning he sat at his desk sorting notes when Daisy appeared with two steaming mugs.

"You look half-frozen," she said, setting one down beside him. "You were at the docks again, weren't you?"

Jonathan smiled a little. "Guilty as charged."

"You ought to be careful down there." She tried to sound casual, but her eyes softened. "People disappear."

"Only sometimes," he teased, attempting levity.

"Jonathan." She folded her arms. "Don't make me fetch Block to talk sense into you."

Her concern surprised him—and warmed him more than the tea. He found himself studying her in a new way: the confidence in her posture, the ember-bright hair escaping her pinned bun, the way she seemed to understand people better than anyone else in the newsroom.

"Thank you," he said gently. "Truly."

She flushed slightly but grinned. "Just don't make Portland write an article about you."

Before he could reply, the front door opened and a rain-soaked trapper stepped inside. His boots clomped across the wooden floor as he scanned the room.

"You the English fellow?" he asked, locking eyes with Jonathan.

Jonathan rose slowly. "I am."

"Got a message for you." The trapper placed a small carved token into Jonathan's hand—smooth river wood marked with symbols he recognized instantly.

Omache's hand.

Omache's sign.

"Your friend says he needs you upriver," the trapper added. "Says trouble's rising like spring floodwater. Says to follow the salmon's path."

Jonathan closed his hand around the token, feeling the weight of both worry and destiny settle in his palm.

Daisy touched his arm. "What does that mean?"

"It means," Jonathan whispered, "my next journey begins sooner than I thought."

PATRICK TIMM

And far beneath Portland's muddy streets, the echoes of trapped voices seemed to rise with the winter rain.

Chapter Thirty-Three

Trouble in the Shadows

"When you die, you will be judged by how much you love, not how much you know." ~Native proverb

The winter rains had grown colder, heavier, almost metallic in their persistence. Each morning Jonathan stood at his small window in Ma Griffith's boarding house and watched the Willamette churn like a restless creature beneath the low gray clouds. Portland seemed to hunch its shoulders beneath the weather, its wooden buildings dripping constantly, its muddy streets filled with wagon ruts deep enough to swallow a boot.

Jonathan, now several months into his new life, felt both settled and unsettled—rooted in the newsroom, yet tugged by threads of mystery beyond its walls. His morning routine, once comforting, had recently begun to carry a strange undertone, as though the city itself whispered secrets behind its rain-soaked shutters. At the Willamette World, he wrote daily—stories of river commerce, pioneer hardships, local tragedies, and even a small feature about the drifting lantern festival the Chinese community held in the winter months.

Block praised him openly. Daisy teased him gently. Danny brought him along on small assignments as though grooming him into the life of a true newspaperman.

Yet Jonathan sensed there was something underneath Portland's surface that no one had fully spoken aloud. Something connected to the river... the disappearances... the bodies.

***

One gray morning Daisy stepped lightly to his desk with a sealed envelope.

"A letter for you, Jonathan. Arrived on the west bound last week."

He recognized the handwriting instantly—Emily.

His breath caught. He carried the letter to the potbelly stove, letting its warmth steady him before breaking the seal. Emily's words were soft, affectionate, filled with news of home and inquiries of his safety. She mentioned walking the foggy lanes near the old mill where they once strolled together. She prayed he was well in the wild American west.

Jonathan folded the letter carefully and held it against his chest for a moment. Homesickness washed over him like a tide. Portland felt very far from London in that instant.

Danny appeared beside him, wiping rain from his slicker.

"Don't get too comfortable, Butler. I've got something for you."

"What is it?"

Danny lowered his voice. "Another man went missing last night. Chinese. Vanished after stepping into a saloon on Front Street. Same place where the first body was found. Police will say nothing, of course."

Jonathan felt a chill, not from the drafty office but from the truth Danny's tone implied.

"Do you think it's... connected?"

Danny raised an eyebrow. "Everything on that riverfront is connected."

Jonathan glanced toward the rain-lashed windows. "What's the name of the saloon?"

"The Starlight." Danny smirked. "Fancy seeing how brave the English are?"

Jonathan straightened. "I suppose we should look."

Daisy overheard, her expression tightening with concern. "Be careful down there," she said quietly. "Men vanish in that part of town. Police turn their heads unless it happens on the east side."

"I'll be cautious," Jonathan replied, though he wasn't entirely sure he believed his own reassurance.

***

The Starlight Saloon sat near the docks, its lanterns glowing dimly through the falling rain. A narrow wooden boardwalk skirted the muddy embankment. Voices drifted from inside—rough, low, wary. Danny stopped short of entering.

"Best you go alone," Danny said. "They know me too well around here."

Jonathan's nerves fluttered, but he squared his shoulders and pushed through the swinging doors.

Inside, smoke hung low. A card game raged in the corner. A few sailors drank in silence. The bartender, a thickset man with a crooked nose, eyed Jonathan suspiciously.

"What'll it be?"

Jonathan took a steady breath. "Just information."

"That costs more than whiskey," the man grunted.

Jonathan placed a coin on the counter. "A man went missing here last night. Chinese. Short, brown jacket. Seen him?"

The bartender's face tightened. "Don't know what you're talking about."

A few men nearby shifted in their seats.

Jonathan sensed the air change—thicken. Someone stood behind him.

A voice whispered, "Best step outside, friend."

Jonathan turned slightly. A tall, gaunt man with sunken eyes and a wet stovepipe hat leaned close.

"You ask the wrong questions in this place, you end up on the wrong boat."

Jonathan swallowed hard. "I'm with the Willamette World. Just seeking truth."

"That's what gets you killed quickest."

The bartender slammed a mug hard on the counter.

"Out. Now."

Jonathan stepped backward toward the door, hands raised slightly. The patrons watched him with the cold interest of wolves sizing up a stray sheep.

Just as he exited into the rain-soaked street, he heard a floorboard creak oddly behind the bar—too hollow, too deliberate.

A trap door.

He backed away, pulse racing.

"Jonathan! This way!" Danny hissed from the shadows of a nearby alley.

The two slipped around a stack of crates just as someone pushed through the saloon doors behind them.

They were being watched.

***

By the time they reached safer streets, Jonathan's breath was visible in the cold night air. Danny smirked, half-applauding, half-scolding.

"You've got guts, Butler, I'll give you that. But those men don't play games. They shanghai for coin. They'll trap a man, drop him through a false floor, and by morning he's halfway to San Francisco."

Jonathan steadied himself. "We need to expose this."

Danny sighed. "Maybe. But we need proof, not rumors."

Proof.

Jonathan knew where he might find some—up the river, among Omache's people, where stories traveled as swiftly as water and truth was spoken plain.

But winter storms barred the way.

For now.

He looked toward the dark river beyond the rooftops, the water shimmering with rain.

A thought formed quietly in his chest—half fear, half certainty:

This city was not done testing him.

And he was not done answering.

Chapter Thirty-Four

East Side Constable

"We do not inherit the earth from our ancestors, we borrow it from our children." ~Native proverb

Winter deepened, not in stormy ferocity but in a slow, lingering gray that seemed reluctant to let go. The Willamette ran high and cold, its current swollen by weeks of rain and mountain snowmelt. Every so often, a fleeting patch of blue appeared between the clouds, hinting that spring waited somewhere just beyond the rim of the world.

Jonathan felt the same way—caught between seasons. One foot in Portland, ink on his fingers and the newspaper's bustle in his ears; the other already leaning upriver toward Omache and the tribes. The carved token in his pocket had become a constant weight, a silent reminder that his journey west was not yet complete.

***

He and Danny sat in a small café near the riverfront one damp afternoon, steam curling from their cups. Outside, wagons clattered past, wheels grinding through slush and mud. Jonathan had just finished a column on the lumber trade when Danny leaned closer.

"I've been thinking," Danny said, lowering his voice. "About the Starlight. About what you heard under those floorboards."

Jonathan's jaw tightened at the memory. "Yes?"

"We need something harder than whispers. Something even Block can't spike."

"What do you suggest? I don't particularly fancy being dropped through a trapdoor to conduct my research."

Danny half-grinned. "No, I suppose not. But there are people who hear more than you or I ever will. People the shanghaiers never notice."

"Such as?"

Danny glanced toward the rain-slick window as if the glass itself might be listening. "East Side constable. Norwegian fellow, name of Larsen. He's got more sense of justice than most men I know. Can't do much on this side of the river, but he hears plenty from sailors who stagger across the bridge after a night in those saloons."

Jonathan stirred his tea slowly. "Do you know him?"

"Met him twice. He's wary of newspapermen, but he hates what's happening on the docks. If you talk to anyone, talk to him."

Jonathan nodded, feeling a flicker of purpose. "Then I shall."

"And Butler?" Danny added. "Best to not go alone."

***

The next day, under a sky the color of tarnished silver, Jonathan crossed the wooden bridge over the Willamette. The river surged beneath the planks, carrying driftwood and the occasional log from upriver camps. East Portland felt quieter, less crowded—fewer saloons, more houses with tidy yards and thin threads of smoke curling from chimneys.

He found the small East Side precinct in a plain building off a muddy street. Inside, a tall fair-haired man in a worn blue coat sat at a desk, sorting through a pile of reports.

"Constable Larsen?" Jonathan asked.

The man looked up, gray eyes sharp but not unkind. "That's me. And you are?"

"Jonathan Butler. I write for the Willamette World." He paused, then added, "The west-side paper."

Larsen's mouth twitched in something that might have been amusement. "Well, that's a brave confession to make in my office. What brings you across the river, Mr. Butler?"

Jonathan hesitated only a moment. "I'm looking for the truth about men who go missing along the waterfront."

The constable's gaze grew more serious. "I see. And what do you think you'll do with that truth?"

"Tell it," Jonathan said simply. "In print."

Larsen leaned back in his chair. "If only ink were as strong as rope. Or as final as a bullet."

He gestured to a chair. Jonathan sat.

"I can't speak for what happens over there," Larsen began, nodding toward the west bank. "Not officially, anyway. But I see the after-effects. Sailors limping off ships months later with stories they're too frightened to repeat. Chinese families looking for brothers and cousins who never come home. River captains suddenly flush with crewmen no one remembers hiring."

Jonathan's stomach tightened. "So it is as bad as they say."

"Worse," Larsen replied. "There are tunnels under that part of town. Old basements connected, bricked passages running from saloons to the docks. Some used to move freight in bad weather. Now used to move... people."

"And the police?" Jonathan asked quietly.

Larsen studied him for a long moment. "On this side, we do what we can. On that side... some do their duty. Some do as they're paid. You understand?"

Jonathan did. Too well.

"Why tell me this?" he asked.

"Because," Larsen said, "you look like a man who hasn't yet learned how to be afraid properly. That's a dangerous quality. But sometimes, dangerous men are useful."

He opened a drawer and took out a folded scrap of paper, sliding it across the desk. Jonathan unfolded it to find a rough sketch—blocks of streets, a few squares marked with an X.

"Those are places you stay away from at night," Larsen said. "Especially a man with an accent and a notebook."

Jonathan frowned. "And if I wished to write about them?"

"Do it from a distance." Larsen's eyes hardened. "And if you ever get pulled below those floorboards, remember—scream all you like. No one above will hear you."

A chill traced Jonathan's spine. He folded the paper and tucked it inside his coat. "Thank you, Constable."

"One more thing," Larsen said as Jonathan stood. "You seem like a man who listens. So listen to this: if you really want to understand this country, don't just stare at the city. Go where the river goes. Talk to those who were here before you. They see things the rest of us do not."

Jonathan thought of Omache's token, heavy in his pocket. "I intend to," he said.

Larsen nodded. "Then maybe we'll both live long enough to see things change."

***

On his way back across the bridge, Jonathan paused halfway and gripped the railing. The river rolled beneath him in restless folds, heading toward the great Columbia and the sea beyond.

He imagined hidden tunnels under the west bank, trap-doors and lanterns, frightened men dragged along damp stone passages.

Then he imagined quiet villages upriver. Fires in winter lodges. The calm, weathered face of Omache. Stories told beneath the stars.

Two worlds. One river running between them.

As he stood there, a strong gust of wind rushed up the channel, whipping his coat and stinging his eyes with spray. It felt almost like a voice—invisible, insistent—pushing him forward.

He knew then that his time in Portland, at least in this first stretch, was nearing a turning point.

He would not abandon the shanghai story. But to understand it fully, he needed distance and perspective—needed to see the river as more than a dark ribbon beneath saloon lights.

He needed to answer Omache's call.

***

That evening, as he returned to the newsroom, Daisy watched him hang his damp coat by the stove.

"You crossed the river," she said, as if stating the weather.

"How did you guess?"

"You have that look." She smiled faintly. "Like you've seen something you can't quite put into words yet."

He hesitated. "I spoke with a constable there. An honest one. He confirmed much of what Danny and I suspected."

"And?" she asked.

"And he told me to go where the river goes if I want to understand this land."

Daisy looked at him for a long, quiet moment. "Then I suppose you'll be leaving soon."

He didn't answer right away. The newsroom hummed around them—Block arguing with the typesetter, Danny swearing at a broken pencil, the press thumping faintly in the back.

At last, Jonathan said softly, "When the weather breaks. When the roads and the river are passable."

Daisy nodded, eyes bright but steady. "Then we'll have to make good use of the days between."

"How so?" he asked.

She smiled. "By giving our readers something worth missing you for."

He laughed quietly, tension easing from his shoulders. "I shall do my utmost."

He returned to his desk and the carved token in his pocket seemed to warm against his palm. The rain began to lighten, and far to the east, above the black silhouettes of the hills, clouds thinned enough to reveal a band of pale, promising sky. Spring was coming and with it, the next bend in the river.

Chapter Thirty-Five

The Call of the River

"All rivers run to the sea, yet the sea is never full. So it is with the heart." ~Native proverb

Winter did not end in a grand gesture; it simply began to fade. The rains softened. The icy bite in the wind eased. Buds appeared on the bare branches along the Willamette as though testing the air, unsure whether it could be trusted. Portland, still muddy and uneven, shed its gray mantle one shade at a time.

Jonathan felt the shift as keenly as the horses along the waterfront. The season was turning—and with it, so was he.

One morning, he stood beside the Willamette as mist rose from its surface in delicate curls. The water still ran fast, but clearer now, touched by early spring sunlight. Jonathan inhaled the cool air and found himself remembering the steady rhythm of the prairie, the smell of sage, the strength of Omache's ponies, and the laughter of the Arapaho around that mountain fire.

He also remembered Larsen's words:

"Don't just stare at the city. Go where the river goes."

He could feel it now—like a wooden ship pulled gently by tide. He belonged here, yes, but not solely here. Portland was a beginning, not an end.

He found Danny later that morning near the pressroom, sleeves rolled up.

"I think I shall be heading upriver," Jonathan said quietly. "Not today. Not tomorrow. But soon."

Danny nodded in that thoughtful way of his. "Can't say I blame you. The city's got two faces, Butler. The further you get from the saloons, the more honest she becomes."

Jonathan smiled. "I dare say the wilderness has been calling to me since I left it."

"Bring back something worth printing," Danny said, handing him a fresh stack of blank paper. "And bring yourself back in one piece."

***

Block cornered him at the front desk later that afternoon, eyebrows arched like cocked pistols.

"Daisy tells me you're thinking of running off into the woods."

Jonathan cleared his throat. "Well, not immediately. But I believe a man cannot write about a place until he truly understands the land around it."

Block snorted, though not unkindly. "If a cougar eats you, Butler, I'm not paying for the obituary."

"I shall keep an eye out," Jonathan replied with a faint grin. His British ease slipped naturally into his tone whenever he felt cornered.

"Good," Block said, gripping his shoulder. "Just leave me with enough stories before you wander into the hills. Folks are finally starting to read the World again."

***

Toward evening, the newsroom slowed. Daisy was sorting letters at her desk when Jonathan approached.

"Heading upriver," she said without looking up, as though she had heard his thoughts before he spoke them.

"You make it sound quite like a funeral march," he teased.

"Only because you look... different lately," she said, lifting her gaze to his. "As if something out there has your name written on it."

Jonathan exhaled softly. "Truth be told, I feel it too. Portland is remarkable, truly—but I came all this way to learn, not merely to settle comfortably."

"And to write," she added.

"And to write," he agreed.

She handed him a folded parcel wrapped in brown paper. "For your journey. It's nothing spectacular."

He raised an eyebrow. "May I?"

She nodded.

Inside was a notebook—leather-bound, stitched by hand. On the first page she had written:

For the words you will discover beyond the city.

—D.

Jonathan felt warmth rise in his chest, unexpected and quietly humbling.

"Daisy... I don't know what to say."

She smiled faintly. "Then don't. Just promise you'll come back."

"I shall," he said, and meant it.

***

The next week was filled with quiet arrangements. He purchased trail boots, a stout coat, and packets of tea wrapped carefully in oilcloth. Danny secured him a small rifle from a trustworthy shopkeeper on the East Side—"less likely to blow your arm off," Danny had said.

Jonathan visited the stage depot, asking about routes toward The Dalles and Hood River—though he already knew he would not be riding the stage. Omache had taught him the real trails, the quieter ones, the ones made by feet not wheels.

He stopped by the waterfront one last time, watching the riverboats paddle against the current.

A weathered fisherman beside him nodded toward the mountains.

"Snow's melting fast," the man said. "River'll rise by a foot or two. But the passes'll open soon enough."

Jonathan nodded. "So I've heard. Do you know much of the tribes upriver?"

"A fair bit," the fisherman replied. "Peaceful folk. Good with their hands. They've been here longer than any of us have roofs."

Jonathan smiled. "Then I look forward to meeting them."

***

The night before he left, Jonathan found a note slipped under his door.

No name. Just a single line:

"Watch the shadows below the Starlight. They haven't forgotten your face."

His pulse quickened. The shanghaiers. He had suspected as much.

But instead of fear, he felt a strange calm.

He folded the note, tucked it into his coat, and blew out the lamp. He would return. He would write the truth. But first—he would follow the river.

Chapter Thirty-Six

Into the Land of Falls and Meadows

"The river is a storyteller. It remembers the old ways long after men forget." — *Old Tribal Saying*

Jonathan left Portland under a soft morning mist, the kind that clung to one's coat and made the world look like an unfinished watercolor. He didn't ride the stage coach nor seek the company of other travelers. Omache had taught him something valuable: If you wish to learn a land, travel slow. Travel close to the earth.

So he traveled by horseback, following the wagon road north out of Portland until it met the broad line of the Columbia River. Spring was unfolding like a careful whisper. New grass pushed through the wet soil. Dogwoods bloomed pale white along the bluffs. The air held the clean, sharp scent of snowmelt rolling down from the high peaks.

The river beside him was wide, powerful, alive.

***

He camped at a bend in the river the first night, making a small fire beneath a crooked cottonwood. As he sipped tea from a dented tin cup, he felt the quiet settle around him the same way it had on the plains—gentle, unhurried, honest.

If only Omache were here, he thought.

He half-expected to hear the Indian's dry humor drifting from the darkness:

"You always make too much noise, Englishman."

But the night carried only the low rush of the river and the occasional hoot of an owl. Jonathan stared into the flames, remembering the long miles of the Oregon Trail, the laughter of tribes around the fire, the storms, the near-death crossings, the immense companionship of a man whose people had been nearly forgotten by the world.

"I shall see you again, my friend," he whispered.

***

On the third day, the Columbia Gorge rose before him — cliffs like ancient fortress walls, waterfalls spilling down as if poured from the clouds. The road narrowed, weaving between river and rising stone.

Every turn was a marvel.

A plume of white mist drifted from a falls that crashed fifty feet into a pool of icy blue. Sunlight broke through the clouds and cast silver across the river's surface. High above, a bald eagle circled, its cry echoing off the basalt walls.

Jonathan slowed his horse, overwhelmed.

"Good heavens," he murmured, "no painting or poem can capture this."

He wrote half a dozen lines in Daisy's leather-bound notebook, words chasing the feeling before it vanished.

As he rounded a thick grove of cedar, he noticed a man crouched at the river's edge, working with a long spear. The man rose as Jonathan approached — tall, straight-backed, wrapped in a woven blanket with geometric patterns dyed deep red and black.

His hair was braided, his eyes dark and steady.

Jonathan stopped his horse.

"Good afternoon," he said gently. "Is this the way toward Hood River?"

The man studied him with neither fear nor haste.

"You follow river," the man said. "Road bends west. Two sleeps from here."

Jonathan nodded. "I thank you. Are you from the village farther upriver?"

"Yes," the man replied. "Wy'am people. Hood River people."

He dismounted, sensing no danger. "My name is Jonathan Butler. I have a friend among the tribes—a man named Omache. I hoped perhaps to see him, or to speak with those he called brothers."

The man's expression shifted at the name.

"You know Omache."

"Yes. He guided me across the Oregon Trail."

"He is good man. Good hunter. Good heart."

The man pointed a few miles upstream. "Go there. Many people gather. You travel safe."

Jonathan bowed slightly—a habit from home, yet it seemed to fit. The man did not smile, but dipped his head in return.

By late afternoon, wind swept through the Gorge — that constant, untamed wind the tribes believed was a living force of its own. Clouds raced overhead. The trail wound past more waterfalls, past fishermen balancing on narrow scaffolds above the rapids, their nets dipping into white foam.

Jonathan marveled at their balance, their confidence.

This is a world I barely understand, he thought, yet I feel as though I've been walking toward it all my life.

***

As dawn broke the next morning, the scenery changed again. The Gorge walls lowered. Meadows opened wide.

Snow-capped Wy'East—Mount Hood—rose ahead like a silent, ancient guardian. Pink morning light draped its slopes.

The sight nearly took Jonathan's breath.

He slowed his horse to a stop.

A single woman stood on a distant ridge, silhouetted against the glowing mountain. Long dark hair. A woven shawl. Her posture was steady, calm, as though she were listening to the land itself.

Jonathan blinked.

And then she vanished beyond the hill.

Was that...? he wondered.

He did not yet have a name for her. He did not yet know her story. He did not yet know what part she would play in his life.

But something deep within him stirred.

The journey upriver was no longer just about news stories, or curiosity, or even the memory of his travels across America.

It was about something calling him forward.

Something waiting.

Chapter Thirty-Seven

The Village Breathes

"Certain things catch your eye, but pursue only those that capture your heart." — *Old Indian Saying*

Jonathan entered the Hood River Valley just as the morning fog lifted from the meadows. The air held a sweetness he hadn't felt since leaving England—a blend of pine, damp earth, and something ancient he couldn't name. Wy'East towered above him, its snowy crown shimmering beneath a sky so blue it seemed freshly washed.

Ahead, along a bend in the river, he saw a cluster of cedar lodges and canvas-topped shelters arranged around a clearing. Smoke curled from several fires. Children played near the water. Older women cleaned fish on smooth flat stones. A pair of young men worked their nets at the riverbank.

Jonathan slowed his horse, not wanting to intrude. Everything felt quiet... but not silent. Watchful, perhaps.

A tall man broke from the group and approached him. Jonathan recognized him — the fisherman he had met the day before.

"You come," the man said simply, gesturing with two fingers. "Tonight is night of sharing. You sit with us."

Jonathan nodded, grateful. "I would be honored."

He followed on foot, leading his horse. Eyes turned toward him — curious, not hostile — but still measuring him as if deciding whether he belonged inside the boundaries of their lives.

***

The Hood River people moved with a quiet grace that reminded Jonathan of Omache, yet each tribe had its own rhythm. Here the women wore woven shawls patterned with reds and greens. Men tied their hair with narrow strips of leather. Smoke from roasting salmon drifted through the clearing, mingling with the crisp scent of cottonwood buds.

Jonathan felt a strange mix of humility and awe.

In Portland, the world seemed to hurry.

Here, the world seemed to listen.

The fisherman led him toward an older man seated near a large driftwood log. His hair was nearly all white, braided in two long lengths bound with carved bone. His eyes were bright but carried a depth that made Jonathan pause.

"This is En-tee-tee-ueh," the fisherman said. "He is chief. He speaks for many."

En-tee-tee-ueh studied him for a long moment.

"You are the Englishman who traveled with Omache."

Jonathan bowed his head slightly. "Yes, sir. My name is Jonathan Butler."

En-tee-tee-ueh nodded once. "Omache has strong heart. He would not bring a fool across the great trail." A thin smile formed at the corner of his mouth. "So perhaps you are not fool."

Jonathan chuckled softly. "I should hope not."

"Tonight we share stories," En-tee-tee-ueh said. "You listen. You learn the river."

Jonathan's chest warmed. "I would like nothing more."

En-tee-tee-ueh pointed toward a basket. "Go. Eat. Make fire warm your bones."

Jonathan stepped back and accepted a wooden bowl from one of the women. Flaked salmon. Roasted roots. Warm berry bread. He sat near a small fire, letting the heat soak into his hands.

He had spent only minutes in the village and already felt the land shift inside him — the same familiar whisper he had known by the prairie fires beside Omache. A whisper older than story, older than time.

***

As he ate, children chased each other along the edge of the clearing. Several young men carved arrow shafts. Women spoke in soft murmurs as they worked. Everything felt calm.

Until Jonathan sensed eyes on him.

He turned his head.

There — beyond the fire's reach — stood the woman he had glimpsed on the ridge that morning.

Her shawl was woven with colors of river moss and sky. Her hair fell in a straight dark sheet down her back, brushed by the wind. She watched him, still and composed, expression unreadable.

Jonathan felt something inside him shift — not a jolt, but a gentle, undeniable tug. A familiarity he could not explain. As though he were looking at someone he had known in another life, or dreamed of on a ship, or felt on the trail without seeing.

En-tee-tee-ueh followed his gaze and said quietly, "That is Lawitha."

Jonathan let the name settle. "She saw me earlier. On the ridge."

The chief's lips pressed into a soft line. "Lawitha sees many things."

"Is she..." Jonathan struggled to find a polite way to ask. "...is she part of your family? A healer? A leader?"

En-tee-tee-ueh shook his head. "She is herself."

Jonathan waited, hoping for more, but En-tee-tee-ueh simply looked into the flames as if consulting something Jonathan could not see.

After a moment, he added, "Her spirit walks ahead of her. You will understand in time."

Lawitha turned and stepped away from the firelight, disappearing into the dark as though she had been shaped from the night itself.

***

Later, as the moon rose over the valley, the villagers gathered around the large central fire. Chiefs spoke of old battles, of lost salmon runs, of the spirits who lived in the river currents and mountain winds. Younger men shared hunting stories. Women sang songs that swayed like the river itself.

En-tee-tee-ueh leaned toward Jonathan. "Now you."

"Me?" Jonathan blinked.

"Your journey," the chief said. "Your storms. Your crossings. Your heart."

Jonathan swallowed. He looked around at the faces waiting for him to speak—patient, open, expectant. And he felt suddenly unworthy, a mere traveler among people whose roots reached deeper than the soil itself.

But he told his story.

The sea voyage. The train across America. Meeting Louise. Meeting Omache. Crossing rivers that nearly took his life. Writing by firelight. Seeing Wy'East for the first time.

As he spoke, the listeners watched intently — not judging, not comparing, but receiving. And for the first time,

Jonathan felt his story being woven into something larger than himself.

When he finished, En-tee-tee-ueh nodded.

"You speak like river," he said. "Sometimes calm. Sometimes fast. Always moving."

Jonathan felt a flush of gratitude.

And then — from the darkness behind the fires — he sensed a presence.

Lawitha. Just listening. Not approaching. Not ready yet.

But near.

Like a wind that knew his name.

Chapter Thirty-Eight

A New Thread in the Loom

"The heart knows the trail long before the feet begin to walk it."
— Old Tribal Saying

A thin veil of river mist drifted through the village at dawn, softening every outline into watercolor. Jonathan woke to the muffled thrum of people beginning their morning rhythms—crackling firewood, the quiet splash of water carried in woven baskets, the soft chanting of a woman grinding roots on a flat stone.

He had slept deeper than expected, wrapped in a bear robe the chiefs had insisted he use. For the first time since leaving England, he felt truly rested. No rattling wagon wheels. No storms rolling over the steppes. No frantic scramble for survival.

Just the river.

Just the mountain.

Just the people moving like they belonged to the land.

***

One of the young men from the night be-fore—Tamanawas, the fisherman who laughed with his whole chest—flagged Jonathan over.

"You hungry," he said, not as a question but as a certainty.

Jonathan followed him to a small firepit where strips of salmon smoked on cedar planks. The aroma alone made his stomach leap.

"Please," . "It smells marvelous."

The man grinned and handed him a piece. "River gives good gifts."

Jonathan closed his eyes at the first bite. "Better than anything at the boarding house."

Tamanawas snorted. "Boarding house food tastes like wet bark."

Jonathan laughed. "Then I've been eating bark for months."

***

As they ate, Jonathan became aware of movement behind him. He turned just as Lawitha stepped out of her mother's lodge, carrying a bowl of crushed herbs. Her long braid glimmered with river droplets, as if she had just come from washing at the water's edge.

She walked toward a line of children who waited patiently near the fire.

Tamanawas nudged Jonathan with his elbow. "She helps people," he said. "Has strong mind. Strong heart."

Jonathan swallowed another bite of salmon, suddenly conscious of his posture. "She seems... respected."

"More than respected," Tamanawas said. "People listen when she speaks. And she sees things. Like your friend Omache."

Jonathan's chest warmed at the mention of the old Indian. "I miss him."

"He will come again," Tamanawas said simply. "River paths cross when they should."

Jonathan nodded, though a part of him wondered if paths always obeyed destiny—or if sometimes they drifted apart without warning.

***

Later in the morning, the village chief with the carved cedar cane approached Jonathan.

"You walk with us," he said. This is my brother Running Horse.

Running Horse gazed into Jonathan's eyes with interest. "You welcome here. Not many white people share our values."

Several villagers had gathered near the edge of the forest. Some carried woven baskets. Others held wooden digging sticks. Lawitha stood among them, her expression unreadable.

"We gather roots," the chief said. "Good food. Good medicine."

Jonathan straightened. "I would be honored."

"You watch," the chief added. "You learn. Do not take too much from ground. Only what you need. Earth remembers."

They led him up a small rise overlooking the valley. From there he could see the whole village—a scatter of smoke threads rising into the pale sky, the river curling like a silver ribbon, Wy'East towering above it all. It struck him that this was sacred ground, in a way his mind could understand even if he lacked the proper vocabulary.

Lawitha knelt near a patch of vibrant green plants. She pressed her fingers to the soil with reverence before loosening it around the roots.

the careful movement of her hands—gentle, patient, respectful. When she noticed him looking, she met his gaze fully for the first time.

"You do this in England?" she asked.

He felt his throat tighten. "No. Not like this. We... we tend gardens. But this feels more like tending a relationship."

A faint smile tugged at her lips. "Yes. The earth listens."

***

That afternoon, Jonathan walked to the river's edge to rinse the dust from his hands. He expected solitude, but found Lawitha there instead, her feet in the shallow water, her braid drifting over her shoulder like a dark ribbon.

She didn't turn as he approached.

"You write many things," she said quietly.

Jonathan blinked. "You've seen me writing?"

She nodded toward the leather-bound notebook tucked in his coat. "Your thoughts are heavy. They make your shoulders bend."

He let out a soft laugh. "Journalists always look worried. Part of the trade."

"You carry more than words." She finally looked at him, eyes deep and steady as the river behind her. "Your heart travels faster than your feet."

Jonathan stared at the ripples along the riverbank, unsure what answer she expected—or what truth he wished to reveal.

"I suppose I'm trying to understand my place here," he said at last.

"You will," she replied. "But the land will tell you, not the city."

Then she stepped past him, her footsteps silent in the grass.

He watched until she disappeared into the trees.

***

That night, after supper with the villagers, Jonathan sat by the fire with his notebook open. The flames painted the valley in warm, flickering gold. In the distance, Lawitha's voice drifted in soft conversation with her mother, followed by gentle laughter that made the air feel lighter.

Jonathan wrote: There is a rhythm to this place unlike anything I have known. It is in the river's pulse. In the mountain's shadow In the quiet strength of the people. And in one voice that lingers in the air long after she steps away.

He closed the notebook and stared into the fire, knowing—without needing to speak it aloud—that something in him had shifted.

And tomorrow, he would discover just how deeply.

Chapter Thirty-Nine

Lesson of Stones

"Wisdom sits in places; it is the land that teaches the heart." —
Old Tribal Saying

The morning broke clear and cold, the kind of crisp river air
that made Jonathan inhale deeper than he meant to. Wy'East
glowed in soft pink light, the snowy crown catching the earliest
rays like embers caught in ice. The village stirred slowly, as if
waking in time with the mountain.

Jonathan felt different today. Settled. Present. As though
the land itself had drawn a tighter circle around him during
the night.

While he finished a small breakfast of smoked fish and
wild berries, the chiefly man with the carved cedar cane approached him again.

"You walk with me," he said simply.

Jonathan rose, brushing dust from his trousers. "Of
course."

The chief led him beyond the village, past the grove of
cedar trees and out onto an overlook where the river bent

sharply before widening toward the open valley. Mist curled along the banks, lifting lazily as the sun warmed the water.

For a long moment they simply stood there in silence.

Finally the chief spoke. "Last night, the council talked."

Jonathan straightened. "About... me?"

"Yes. You come from far. You carry words. Words change people. Sometimes help. Sometimes hurt."

Jonathan swallowed, unsure where this was headed.

The chief tapped the earth with his cane. "Omache tell us you listen. That you watch. That your heart moves slow and careful. This is good."

"I hope so," Jonathan said quietly. "I certainly try."

"You will come again," the chief continued. "In summer. When river wakes. When trails safe."

Jonathan blinked. "You want me to return?"

"Yes. There is more for you here. More to learn. More to give." The chief looked at him with an expression that pierced deeper than words. "But first you go back to city. Finish your writings. Strengthen your feet before your heart pulls you up-river for good."

For good.

The phrase clung to him like the soft morning mist.

***

As they walked back toward the village, a sudden gust of wind rattled the branches overhead. The chief paused, eyes narrowing at the shift in the air.

"Storm coming," he said. "Not from sky. From people."

Jonathan frowned. "What do you mean?"

The chief shook his head. "City grows hungry. Men hungry. They look at land, river, gold, timber. They take too much. They see tribes as stones in river—something to kick aside."

Jonathan felt a coldness settle at the base of his spine. "I've sensed some tension in Portland. But not here."

"Here too," the chief murmured. "Trouble moving north. Soldiers from The Dalles make plans. Not all friendly. Remember what you hear. Remember what you see."

He nodded slowly, unable to shake a feeling that the chief was preparing him for something larger than a return visit.

***

Later that afternoon, Jonathan found Lawitha at the river's bend, arranging smooth stones in a careful pattern. He approached quietly, not wanting to disturb her work.

She glanced up. "You are leaving soon."

"How did you know?" Jonathan asked.

"My father spoke with you," she said simply. "His cane tells stories when he returns from a walk."

Jonathan sat beside her, knees in the warm sand. "He asked me to return in summer."

"You should." She placed another stone, her fingers nimble and deliberate. "The river knows your name now."

Jonathan smiled a little. "And what are you doing here?"

"Listening," she said. "Stones remember what the river forgets."

He tilted his head. "You speak in riddles sometimes."

"Not riddles." She held up a polished black stone. "This one comes from far away. Avalanche many winters past. Carried by snow-water, melted, then pushed by river. It holds stories of mountain... not of the village."

Jonathan ran his thumb over the stone's surface—smooth, cold, ancient.

"Everything travels," she said. "Even people who never planned to."

Her gaze drifted to him then, calm but searching. Jonathan felt something settle between them—quiet, steady, unmistakable.

***

That evening the villagers gathered again for the night meal. Laughter drifted through the camp, and the cedar fire painted golden circles on every face. Jonathan felt the warmth of it settling into him in a way he hadn't expected.

After the meal, the chief stood and raised his hand. The crowd quieted.

"Our white brother returns to the city tomorrow," he announced. "He will return in summer, when river calls again."

Faces turned toward Jonathan—nodding, smiling, accepting.

Lawitha didn't smile. Instead she watched him with an expression that felt like a question he wasn't yet ready to answer. When the crowd thinned, she approached him.

"Do not forget what you felt here," she said softly. "City words make men blind. But mountains open the eyes."

Jonathan touched the small black stone she had given him earlier. "I won't forget."

She stepped back, her silhouette outlined by the firelight. "Good. Then river will remember you."

As the flames crackled and Wy'East glowed faintly under starlight, Jonathan felt something shift inside him—not a farewell, but a beginning. And somewhere deep behind the trees, a faint coyote howl echoed through the valley, as if agreeing.

Chapter Forty

Preparations began quietly

"You must live your life from the inside out. Only then can the path reveal itself."
— Native Proverb

The last of the spring rains gave way to long, bright days that stretched lazily over Portland. The river ran high and cold with the last of the mountain snowmelt, and warm breezes drifted through town carrying the scent of fresh-cut timber and wildflowers blooming along the foothills. Summer hadn't quite arrived, but the season hovered close, like a promise waiting to be spoken.

Jonathan felt it before he understood it—a restlessness moving behind his ribs, a tug in his chest whenever he gazed east, toward the blued shadows of the Columbia Gorge.

He wrote his stories, he attended meetings, he exchanged lively quips with Daisy and good-natured ribbing with Danny. Yet each afternoon he found himself watching the river, imagining its winding path through steep basalt cliffs toward the far-off land where Omache's people lived.

The chief's words returned to him often, "Come back in the summer."

Spring had passed. Now the land was opening its hands.

***

One warm afternoon, Block waved him into the office with his usual brusque enthusiasm.

"You've found your stride, Jonathan," he said, pushing a stack of newspapers aside. "Your last piece on the logging camps? Folks loved it. Gives them pride, you know? Seeing their work through an outsider's eyes."

"I'm grateful," Jonathan replied, trying to ignore the uneasy flutter in his chest. "This place... it's changing me, I believe."

Block leaned forward, narrowing his eyes slightly. "You've been looking upriver a lot lately."

Jonathan blinked. "You've noticed?"

"Hard not to. You stand out there at noon like you're listening for a voice only you can hear." Block folded his hands. "If you need a little time away—go. Just don't get yourself lost, lad. The frontier bites hard."

Jonathan nodded, grateful. "I'll return with stories... and perspective."

"You'd better," Block huffed. "We're trying to sell papers, not poetry—though your poetry is selling just fine these days."

Jonathan laughed, feeling lighter than he had in weeks.

***

He visited the general store and purchased a small axe, a skinning knife, two coils of rope, a tin of gun oil, extra cartridges for his pistol, and a new waterproof journal. The shopkeeper raised an eyebrow.

"Heading upriver, are ya?"

Jonathan paused. "How can you tell?"

"Only two sorts buy rope and cartridges together—loggers and travelers. You ain't a logger."

Daisy noticed next. She watched him roll up a map one afternoon and dust off his wool coat.

"You're leaving for a spell," she said, not a question.

Jonathan exhaled through a soft smile. "Just a short journey. There are stories upriver. People I need to see."

"Be careful," she warned, eyes narrowing. "Portland's one kind of wild. That Gorge is another. And don't talk to strangers at the docks unless they're wearing an Eastside badge."

Jonathan chuckled lightly. "I've learned that lesson."

Danny, however, handled the news in his own dramatic fashion.

"You're going where?" he practically shouted, waving his arms. "Up the Gorge? Alone? You'll get eaten by a cougar or kidnapped by loggers!"

"Kidnapped by loggers?"

"It happens!" Danny insisted—though it almost certainly did not. "At least take a whistle."

Jonathan promised he'd consider it.

But that night, alone at his boarding house window, he looked again toward the dark outline of the mountains. A silver ribbon of moonlight danced along the Willamette, drifting north toward the great river beyond.

He felt it now—not just restlessness, but calling.

The same calling that had drawn him across half the world.

The same thread that had led him to Omache, and the chief, and the valley waiting for him upstream.

Tomorrow he would inform Block and Daisy of the exact date.

In three days, he would secure passage on a riverboat heading east.

And in early summer, Jonathan Butler would follow the river into the unknown once more—toward the land of his Indian brothers, toward the stories he was meant to write, and toward the woman whose name he still dared not speak...not even to himself.

Chapter Forty-One

Summer had come at Last.

"The river is the storyteller of the land. Listen long enough, and it will carry you home."
— Old Tribal Saying

The morning Jonathan left Portland, the city felt strangely hushed—as if the river itself were holding its breath. Summer sunlight spilled across the Willamette, turning the water into rippled silver. He arrived at the dock just as the eastbound riverboat Hesperus groaned awake, ropes tautening and steam hissing in the cool air.

He wore his best shirt, his derby brushed clean of dust, and his journal tucked beneath his arm. In his coat pocket were Omache's last gifted items: a small pouch of sage, a carved wooden bead, and the memory of the Indian's hand on his shoulder that final morning.

"Good fortune, Jonathan," Daisy had whispered before he left the office the prior afternoon.

"Return with a story worth printing."

Block simply grunted and waved him off. Danny insisted on giving him a tin whistle "in case a cougar tried to eat him."

He kept it—if only for Danny's enthusiasm.

As the Hesperus chugged upriver, Jonathan leaned against the railing and watched Portland shrink behind him—boardwalks, sawmills, low brick buildings, and the swarming busyness of a young city on the cusp of becoming something greater.

He felt no fear. Only a deep, steady pull inward, as if each bend of the river turned a page in a book not yet written.

***

The boat cut through calm morning waters, the Gorge rising slowly around them like the great stone gates of an ancient kingdom. Steep cliffs dressed in fir trees towered above. Waterfalls appeared suddenly, thin white ribbons spilling from emerald heights. The air grew cooler, cleaner—filled with the crisp scent of cedar.

Jonathan wrote as he traveled, sketching the rocks, describing the thunder of the falls, the cry of an eagle circling far above. Several passengers leaned over the rail to admire the view, but Jonathan felt something deeper—an echo, as though the land recognized him.

This is where you belong, it seemed to say.

Welcome back.

When the boat stopped at a modest landing near the Hood River, he stepped off with his pack and supplies, boots crunching on the small stones of the shoreline. The captain tipped his cap.

"Only one goin' off here today. Tribe's a fair ways back in the valley."

"I know," Jonathan replied, gripping his journal. "I've been invited."

The captain raised an eyebrow but didn't pry.

***

He followed the narrow trail inland, weaving through groves of cottonwood and pine. A bright breeze came down the valley smelling of summer grass and distant snowfields. His footsteps stirred memories—Omache's calm steady voice, the chief's dark eyes, the sound of drums drifting across the evening air.

Hours passed. The land opened, revealing a broad green valley backed by the white gleam of Wy'East's distant slopes. Smoke from cookfires curled into the sky. Children's laughter echoed faintly.

The tribe.

He felt his heartbeat rise, though he did not know why.

As he approached, a few villagers spotted him first. They did not retreat or stiffen; instead, they murmured to one another, recognizing the Englishman who once traveled with Omache. A couple of young braves waved him forward.

Then he saw her.

Standing slightly apart from the bustle, near the edge of a meadow where tall grass rippled like water, was Lawitha.

Her hair caught the sunlight, long and dark, woven with two thin braids near her temple. She wore a soft doeskin dress edged with intricate beadwork the color of early dawn. She had been gathering herbs, a small woven basket at her side.

For a moment Jonathan forgot how to breathe.

Lawitha turned at the sound of footsteps. Their eyes met—his blue and travel-weary, hers deep and bright as river stones warmed by sun. Recognition flashed across her face, soft but unmistakable.

She walked toward him with calm grace.

"You have returned," she said quietly.

Her voice was exactly as he remembered—gentle, steady, like a stream flowing over smooth stones.

"Yes," Jonathan managed, his throat unexpectedly tight. "The chief... Omache... the valley... all of it has called me back."

A faint smile touched her lips. "The land remembers those who walk it with respect."

Before he could respond, the chief appeared from behind one of the lodges, leaning on his carved staff. His eyes, sharp even with age, studied Jonathan.

"You came in the right season," the chief said. "The river speaks loudest now. And there is much for you to learn."

Jonathan bowed his head slightly. "I am honored to be welcomed again."

The chief nodded approvingly. "Come. The people will greet you. Tonight we will share the summer fire. Tomorrow, your journey here begins."

Behind the chief, Lawitha glanced once more at Jonathan—a look not of mere recognition this time, but of something deeper forming in its first quiet breath.

***

That evening, Jonathan sat among them, listening to stories, drums, and laughter. Smoke curled into the twilight sky. Lawitha moved gracefully between fires, offering food, speaking softly with the women, casting an occasional, shy glance in his direction.

Jonathan felt the pull of this place settle firmly inside him.

He was not merely visiting, but arrived at the next turning point of his life.

And somewhere beyond the fires, beyond the drumbeats, the mountain loomed—silent, ancient, watching.

Summer had come at last.

And so had he.

Chapter Forty-Two

New Skills, Rough Hands

"A heart is not judged by the color of its skin, but by its deeds in the face of the Great Mystery."
— Old Plateau Saying

Jonathan slept more deeply that night than he had since England. It was the kind of sleep that comes only in places where the air is clean and unbroken, where the river sings you into dreams. When he opened his eyes at dawn, the world beyond the lodge was wrapped in soft mist drifting low across the riverbank. Somewhere an early bird called, the sound bouncing off the tall basalt cliffs.

Outside, the village was already alive with quiet morning bustle. Women stirred cookfires, thin spirals of smoke rising into the pale blue. Children splashed at the river's edge. A pair of braves sat cross-legged on a drift log, speaking in low tones between puffs of long-stemmed pipes.

And among them—Lawitha. Standing ankle-deep in the river, brushing water through her hair with her fingers, the morning sun turning the droplets on her braids to small, trembling stars.

Jonathan paused halfway through tying his boots. Something about her presence eased him and unsettled him at the same time, a gentle contradiction he didn't know how to name.

Omache was sitting on a flat rock shaping a piece of river willow with his knife. Without looking up he muttered, "You stare like hungry wolf, white brother."

Jonathan startled. "Omache! I am so glad to see you my good friend." He went down and sat beside him. He smiled as he looked at the Indian. "I was merely—well—observing the scenery."

Omache snorted. "Scenery has long black braids and strong eyes." He flicked a shaving of wood into the fire pit. "Be careful. Heart is tricky thing. River current strong."

Jonathan tried to reply but his words tangled somewhere between pride and embarrassment. He settled for tightening his boots a bit more aggressively than necessary.

Breakfast was simple—fresh trout roasted over coals, roots, berries, and tea steeped with mint gathered along the riverbank. Lawitha sat nearby, speaking gently with the chief who had first greeted Jonathan the day before. Occasionally her gaze drifted toward him—curious, but not bold. A quiet study, as though trying to decide what sort of man he was beneath the derby, the English diction, and the ever-present notebook.

After the meal, Jonathan helped where he could—carrying water, retrieving driftwood for the fire, sorting tools he hoped to use in the coming weeks. The tribe had a particular way of moving through their tasks, almost choreographed, each knowing their part without being told. He admired that sense of belonging, that unwritten rhythm.

In late morning, the Chief beckoned him toward the shade of a cottonwood.

"You came to learn," the Chief said, lowering himself onto a woven mat. "Not just words. Not just stories. You wish to learn how a man lives with the land, not on top of it."

Jonathan nodded.

"You help us make smokehouse today," the chief continued, "and tomorrow you learn river paths with Lawitha."

The statement struck Jonathan in two ways First—that he was being trusted. Second—that he would be spending an entire day with the woman whose gaze had stirred something deep in him.

He swallowed. "What shall I do first?"

"Cut cedar." The chief pointed toward a pile of logs. "Not too big. Not too small. Cedar is like a stubborn man—you take too much at once, it will split crooked. Take your time. Listen to the grain."

The instructions felt like more than instructions.

Jonathan set to work alongside several village men. The day grew warm, and the scent of freshly split cedar filled the air—rich, sharp, ancient. Sweat dripped down Jonathan's temples, mixing with dust and effort. But he felt useful. Grounded. Stronger in a way the newspaper office could never provide.

Every now and then, Lawitha passed by carrying baskets or tools. Each time she offered a faint smile, soft as a feather brushing the edge of a page.

By late afternoon, the frame of the smokehouse stood solid and straight. The men nodded, satisfied. Even Omache—even he allowed a small grunt of approval.

"You do well," he said. "Hands soft when you left Portland. Harder now."

Jonathan flexed his fingers, stiff and aching. "Feels good," he admitted.

That evening, the village gathered around a larger fire. Stories rippled through the circle—tales of past hunts, of brave ancestors, of battles fought without arrows, only wisdom. The flames cast warm amber light across every face, and Jonathan felt—for the first time since England—that he might belong somewhere again.

Lawitha sat near him, not too close, not too far. When she spoke, it was to share a small legend of the river—how salmon carried prayers between the living and the spirits. Her voice was calm, melodic, intimately tied to the world she described.

Jonathan listened as if hearing a new language entirely.

A language he wanted to learn.

A language that felt strangely like home.

By the time the fire burned low and stars crowded the heavens, Jonathan knew: Tomorrow—traveling upriver trails at Lawitha's side—would change something in him. Perhaps something small. Perhaps something irrevocable. He wasn't sure which fate he hoped for. But he knew he wouldn't miss it for anything.

Chapter Forty-Three

River Walk with Lawitha

"All rivers carry two journeys—one across the land, and one through the heart."— Old Nez Perce Saying

Their summer camp rested far up the Hood River Valley, tucked between green slopes and the white shoulders of Wy'East. From here, Lawitha said, they would follow the narrow trail downriver to where the Hood River emptied into the great Nichi-Wana. Only then would they turn east and walk the paths of the Columbia.

Morning broke clear and bright, without a single cloud clinging to the basalt cliffs. A soft breeze drifted off the river, cool and sweet with the scent of cottonwood sap. Jonathan stood at the edge of the village with his boots in the dust, watching Lawitha prepare for their day upriver.

She moved with easy, unhurried confidence—braiding her hair, tying a small knife to her belt, fastening a woven pack across her shoulder. A quiet strength radiated from her, the kind that didn't need to be announced.

"You carry notebook?" she asked without looking back.

"Yes," Jonathan replied, patting the small leather journal tucked into his coat. "Old habits, I suppose."

She nodded. "Good. The river teaches. But only those who remember."

Omache walked over, grinning beneath his weathered features. "Try not fall in river today," he muttered, adjusting Jonathan's pack for him. "Water cold. Words get wet."

Jonathan rolled his eyes playfully. "I'll do my best."

They set off along a narrow trail skirting the riverbank. The Columbia glimmered bright silver, moving fast but smooth, like a great animal keeping one eye always open. The cliffs rose hundreds of feet above them, swirled with ancient layers that no English book had ever prepared Jonathan to understand.

For a time, they walked in silence. Not an empty silence, but one shaped by wind and birdsong and the far-off crash of water against stone.

At a bend in the trail, Lawitha pointed across the river. "There," she said. "My people tell story of that cliff. Great Eagle rested there after battle with Wind-Spirit. His wings beat so strong the river changed its path."

Jonathan studied the cliff—its sweeping curved face, the places where rock had sheared off as though something tremendous had once struck it.

"It does resemble a wing," he said softly.

Lawitha smiled at the ground. "You see with heart, not only eyes. Many do not."

They continued on until the trail narrowed, weaving through a stand of tall pines. The air grew cooler. Shafts of sun pierced through the branches overhead, turning the dust into drifting golden motes.

"Tell me about England," Lawitha said at last. "Your home. Your people."

Jonathan exhaled, touched that she'd asked. "It is... very different. Grey skies, old stone buildings, narrow streets. Beautiful in its own way, but ordered. Predictable. I suppose that was the life meant for me." He paused. "Or the life I was expected to live."

"And your heart?" she asked.

He hesitated. "My heart... chose something else. Or perhaps the road chose for me."

Lawitha seemed to understand. "River chooses path," she said, "but water moves because something inside it must travel."

They reached a broad overlook where the trail widened, offering a sweeping view of the Columbia rolling westward toward the sea. Jonathan sat on a flat stone, breath caught by the beauty below.

Lawitha sat beside him—closer than before.

"Show me your writing," she said gently.

Jonathan blinked, surprised. Few had ever asked. Slowly, he opened his notebook and handed it to her. She traced the inked lines with the tip of her finger, careful and thoughtful, as though reading something alive.

"You write from feeling," she said. "Not just mind. That is good."

He swallowed. "I try."

She handed the notebook back. Their fingers brushed for a brief moment—light as a falling leaf. Jonathan felt the spark of it all the way to his chest.

"You have river inside you," Lawitha said, rising to her feet. "Always moving. Never still long."

Jonathan stood as well, his voice quiet. "And is that good?"

Her eyes lifted to his—warm, steady, unafraid. "Yes. Good. But river needs strong bank to guide it."

They continued upriver until midday, learning plants, reading tracks, listening to wind as though it carried secrets. At a shallow tributary, Lawitha knelt and cupped water into her hands.

"Drink," she said. "Old spring. Good for guiding thoughts."

He did. The water was cold, pure, startling in its clarity.

As they began their return, Jonathan found himself walking closer to her—not out of intention, but instinct, as though some invisible thread gently drew them side by side.

Only once did Lawitha pause, turning to him with a look both soft and searching.

"You walk two worlds," she said. "England behind you. Portland before you. You must choose how to live between them."

Jonathan swallowed. "I don't know yet."

"You will," she said, and continued down the trail.

But Jonathan stayed still for a long moment, watching the river shimmer below and feeling something shift inside him—quietly, deeply—as if the current had just found a new course.

Chapter Forty-Four

Write the Truth

"The rivers remember everything. Even the footsteps that do not touch their waters."
— *Wasco Proverb*

Jonathan woke before sunrise, stirred by something he couldn't name. Not sound, not dream — more like a tug from the land itself. He stepped from his tent and found the valley hushed beneath a velvet sky, the eastern rim just beginning to flush pink.

Lawitha was already awake.

She stood near the edge of the meadow, facing the dark outline of Wy'East. Her silhouette was steady, peaceful — as though she were speaking to the mountain and it was listening.

Jonathan approached quietly, unsure whether to disturb her.

"You rise early," she said without turning.

"Not usually," he replied. "But this place... it feels alive. Like it calls you up before the sun."

She glanced at him then, a slow nod. "Land does that. When it knows who listens."

Jonathan looked down at the valley. The Hood River glinted in soft morning silver. Pines whispered along the slopes. Mist curled low like drifting breath.

"It's strange," he said. "I spent months crossing America, and yet this is the first place that feels... almost familiar."

Lawitha studied him for a heartbeat. "Part of you belongs here."

Jonathan exhaled, surprised by how right her words felt. "And yet I don't know what that means."

"You learn," she said simply. "Place teaches. People teach."

A pause. "You teach, too."

They shared a quiet moment — not heavy, just full.

Before they could speak more, a young boy from the village hurried toward them, his breath puffing in the cool dawn air.

"Lawitha," he said in Chinook Wawa. "Your father asks for you."

She nodded and turned to Jonathan. "Come. He wishes to speak with you too."

Jonathan followed her across the meadow to where the chief sat near the fire pit, wrapped in a thick wool blanket. His face was carved with age and kindness, eyes sharp as river stones.

He gestured for Jonathan to sit.

"You travel back to Portland soon," the chief began. "But not same man who came."

Jonathan swallowed. "I think that's true."

"You listen well to river. To trail. To people," the chief said. "Good. Many white men come here and hear nothing."

Jonathan bowed his head slightly. "Your people have taught me more in weeks than my schooling ever did."

The chief seemed pleased. "Then you will hear this, too..."

He leaned forward, voice low but firm:

"Write truth. Not just what white men wish to read. Write so their children may know this land was loved before they came. Write so they remember we lived, and why."

Jonathan felt the weight of it — not as a burden, but as a calling.

"I give you my word," he said quietly. "I will write what is true."

Lawitha's gaze flickered to him, something unspoken there — gratitude? Pride? Something else?

The chief nodded once, satisfied. "Good. Before you go, you take gift."

He motioned to a bundle beside him. Lawitha opened it and lifted a small carved figure — a river otter, smooth and delicately shaped from dark cedar.

"Otter is clever," the chief said. "Moves between water and land. Between worlds. Like you."

Jonathan accepted it with care. "I... I don't know what to say."

"Say nothing," the chief replied. "Just remember."

***

The day warmed as they walked back to camp. The village was stirring — smoke rising, voices soft, children laughing. Jonathan felt a pang in his chest, unexpected and hard to place.

"Lawitha," he said softly, "I don't know how to leave this place."

She didn't answer at first. Then: "You do not leave," she said. "Not all of you."

Their eyes met. A quiet spark passed between them — something acknowledged but not spoken. Not yet.

"Will you come upriver again?" she asked.

"Yes," he said without hesitation. "As the weather allows."

She smiled then — small, but warm enough to last for miles.

"Good."

The sun rose higher. Jonathan packed his few belongings. Several tribe members offered shy farewells, gifts of dried berries, a woven cord, a small pouch of tobacco for Omache.

At last, Jonathan and Lawitha stood facing each other.

He cleared his throat. "I will miss... all of this. And you."

Lawitha touched the carved otter still in his hand. "River brings back what it carries," she said. "If heart is true."

Jonathan felt something catch in his chest. "Mine is."

"Then river knows the way," she said.

And with that, she stepped back, letting the morning carry him toward whatever Portland — and his unwritten future — would demand next.

But as Jonathan walked toward the trail, the cedar otter warm in his palm, he felt certain of one thing:

He would return.

Chapter Forty-Five

Touching Base

"The soul would have no rainbow if the eyes had no tears." —
Native Proverb

Jonathan arrived back in Portland under gray skies, the clouds sagging low over the river like a weary shawl. The Willamette current moved thick and steady, carrying flecks of driftwood toward the distant sea. He stepped off the steamboat with a strange weight inside him—half relief at being home, half reluctance at leaving the quiet, ancient peace of the upper valley.

At the Willamette World office Daisy greeted him first, her eyes widening the moment she saw the river dust still clinging to his coat.

"Well heavens, look at you—you've brought half the valley back with you," she said, brushing at his sleeve as she ushered him inside.

Jonathan smiled faintly. "I've seen things up there no man can forget, Miss Daisy."

She tilted her head, reading more than he spoke. "Then you best write it down before it slips out of your grasp."

Her words struck him more deeply than she could know.

Danny came barreling through the doorway from the pressroom, half-laced boots thumping on the floorboards. "Hoy, Butler! Welcome back! Rumor is you were off consorting with mountain spirits."

"Not spirits," Jonathan replied, settling his hat on the hook. "People. Starving for their story to be told."

Danny blinked in surprise, then nodded slowly. "Then I reckon you're the man to tell it."

Block soon called Jonathan into his office, pipe glowing like a lighthouse ember in the dim paneled room.

"Well?" he asked without ceremony. "Learn anything of value up there, or did you spend the time courting deer and dawdling in meadows?"

Jonathan placed both hands on the chair in front of him, steadying himself. "Mr. Block... I saw a people on the edge of losing everything. Not by nature's hand, but by ours."

Block lowered his pipe, expression tightening. "Careful now. You start pointing fingers too boldly, you'll find yourself the subject of next week's editorial."

"With respect," Jonathan said softly, "the truth ought not fear being printed."

A long pause. Block leaned back in his chair, exhaled smoke, and studied him with a shrewd but not unkind eye.

"Well then. Write it as you see it. You're green, but you've got a spine. Don't lose it."

He waved him away with the pipe stem. "Off you go before I start feeling sentimental."

Jonathan nearly laughed. Block never felt sentimental. But the older man's concession mattered all the same.

***

Those first days back settled into a quiet rhythm—ink-stained mornings, long walks along the wharves gathering impressions, and late evenings scratching words into his growing ledger of stories. Yet even surrounded by the bustle of Portland—steam whistles, horse carts, the smell of sawdust from the mills—Jonathan felt his thoughts drifting again and again to the valley upriver.

To Lawitha's calm voice.

To Running Horse's steady gaze.

To the chief's hand upon his shoulder beneath the pines.

At night in his narrow room at Mrs. Griffith's boarding house, he stood at the small window overlooking the river. The rain drummed gently on the roof while the Willamette glimmered faintly in the lamplight below. More than once he imagined following its path north, then east, back to the place where the air smelled of pine resin and mountain snow.

He closed his journal one evening with a decisive snap.

"I will return."

Not simply to write.

Not simply to observe.

But because a piece of his heart had taken root there, among the people who had treated him not as an intruder but as one of their own.

He tucked the journal beneath his pillow, folded his hands behind his head, and listened to the soft murmur of rain.

The Willamette flowed onward in the dark, carrying its secrets toward the sea—and carrying his promise with it.

Chapter Forty-Six

The Watch

"The heart should be like a river — open, willing, and always finding its way home." — *Yakama Proverb*

Jonathan arrived in the upper Hood River Valley beneath the long light of mid summer, the kind that fell through the pines in thin gold ribbons. The air was sharp with the scent of fir bark warming in the sun, and somewhere down the slope the Hood River murmured over stones, carrying snowmelt toward the Columbia.

Running Horse spotted him first.

"Jonathan returns," he said simply, lowering a bundle of salmon drying on a rack.

Word traveled quickly through the camp. Faces appeared between the pine trunks, voices calling his name with quiet warmth. When Lawitha stepped from the shadows of a cedar, her braids shining like dark river water, Jonathan felt something in his chest settle into place—as though the weeks in

Portland had only been a long inhalation, and this moment was the exhale.

"You came back," she said softly.

"I said I would," he replied.

She touched his sleeve—just a brush of fingers, but enough to erase the long distance between them.

***

The cabin stood exactly where they had chosen it in early spring, on a rise overlooking the meadow, with Wy'East's snowy crown rising solemnly behind it. Jonathan paused in the doorway, stunned by what had been done in his absence.

Running Horse had finished the cedar roof and fitted the shutters. A stone chimney rose solid and proud at one corner, smoke trailing into the blue sky. Inside, the single room smelled of cut wood, warm pine, and the faint sweetness of dried mint tied in bundles from the rafters.

Jonathan turned slowly, overwhelmed. "It's... perfect."

"You dream it," Running Horse said. "We help make it so."

Lawitha stepped beside Jonathan, her eyes shining with pride. "This place will keep your stories safe."

He swallowed. "And hopefully a part of me too."

***

They spent the afternoon readying the cabin for the night—stacking firewood, hauling fresh water, brushing pine needles from the stone step. Lawitha worked quietly beside him, humming an older song, the kind he never fully understood but always felt in the spine.

As the sun slipped behind Wy'East and turned the sky a soft lavender, Running Horse said his goodnights and disappeared into the trees, leaving only the sound of crickets rising from the meadow.

In the quiet that followed, Jonathan lit a small fire inside the cabin. The glow touched the wooden walls with honeyed light, dancing in the grain like living lines of a story still being written.

Lawitha stood at the open doorway, watching the first stars appear.

"You build a home with your hands," she said. "But also with your heart."

He stepped toward her, unable to hide the tremor in his voice.

"It seems my heart has been here for some time now."

She turned, her dark eyes catching the firelight, soft and unguarded. "Then you are not lost."

Without speaking further, she reached up and brushed a curl of hair from his forehead. Her fingers were warm, steady. Jonathan cupped her hand gently, holding it against his cheek.

"Lawitha..."

But he didn't finish the thought.

She leaned into him, their foreheads touching for a long, still heartbeat. Then her arms slipped around his shoulders, and he drew her close. Their kiss was unhurried—soft, deep, and filled with the unspoken promise of a future they both dared to imagine.

Later they lay side by side atop the simple cedar-framed bed, blankets pulled over them, the fire crackling a quiet lullaby. They didn't sleep at once. They spoke in hushed tones—about the river, about her people, about dreams neither had confessed aloud before this night. His arm around her waist, her head resting lightly on his chest, the whole world seemed to shrink to the small, glowing space they shared.

Outside, the night moved gently through the pines.

Inside, the cabin held its first memory of love.

Jonathan knew he couldn't remain forever. His work in Portland called to him. But as Lawitha drifted into sleep against him, he made a promise to himself — a vow as sure as the mountain outside the window: he would always return.

And he did. Over time, Jonathan traveled often between Portland and the river valley, spending long seasons in the cabin. There he wrote much of his poetry and musings, and recorded the tribe's desperate struggle to remain in their homeland as white settlers pressed steadily into the territory.

And one day he would bring something more than words.

***

Jonathan left for Portland as the morning broke cold and still, a thin mist drifting through the cottonwoods. Lawitha waited near the edge of the clearing, her shawl drawn close, the faint breath of dawn rising about her. Neither spoke for a time; words had already lost their meaning.

At last she reached into the folds of her dress and brought forth a small bundle wrapped in soft deerskin. When she placed it in his hand, he felt the weight of metal, smooth and cool.

"It came from a trader long ago," she said softly. "My father kept it for the sound it made. He said it held the white man's heartbeat."

Jonathan turned the silver watch over, and the morning light caught the fine engraving upon the back: *To J.B., with love — Lawitha*. The letters gleamed, newly cut and certain. For a moment he could only stare, his throat tightening.

"So you will not lose the hours between us," she whispered.

He pressed her hand in silence, then slipped the watch into his coat pocket. The trail to the Columbia waited, and the sound of the river could be heard. He told her he would return in 14 days.

Decades later, when time and tarnish had dimmed its silver face, another man would hold it in his palm and wonder at the name engraved there—never knowing how deep its promise once ran.

Chapter Forty-Seven

Brilliant as Diamonds

"Where your heart walks, your steps will follow." — *Nez Perce Saying*

Jonathan returned to Portland with the scent of cedar still clinging to his clothes and Lawitha's quiet warmth still lingering in his thoughts. The trip downriver took two days, the boat rocking gently as it passed basalt cliffs, waterfalls like threads of silver, and drifting wood that turned lazily in the current.

He spent most of the journey leaning on the rail, touching the pocket where her braid wrap—woven with red thread and a small eagle feather—rested safe against his chest. His heart wandered back to the cabin again and again: the glow of the fire, the way her head rested softly on his shoulder, the promise he carried wordlessly.

In Portland, late afternoon sunlight slanted across the streets. The smell of sawdust and horse manure mixed with the odor of the river at low tide. Life moved quickly here—new storefronts going up, scaffolding rising, loud voices on every corner—but Jonathan felt slightly apart from it all, like a man returning from a sacred ceremony only to find the world unchanged.

He walked straight to Alexander's Jewelers — the small downtown shop where time itself seemed to linger behind the glass. Inside, the faint ticking of clocks filled the quiet air. Alexander stood behind the counter, polishing a gold watch.

"Ah! Mr. Butler," he said, recognizing him at once. "Back from your wilderness adventures, are you? You've the look of a man who found something... or someone."

Jonathan felt his cheeks warm.

"One could say that."

"Well then," Alexander said, leaning forward with a knowing expression, "shall we look at rings?"

Jonathan nodded. The jeweler brought out a small tray lined with velvet, where bands of gold and silver nestled like sleeping light.

His gaze settled on a solitaire diamond — an old-mine cut that flared in the sunbeam spilling across the counter. Light danced up the wall, across the ceiling. Jonathan reached for the men's band. It slid onto his finger as if made for him.

"That diamond ring was handcrafted in Georgia," Alexander said, voice bright as sunlight on snow. "Eighteen-karat rose gold. One-carat diamond, old-mine cut. Nearly colorless, clarity eye-clean."

Jonathan smiled and nodded. He touched the ring once, as if to reassure himself it was truly there, and felt a ripple of nervous excitement sweep through him.

"I'll pay you now," he said, "but could you keep it here for a while? I'll drop back and pick it up."

Alexander's smile deepened. "You've made an excellent choice, Jonathan. I'll keep it safe for you."

Alexander closed the case and turned the small brass key in its lock. The faint tick of a wall clock filled the silence, steady as breath. Jonathan lingered a moment, watching dust drift in the sunbeam that cut across the counter, before nodding his thanks and stepping back into the afternoon light.

He left the shop and walked briskly through town toward the newsroom. Shively was speaking with Danny when Jonathan burst through the door.

"Well now," Shively said, eying him. "You look like a man with purpose."

Jonathan lowered his voice. "Richard, I need your help."

Shively raised a brow, leaning closer. "With what, my boy?"

"She deserves to know," Jonathan said. "I want to return and I want to ask her for her hand."

Shively clapped him on the back. "I'll stand by you. And when you return upriver again, I'll make sure the paper gives you the time."

Jonathan exhaled slowly, relief warming him from within.

"There's just one thing, Richard."

"What's that?"

"I want to tell her properly. With words that honor her. I need to write the truth about her people first. The chief asked me to. It feels right that my heart speaks through my work before I ask for hers."

Shively nodded, understanding.

"Then let's get to it. Portland needs those words."

Jonathan spent the evening writing steadily at his desk, pouring his thoughts about the upriver villages onto paper—their dignity, the hardships they faced as the government tightened its grip, the beauty of their traditions, and the quiet wounds history never recorded.

He worked until the lantern burned low.

Before leaving for the boarding house, he thought of the brilliance of the wedding ring.

His heart thudded once, solid and certain.

"Soon I will go back," he whispered to the empty newsroom.

"And this time... I will not return alone."

Chapter Forty-Eight

England Calls

"Sometimes the longest journey is the one that returns you to where you began." — Old Tribal Saying

The weather turned warm and golden in Portland. Late summer light filtered through the newsroom windows, warming Jonathan's desk and settling gently over his stack of notes about the upriver tribes. Every column he wrote drew more attention. Readers posted clippings on the mercantile bulletin boards, carried them to saloons, whispered about "the Englishman who tells the truth."

Block was pleased. Daisy encouraged him. Danny ribbed him with good-natured envy.

And all the while the ring rested in Alexander's safe, he could feel its presence like a second heartbeat.

Soon, he told himself.

Soon I will return to her.

He had already purchased supplies for the trip: pencils, notebooks, a fresh shirt, smoked meats, and a new blanket as a gift for Lawitha. By week's end he would board the river-boat and head upriver. He felt it so strongly that each sunrise seemed to carry him closer to her.

Until the wire arrived.

It came just after noon. Daisy hurried toward him from the front counter with a piece of folded paper and a strange tightness in her voice.

"Jonathan... this came through. It's from England."

He took it slowly, the room suddenly hushed around him, the edges of the moment blurring like mist over the river.

He opened the telegram.

FATHER GRAVELY ILL . STOP . MOTHER RE-QUESTS YOU RETURN AT ONCE STOP. URGENT . STOP — BUTLER

Jonathan's breath left him entirely. The newsroom sounds faded—the clatter of type, the rumble of presses, the murmur of voices. His world narrowed to the small sheet of paper trembling between his fingers.

His father.

The man who'd taught him Latin by lamplight.

Who'd supported his writing when no one else under-stood it.

Who'd stood on the London dock waving as Jonathan boarded the ship for America.

Daisy placed a hand gently on his arm. "I'm so sorry."

Shively was at his side moments later. "Let's step outside, lad."

They walked onto the boardwalk. Jonathan leaned on the railing overlooking a jumble of carts and wagons. The river breeze carried a faint smell of tar and cedar.

"I have to go," he whispered.

Shively nodded. "Yup. You do."

"I promised them I would return." His voice strained. "The tribe... Lawitha... I told them I would come back in 14 days."

"And you will," Shively said. "Not now but in time."

Jonathan glanced at him, eyes wet, jaw tense. "Richard, will you take a message upriver? Tell them why I cannot come. Tell Lawitha I—"

His voice cracked, and he looked away toward Mount Hood's far blue shadow.

Shively finished softly, "—tell her you did not abandon her."

Jonathan swallowed hard. "Yes."

"I can go in a week's time," Shively said, placing a hand on his shoulder. "I'll deliver your words myself."

Jonathan nodded slowly, steadied himself, and looked up at the river one last time. A river that had led him to a new life, a new love, and a future he thought he could grasp.

Now it was slipping through his fingers like the current.

He returned to his desk and began writing furiously — letters, instructions, pages for the paper, notes for the journey. By evening he had purchased his steamer ticket to London and packed his single trunk.

That night, alone in his boarding room, he penned a log letter for Lawitha and would give it to Shivery to deliver.

PATRICK TIMM

He closed his fingers around it, whispered to the empty room:

"I will return." Whether the world would let him...he did not know.

Chapter Forty-Nine

What Time Forgot

"The soul would have no rainbow if the eyes had no tears." —
Traditional Native Proverb

Late summer settled warm and gentle across the Columbia
Valley, but Jonathan was gone before the first heat could shimmer on the river stones.

A morning mist clung to the Willamette docks as the
steamer hissed and groaned under the weight of cargo and
passengers preparing for the long voyage to San Francisco, then
across the ocean. Jonathan stood on deck in a plain traveling
coat, hat brim low, the outline of his trunk beside him. He kept
his back straight, but a heaviness settled in his eyes—something Daisy noticed as she waved from the wharf.

Shively stood beside her and clenched his coat pocket
with the letter Jonathan had penned for Lawitha.

"You'll write when you can," Shively called up.

"I will," Jonathan answered, though part of him wondered if his words could ever travel as swiftly as his heart wished.

The steamer whistle shrieked. Ropes fell. The deck shuddered.

On the Columbia, Jonathan looked upriver—toward the mountains, toward the little cedar cabin hidden in the Hood River valley, toward the tribe, toward her. He imagined Lawitha there, stepping lightly through meadow grass, her braids catching the wind, unaware of the storm that had torn him away.

He touched the small carved figure — a river otter inside his pocket that Lawitha and her father gifted him, holding it as though it might steady him.

"Goodbye, my friend," Shively called.

Jonathan hesitated, then replied quietly, "Take care of them for me."

The boat pulled away, leaving a wake that rippled back toward the city and broke gently against the pilings.

***

A week later, true to his word, Shively boarded a small sternwheeler and headed up the Columbia. The river narrowed, cliffs rose tall and sheer, the wind carried a wild edge.

He felt then letter inside his vest, but each mile upriver made it heavier.

At Hood River he disembarked, expecting familiar canoes along the shoreline or smoke from the summer campfires rising through the pines.

There was nothing.

No voices.

No footprints.

No children racing near the water.

No sign of horses tethered in the shade.

Only silence.

He walked the old path toward the summer encampment. The meadow lay empty, grass grown high where once women gathered roots and men repaired nets. The fire pit was cold, scattered with a few charred stones. A lone eagle feather drifted in the breeze, catching on a tuft of dry weed.

Shively stood still, hat in hand.

A knot formed in his throat.

Two hunters, older men, approached from the trees above. Their eyes were wary but not unfriendly. One recognized Shively from earlier visits; he lifted a hand in greeting.

"Where is everyone?" Shively asked softly.

One man answered with a tired heaviness.

"Soldiers came. Took most to Warm Springs. Some escaped into the high valleys. Some fled across the river. Many... gone."

Shively closed his eyes for a moment, steadying himself.

"I have a message," he said. "For Lawitha."

The man shook his head.

"She left before dawn. We do not know where. She expected someone."

He looked directly at Shively.

"He did not come."

Shively opened his mouth to speak but found no words. He gripped the letter through his coat, feeling the weight of broken promises not his own.

The second hunter stepped closer.

"You tell him... her heart broke quietly. That is all."

The wind stirred the meadow grass, bending it like a sigh.

Shively nodded, swallowing the ache rising in his chest. "I will tell him," he whispered.

But even as he said it, he knew Jonathan might never return. Life had a way of pulling men across oceans and holding them there.

He left the meadow and walked to the river's edge. The water glimmered beneath the morning sun, restless and unyielding, carrying stories east and west but never returning any.

Shively stood there a long-time holding Jonathan's letter. For someday, for someone, for somehow. For a man who left with every intention of coming back.

***

Weeks later, Shively sat at Jonathan's empty desk as the newsroom buzzed around him. He opened Jonathan's final draft—an unfinished column titled "People of the River: Voices the West Must Hear." His handwriting was clean, strong, earnest. The heart of a man who wanted to bridge two worlds.

Shively placed a hand on the page.

"I'll publish it, lad," he murmured. "Your words will get there before you do."

He folded the column and carried it to Block's office.

Outside the window, the rain returned—soft and steady, like a memory settling over Portland.

***

Jonathan Butler crossed the sea.

Lawitha vanished from the river.

The cabin waited in the valley — empty, but not forgotten.

A letter remained in a vest pocket, close to Shively's heart.

History, somewhere far ahead, would bring Jack and Lisa to the edge of that unfinished love.

The story was not done.

Part III Journey Complete

Chapter Fifty

Waiting for Spring

"The wind does not break a tree that bends." — Lakota Proverb

The storm on Mount Hood had passed nearly a month ago, yet Jack still felt it living somewhere in his bones. Not in a fearful way—more like an echo, a soft vibration that rose and fell with the weather. Whenever the wind rolled down from the high snowfields, he would pause without thinking, listening the same way a man listens to a familiar voice calling his name from another room.

Lisa noticed it on the days she visited. Sometimes she'd find him standing near the back deck, eyes fixed on the far white crest of Mount Hood. Other times he'd be tracing the old trail map with his fingertip, following the same path he and George had climbed through snow and shadow.

But he never said much about it. Men like Jack seldom did. Instead, he carried the memory of that night quietly, like a lantern tucked beneath his coat—something that kept him warm and watchful without needing explanation.

Winter in the Gorge had been long that year. Long enough for the mountains to gather silence like wool, long enough for the river to run dark and slow. When March slipped in, the clouds began to lift just enough to show the mountain's shoulders again, pale and sharp against the dull sky. Spring wasn't here yet, but its breath was beginning to stir.

On a breezy Thursday afternoon, Jack pulled into his driveway and shut the truck door with that familiar hollow thump. He stood for a moment, letting the wind push past him, the scent of damp cedar rolling in slow waves. The house was warm when he stepped inside, the fire low in the stove.

He wasn't expecting company, but Lisa's voice floated from the dining room—soft, calm, as if she'd been letting herself settle after a long day.

She'd stopped by after work, the way she sometimes did when she needed a breather from Portland traffic. Her coat hung neatly over the chair, and she was sorting through a few envelopes she'd brought with her.

"You're home early," she said, glancing up with a small smile. "Roads are rough east of Corbett?"

"Yeah. Figured I'd get ahead of it."

She nodded. Though she wasn't living with him, moments like this had become a comfortable rhythm—quiet afternoons, shared space, no pressure. Just presence. And yet she still watched him closely, sensing the shift the mountain had left in him.

Jack dropped his coat on the hook and took the chair beside her. "George called," he said. "I should go back up there for a short visit."

Lisa stilled the envelope in her hand. "Are you ready?"

He considered the question. Not with fear—more with honesty.

"I think I need to see it again," he said. "Without the storm. Without the fog."

She reached across the table and lightly touched his hand. A simple gesture. Support without assumption.

"Then you should go," she said. "And when you're ready... I'll go with you."

A warmth passed between them—steady, unhurried, deeply respectful of the boundaries they were still figuring out.

Lisa stood and opened the curtains. Evening light slid across the floor, turning the room into a soft wash of gold. The wind outside brushed against the house like an old friend testing the latch.

"Feels like things are changing," she murmured.

Jack stood beside her, following her gaze to the pale crown of Mount Hood rising beyond the river.

"Yeah," he said quietly. "Feels like the mountain's calling again."

Neither spoke after that. They didn't need to. The wind carried enough voices on its own.

Outside, the last of winter sagged gently into the waiting arms of spring.

And far upriver, in the deep quiet places where stories sleep and blood remembers, something ancient began to stir—slow, patient, inevitable.

Chapter Fifty-One

Lisa's Awakening

*"The life of a man is a circle from childhood to childhood, and
so it is in everything where power moves."*
— *Black Elk, Oglala Lakota*

Lisa had grown used to the sound of the city breathing outside her little Northeast Portland bungalow. Out here, the wind didn't roar like it did on the mountain; it threaded itself through maple branches, sighed along eaves, and carried the distant hum of buses and late-shift traffic. On most nights, that quiet, familiar noise helped her sleep.

Lately, it wasn't enough.

She woke more often than she liked to admit, heart beating a little too fast, with the strange sense that she'd just come back from somewhere high and cold. Sometimes she could almost smell snow and pine. Sometimes she was sure she'd heard a drumbeat far away, steady as a heartbeat, pulsing through the dark.

By morning, it all felt ridiculous. She made coffee, fed the cat, checked email. Normal life reassembled itself one small routine at a time.

But something underneath had shifted, and she knew it.

On Saturday afternoon, Wakanda arrived the way she always did—as if the house were already halfway hers. She breezed in with a gust of March air and a paper bag that smelled like cardamom and curry.

"I brought food, because you clearly can't be trusted to eat anything but toast when you're stressed," Wakanda announced, kicking the door shut with her heel.

"I am not stressed," Lisa said, taking the bag anyway.

"Oh, okay," Wakanda said. "Then this is just... preventative rice."

They set the food out on the small kitchen table, sunlight slanting through the window and catching in Wakanda's hoop earrings. A thin, restless breeze pushed at the glass now and then, rattling a loose corner of the old window trim.

Wakanda stopped mid–scoop of rice and tilted her head. "You've been quiet in your messages," she said. "And not the good kind of quiet. Talk."

Lisa tried to brush it off. "It's just been a weird month. Long winter. Too much time in my own head."

"Mm-hmm." Wakanda arched an eyebrow. "Is this 'too much time in my head' before or after you go stare at the mountain from Jack's back deck?"

Lisa laughed once, caught. "You make it sound creepy."

"I make it sound like you," Wakanda said. "Which is my job."

They ate in comfortable silence for a few minutes. The curry warmed Lisa from the inside out, but it didn't quite touch the little knot she'd been carrying for weeks now, somewhere between her ribs and her throat.

Finally, Wakanda pushed her plate away and folded her arms on the table. "Okay. Out with it. The real thing. Not the 'oh, I'm fine' version."

Lisa stared at her hands. Her fingers had a faint tremor she hadn't noticed before.

"I keep... feeling things," she said slowly. "And I don't mean feelings-feelings. I mean... like I'm walking around with someone else's memories stuck in my skin."

"That's specific," Wakanda said gently. "Go on."

"Sometimes, when I look at Mount Hood—" she caught herself, then corrected, "—when I look at the mountain, I feel like I've been there a thousand times. Not just hiking, not just day trips. It's like... I know the tilt of certain rocks, the way the wind sounds in one particular stand of trees. I get flashes. Déjâ vu. Dreams that feel like they're remembering me instead of the other way around."

She glanced up, half expecting Wakanda to tease her out of it. Instead, she found her friend watching her with a steadiness that made it easier to keep going.

"And it's not just the mountain," Lisa said. "Sometimes I hear the wind at night, and it feels... personal. Like it's saying my name. I know how that sounds."

"It sounds like you're describing something real," Wakanda said quietly. "Even if you don't have a label for it yet."

Lisa let out a slow breath. "I thought maybe it was just stress. After what happened up there with Jack and George, the storm, the... everything. Maybe my brain is trying to make sense of it and using dreams as a dumping ground."

Wakanda leaned back in the chair, studying her. The breeze nudged the window again, a soft, persistent tapping.

"Lisa," she said finally, "I know what stress looks like on you. Stress is you making color-coded to-do lists and cleaning your bathroom grout at eleven at night. This—" she motioned at her, at the room, at the invisible weight in the air "—is not that."

Lisa tried to smile. "Then what is it?"

Wakanda's expression softened, a mix of humor and concern. "Girl... something is waking up in you. And it ain't the weather."

Lisa laughed despite herself, a quick, shaky sound. "You realize that's not exactly comforting?"

"Who said I came here to comfort you?" Wakanda said. "I came to tell you the truth. That's the risk of befriending someone who believes in both therapy and weirdness."

She reached across the table, laid her hand over Lisa's. Her palm was warm, steady, an anchor.

"Listen," Wakanda said. "You went up that mountain one person and came down... not a different person, exactly, but more of who you already were. Something about that place, that storm, that whole... situation with Jack and George—it turned on a light that had been dim for a long time. Maybe longer than this lifetime, if you want to go there."

Lisa swallowed. The words rang uncomfortably close to something she'd been afraid to say out loud.

"What if I'm imagining it?" she asked. "What if this is just me being overly dramatic because I finally had an adventure and my brain doesn't know what to do with it?"

"If you were making it up, you'd be having way more fun with it," Wakanda said dryly. "You'd be posting moody mountain selfies and writing poetry about pine needles. Instead you're trying to pretend it's nothing, which tells me it's absolutely something."

Lisa let her gaze drift to the window. From here, she couldn't see the mountain, but she knew exactly where it sat beyond the city, beyond the river, watching.

"I don't know what to do with it," she admitted.

"You don't have to know yet," Wakanda said. "But you do have to stop stuffing it in a box and shoving it under the bed."

Lisa hesitated. "Jack doesn't even know all of this. Not the dreams. Not the..."

"The pull?" Wakanda supplied.

"Yes." Her voice came out barely above a whisper. "The pull."

Wakanda's eyes flashed. "Okay, no. That part? You cannot keep that from him. Not if you two are going to keep... whatever this is... moving forward."

"It's not that I don't trust him," Lisa said quickly. "I just don't want him to think I'm losing it. He's already carrying enough from that night. I see it in the way he looks at the mountain."

"I'm not saying dump it on him like a therapy session," Wakanda said. "I'm saying let him in. Even if it's just a tiny crack at first. 'Hey, Jack, sometimes I dream about the ridge,' is better than 'Everything's fine, pass the salt.'"

Lisa smiled weakly. "You make it sound so simple."

"It's not simple," Wakanda admitted. "But it is honest. And you owe yourself that much."

They sat with that for a moment. The house creaked, settling. Somewhere down the street, a dog barked. The ordinary life around them went on, unaware of the strange, invisible tide tugging at the edges of Lisa's awareness.

"Have you thought about going back?" Wakanda asked quietly. "Not just with Jack, but for you?"

Lisa nodded. "Jack and George are talking about another trip. A calmer one. No blizzard, no near misses. Part of me wants to go. Part of me wants to run the other way."

Wakanda grinned. "Classic sign you're supposed to go."

"That is not helpful," Lisa said.

"Sure it is. Look." Wakanda leaned forward, elbows on the table. "There is a difference between fear that's trying to protect you and fear that's just afraid of growth. Only you can sort out which is which. But from where I'm sitting? The mountain isn't trying to swallow you. It's calling you. There's a difference."

Lisa felt goosebumps rise along her arms. She rubbed them away, but they lingered.

"You really think I should go back up there," she said.

"I think," Wakanda said slowly, "that you're already there half the time, in your head and your dreams. Maybe your body just needs to catch up. When you do go—because I think you will—go with your eyes open. And don't pretend it's just another hike."

Lisa looked at her friend—the open face, the sharp humor, the deep, steady compassion underneath it all. Wakanda had always been the one who could sit with both the practical and the mystical without flinching.

"What would I do without you?" Lisa asked.

"Probably implode," Wakanda said cheerfully. "Or worse, start journaling in vague metaphors and never show anyone."

She squeezed Lisa's hand once more, then released it. "Promise me one thing."

"Only one?" Lisa tried to tease.

"For now." Wakanda's tone softened. "Don't keep this locked away from Jack. He deserves to know what's really moving around inside you. And you deserve to be known. All the way."

Lisa drew a slow breath in, held it, and let it out. "Okay," she said. "I'll try."

"Good," Wakanda said. "Because I'm not above calling him myself and saying, 'Hey, mountain boy, your woman is having spiritual side effects.'"

"Do not dare," Lisa said, but she was smiling now, fully.

Wakanda stood and wandered to the living room window, peering past the bare branches of the street trees toward the far, unseen east.

"You know," she said, "next clear day, you should drive somewhere you can actually see her. The mountain. No errands, no excuses. Just... look. Listen. See what comes up."

Lisa joined her at the window, standing shoulder to shoulder.

"I will," she said. And for the first time in weeks, the thought didn't scare her as much as it steadied her.

Outside, the wind shifted, sliding down from the high country, threading its way through the city's streets and rooftops. In a small house in Northeast Portland, two women stood together in the quiet, one carrying questions she could finally name, the other bearing witness.

Somewhere far above the clouds, Mount Hood waited, patient and unmoving.

And deep inside Lisa—beneath reason, beneath memory, beneath the daily tasks that filled her hours—something old and wordless turned toward that waiting, as if answering to its own true name.

Chapter Fifty-Two

Returning to the Cabin

"When the wind returns, so do the memories it carries."
— Old Indian saying

Lisa woke before her alarm, heart already beating with that strange mix of excitement and unease that had become familiar ever since the mountain storm. For a moment she lay still in the half-dark of her little house in northeast Portland, listening to the faint hum of traffic and the whisper of wind outside her window.

It felt like the wind she remembered from higher up—thinner, older somehow.

She slid out of bed and crossed to the window. The sky over the city was still a dull charcoal, but far beyond the roofs and streetlights, she could sense rather than see the outline of Wy'East—no, Mount Hood, she reminded herself. Present day. Her life. Her time.

And yet.

On the dresser, the old pocket watch lay where Jack had left it the last time he visited. Just looking at it made her fingertips tingle, like her skin remembered the cold weight of it before her mind did.

Her phone buzzed.

WAKANDA: You up, mountain girl?

LISA: Barely. Packing now.

WAKANDA: Uh-huh. Send pics. And tell that man of yours if he doesn't bring you back in one piece, he's answering to me.

LISA: We are NOT using the phrase "that man of yours."

WAKANDA: Mmm-hmm. Keep telling yourself that. Call me from the trailhead. Seriously.

Lisa smiled despite the knot in her stomach.

LISA: I will. Promise.

She set the phone down and picked up the watch. It was cool against her palm, the metal dulled with age, the chain coiled like a thin, sleeping snake. The first time she'd seen it, she'd thought it was just an heirloom, another piece of old history Jack carried around out of habit.

Now she knew better.

"Okay," she whispered to the empty room. "One step at a time."

She slipped the watch into a small inner pocket of her jacket, finished packing her daypack, and locked up the house. The air outside smelled of wet pavement and budding trees, a city version of spring. As she drove west, the mountain in the rear view mirror slowly rose from the horizon, pale and patient, like it had been waiting for this day a very long time.

***

Jack was already outside when she pulled into his driveway, steaming mug in hand, breath curling in the cold air. He gave her that small, steady smile she'd come to rely on, the one that said more than words ever did.

"You sleep?" he asked, taking her pack from the back seat.

"Some," she said. "You?"

"Some," he admitted. "George called last night. Wanted to know if we were really going."

"And you said...?"

"I said yes." He opened the tailgate and set her pack beside his. "First we see it again. Just us. Clean. Then we bring him back into it."

Lisa nodded. That felt right—like the way you walk into a familiar room before turning on the lights, just to remember where everything is.

She pulled out her phone. "Wakanda's expecting proof of life."

Jack huffed a quiet laugh. "Of course she is."

They snapped a quick, slightly crooked selfie: Lisa's knit hat pulled low, Jack's eyes narrowed against the pale morning glare, the faint line of the mountain rising behind them. Lisa sent it with a simple caption:

LISA: Still in one piece.

Almost instantly, the three dots appeared.

WAKANDA: Good. Keep it that way, mountain boy.

WAKANDA: And Lisa... listen to yourself up there, okay? Call if you get weird feelings. I mean extra weird.

Lisa swallowed.

LISA: Got it. Love you.

She tucked the phone away. Jack watched her, face thoughtful.

"She worried?" he asked.

"She knows something's... shifting," Lisa said. "She doesn't know the details. Just that the mountain got into us more than we realized."

"She's not wrong," Jack said softly.

Lisa reached into her coat pocket and held out the old pocket watch. "You left this at my place," she said softly. Jack hesitated before taking it, the weight familiar in his hand. "Thought you should have it back," she added. He slipped it into his jacket pocket — the same place he always kept it — and nodded once, as if accepting more than just the watch. "Thanks," he said.

***

The drive up into the foothills was quiet but not heavy. A light powder dusted the higher trees, the last scraps of winter clinging to the shaded slopes. Sun broke in thin bands through the clouds, flashing across the windshield in brief, blinding strokes.

Lisa traced a finger along the edge of the folded map between them. She knew the route now, not only on paper but in her body—the twists of the narrow road, the lean of the truck around each bend, the way the mountain's presence grew stronger the closer they came.

"Do you ever feel like we're not just going somewhere," she asked, "but... back to something? Like the road remembers us."

Jack let out a slow breath. "Yeah," he said. "That's exactly how it feels."

They parked near the same trailhead where the storm had first turned the world sideways. Today the sky was clearer, the clouds thin and high. The air held that bright, sharp chill that made every sound carry.

Lisa hoisted her pack and stood for a moment, letting the quiet settle around them. A jay called somewhere in the distance. The crunch of their boots on the frozen ground sounded louder than it should have.

"Ready?" Jack asked.

"No," she said honestly. "But let's go anyway."

He smiled, and that was enough.

They entered the trees.

***

The forest closed around them with familiar arms. Tall firs and hemlocks rose on either side, their trunks dark and damp, moss glowing in soft patches where the light broke through. The trail wound gently upward, not steep yet, just persistent.

After a while, Lisa realized her breathing had fallen into the same rhythm it had that first time. Step, breath, step, breath. The smells came back too—wet bark, cold earth, something faintly metallic and mineral whenever the wind shifted from higher up.

Jack walked a few paces ahead, his posture easy but alert. At one point he touched his chest, where she knew he kept the watch in a small inner pocket, mirroring her own.

"Is it... doing anything?" she asked.

"Not yet," he said. "Feels... aware, though."

She almost laughed. "How does a watch feel aware?"

He glanced back at her. "You tell me. You're the one who said the mountain was listening."

Touché.

They crossed the small creek where icy water slipped over smooth stones, then the narrow saddle where the wind funneled down in sharper gusts. With every turn, Lisa's sense of time thinned a little more. Memories from Jack's last trip rose unbidden—the wall of snow, the whiteout, the strange, light-filled silence when everything had gone still.

Today, there was no blizzard. No roar.

But the silence still carried something.

After an hour, the trail bent toward a ridge she recognized. Beyond it, somewhere ahead, lay the clearing where the old cabin had once stood—or would stand—or still stood, depending on which way you turned the thought.

Her palms prickled.

"Jack," she said quietly.

"I know," he answered without turning around. "I feel it too."

The wind shifted.

It wasn't dramatic at first. Just a slight change in temperature, a faint scent of woodsmoke that didn't quite make sense. The hair on Lisa's arms rose beneath her jacket. Jack slowed, then stopped altogether, head tilted like he was listening for a voice just out of earshot.

Lisa moved up beside him.

Ahead, the trail continued as always, a simple cut through ferns and fallen needles. But the light had changed—subtle, like someone had turned the brightness down just a notch and warmed the edges. Colors seemed deeper. The green of the moss, the brown of the trunks, the pale band of sky overhead—all of it richer, more present.

"Do you hear that?" she whispered.

"At first I thought it was just the wind," Jack murmured. "But it's... layered. Like there's something underneath."

She closed her eyes.

Under the steady rush of air through branches, she heard it: the faint crackle of a fire that wasn't there, the low murmur of voices, the muffled clink of something metal. For a heartbeat she smelled stew, herbs, smoke on cloth.

Her chest tightened.

"The cabin," she said. "We're close."

Jack reached into his jacket and drew out the pocket watch. It lay on his palm, its silvered case catching the strange light. The hands on its face were ticking normally—then, as she watched, they shuddered once and stopped.

The forest went completely still.

No wind. No jay calling. No distant drip of water.

It was as if the world had paused to take a single, long breath.

Lisa's ears rang with the sudden quiet.

"Jack..." she began.

He closed his fingers gently around the watch. "We don't force it," he said, voice barely above a whisper. "We just walk. Same as before. If the mountain wants us there, it'll open the way."

She nodded, throat tight.

Side by side, they stepped forward.

***

The path didn't change under their feet. Dirt, roots, a slick patch of old leaves. But with each step the feeling of being between things deepened. Lisa had the odd sensation of walking along the surface of a river while a much stronger current moved beneath her, waiting for the moment to pull them in.

Then the trees thinned.

They stepped out into a small clearing, and Lisa's breath caught.

In one way, it was exactly as she'd seen it last summer on that historical survey hike: a gentle rise in the ground, the faint outline of old foundation stones half-sunk into moss, a rusted hinge half-buried near a blackberry bramble. The place where a cabin had once been.

But layered over that, like a reflection laid on top of itself, was something else.

For an instant—just an instant—the outline sharpened. The air above the foundation seemed thicker, holding shape. Lisa could almost see the ghost of a roofline, the dark suggestion of rough-hewn logs, smoke curling from a chimney that wasn't there.

Her heart hammered.

"Do you see it?" she whispered.

Jack's eyes were fixed on the empty space. "Yeah," he breathed. "It's like it's... trying to come into focus."

The watch in his hand warmed suddenly, as if someone had laid it in sunlight.

Lisa could feel the answering heat against her own ribs where her jacket pocket pressed against her. For one dizzy moment she didn't know if she was standing in March, or a hundred years ago, or both at once.

The wind exhaled.

Sound rushed back in a flood—branches, birds, the distant whisper of snowmelt. But beneath it all, that other layer remained: a faint clatter, a woman's far-off laughter, the low hum of a man's voice speaking in a language older than the trail.

Lisa's eyes stung.

"They're here," she said, not sure how she knew. "Or... we are. Or all of us."

Jack shut the watch with a soft click.

"We don't push it," he said again, more to himself than to her. "We just stand where we're meant to stand."

They moved slowly to the center of the clearing. The air felt thicker there, more aware. Lisa reached out a hand without thinking, fingers splayed, and for a heartbeat she felt rough wood beneath her palm instead of empty air—the chill of a door that hadn't been opened in a very long time and yet was not quite closed.

She gasped.

"Jack—"

"I've got you," he said quickly, one hand firm at her back.

The sensation flickered, then steadied, like a lantern in wind. Lisa could almost see the door now, could almost see her own hand hovering just above an iron latch, the grain of the wood worn smooth by other fingers long ago.

Images flashed through her mind: Jonathan's weary smile, Lawitha's dark eyes lifted to the mountains, a child's small hand gripping a carved feather.

Tears burned hot and sudden.

"This is it," she whispered. "This is where it all braided together. Them. Us. Everything."

Jack's voice was low and reverent. "Then maybe that's why we're here. To see it clearly this time. To stand in the right place long enough for it to remember us."

Lisa let her hand fall back to her side. The phantom door remained, a shimmer at the edge of sight.

She stepped back, breathing hard.

"Not all at once," she said, surprising herself with the certainty in her own voice. "If it pulled us straight through right now, we wouldn't understand any of it. We'd just get lost again."

Jack studied her, something like pride and awe mingling in his eyes.

"That's what George keeps saying," he murmured. "The mountain doesn't rush the ones it calls. It stretches time instead. Gives you room to choose."

They stood there until the shimmer softened, until the sounds of the present-day forest grew louder than the echoes underneath. Slowly, the weight in the air lightened. The watch cooled in Jack's hand. The faint smell of stew and smoke faded back into damp earth and fir needles.

At last, Lisa exhaled.

"So," she said. "We found it. Or it found us. But we didn't step all the way through."

"Not today," Jack said. "Today we came to remember the door."

"And tomorrow?" she asked.

He looked up toward the high ridge where the snowfields began, where clouds drifted like slow-moving spirits.

"Tomorrow," he said quietly, "we talk to George."

Lisa nodded.

As they turned to go, she glanced back one last time. For just a heartbeat, she saw it—the full cabin, solid and bright in the filtered light, smoke rising in a thin blue thread into the trees. A woman stood in the doorway, her dark hair braided, her eyes steady and sad and kind.

Then the wind shifted, and the vision was gone.

Lisa swallowed hard.

"I'll call Wakanda from the truck," she said, voice trembling but sure. "She's going to want to know that the mountain's not done with us yet."

Jack smiled, and together they walked back into the trees, the trail carrying them forward even as something deep in the earth turned its face toward the past.

Chapter Fifty-Three

George's Knowledge

"Wisdom is not spoken when it arrives, but when it is needed."
— Old Indian saying

Jack and Lisa arrived at George's place just after noon, the clouds hanging low over the foothills like damp wool. A faint drizzle clung to the edges of the porch roof, tapping softly as they climbed the steps. Inside, the old woodstove breathed a slow warmth into the room, the kind that settled deep into your chest.

George greeted them with his usual quiet nod, but there was something else in his eyes today — a kind of anticipation, as though he'd been waiting for the right moment to show them something.

"Come on back," he said, motioning toward his study.

Lisa followed, her gaze trailing along shelves lined with old maps, trail guides, and framed photographs. Jack stepped in behind her, slipping a hand into his coat pocket, fingers brushing the smooth shape of the pocket watch he always carried now. He didn't take it out — he rarely did — but its presence was a constant reminder of the connection he couldn't fully name.

George cleared a space on the desk and set down a weathered leather-bound journal. Its cover was scuffed and softened with age, edges worn like old river stones.

"This," George said quietly, "belonged to Jonathan Butler."

Lisa's breath caught.

Jack leaned closer. "Where did you get it?"

George hesitated before answering, as if the truth carried its own weight. "From Elias Crowther. Remember him? Lived up in Parkdale — that old historian who collected pioneer journals, mountain lore, anything tied to early settlements around Mount Hood."

Jack nodded. "Yeah. He passed, what... seven, eight years ago?"

"Six." George rested a hand on the journal. "I helped his niece clean out the house. Crowther had boxes of writings, artifacts, personal accounts... and this was tucked inside one of them. Took me a long time to realize what I had."

Lisa stepped closer, fingertips brushing the fragile leather. "Jonathan Butler... he lived in the 1800s. Why would his journal end up here?"

"Because Crowther was thorough," George said. "He tracked down families, descendants, abandoned homesteads. Anything tied to Wy'East. Perhaps it was in the possession of that Shivery fellow who Jonathan entrusted his belongings. Or it was stowed away in the old offices of the newspaper. Or perhaps sent from England after Jonathan had passed. Somehow Crowther acquired the journals and kept them safe."

Jack let out a slow breath. "So this is real."

"Very real." George opened the journal carefully, revealing pages filled with tidy, looping ink. "And what's in here... it's not just daily logging or weather notes. Jonathan wrote about dreams. Signs. A feeling of... returning. Like something was calling him through the years."

Lisa felt a chill slip over her shoulders. "Calling him?"

George nodded. "Some of what he describes... matches things you both have felt. Things neither of you could quite explain."

Jack's jaw tightened. He didn't speak, but Lisa felt the shift in him — quiet recognition.

George turned another page. "Jonathan believed the mountain was holding something for him. Something he could only understand by going back."

"Back where?" Lisa whispered.

George closed the journal gently. "That's the question he never answered."

They stood there in the dim light of the study, the journal resting between them like a bridge across time.

Outside, the wind stirred the eaves — soft, searching, familiar.

And without needing to speak it aloud, all three of them felt the same quiet truth settle in the room:

The story wasn't finished. Not for Jonathan. And not for them.

Chapter Fifty-Four

Wedding Plans at Timberline

"A good friend is a sheltering tree." — *Cherokee Proverb*

The sky over Portland held a soft spring brightness, the kind that made everything feel just a shade more possible. Lisa stood in front of the wide mirror in her bedroom, holding up a dress she wasn't sure she liked, when Wakanda let herself in without knocking.

"Please tell me you're not thinking about wearing that," Wakanda said, her voice teasing but warm.

Lisa snorted. "It's just a try-on."

"It's just a disaster," Wakanda corrected, plucking the dress from Lisa's hands and tossing it onto the bed. "We're finding something that makes you glow. Not something that makes you look like you're auditioning for a prairie ghost reenactment."

Lisa laughed, the first real laugh she'd had all week. "Okay, okay. But I still don't know if Timberline is the right place."

"Oh, it is," Wakanda said without hesitation. "It fits you. All that wood and stone. That history. And that view? Girl... it's like the mountain itself says 'welcome home.'"

Lisa felt that strange stirring again—the one she couldn't quite name. "It does feel... right."

Wakanda's expression softened. "You've changed lately, you know. Not in a bad way. Just... deeper. Like there's something ancient sitting behind your eyes. Something waking up."

Lisa didn't know how to answer. "I don't feel different."

"You don't have to," Wakanda said, reaching out to adjust a strand of hair over Lisa's shoulder. "I can see it for you."

The doorbell rang, shaking them out of the moment.

"That'll be Jack," Lisa said, heading toward the hallway.

"Perfect," Wakanda whispered theatrically. "He can vote on the dresses. Or at least pretend to."

Jack stepped inside with a small stack of brochures under his arm. "Found the lodge's updated wedding packet," he said, offering it to Lisa. "Thought it might help."

Wakanda snatched it before Lisa could touch it. "Let me see. Ooh—look at this ballroom. And the terrace. And these flower setups! Lisa, this is your place. I'm telling you."

Jack just chuckled. "I stay out of flower discussions. Way too dangerous."

Wakanda pointed at him. "You stay out of a lot of things. Except losing yourself in maps. Lisa told me you spent two hours yesterday staring at elevation lines."

Jack shrugged, unbothered. "They're accurate elevation lines."

Lisa rolled her eyes fondly. "See what I deal with?"

The three of them gathered around the dining table as Wakanda spread out the brochures, her commentary bouncing between sharp humor and genuine excitement. Lisa felt a warmth settle over her—something like home, something like belonging.

Then Wakanda paused mid-sentence, looking at Lisa with sudden seriousness.

"I mean this," she said quietly. "I've never seen you like this before. You're... brighter. Whole, somehow."

Lisa felt her cheeks warm. "I don't know what's happening to me."

"You don't have to," Wakanda murmured. "But you need to talk about it. With each other. Don't start keeping things bottled up."

Jack's gaze lifted to Lisa. Something unspoken passed between them—soft, steady, familiar.

Wakanda clapped her hands once. "Alright! Enough feelings. Back to dresses."

Lisa laughed again, the sound easing the tension.

Outside, a thin veil of clouds drifted off Mount Hood, revealing its bright snow crown. The mountain seemed to watch them through the window—calm, patient, waiting.

Chapter Fifty-Five

The Journal Reveals the Past

"A story lives on only when someone is willing to listen." — Nez Perce Proverb

Jack sat at the small kitchen table, the leather-bound journal resting between his hands like something both fragile and alive. The cover was worn to a warm brown sheen, the corners slightly frayed, the spine softened by time and touch. Lisa stood beside him, leaning in with a quiet curiosity that trembled on the edge of wonder.

George had barely stayed long enough to hand it over.

"All I'll say," he'd muttered, rubbing the back of his neck, "is that the man who kept this... saw things. Felt things. And he wasn't wrong."

Then he'd left without another word.

Now the house seemed to hold its breath.

Lisa slid into the chair next to Jack. "I can't believe this belonged to Jonathan Butler."

Jack nodded.

She touched the journal gently, her fingers brushing the old leather. "It feels… important."

Jack opened it carefully.

The pages were filled with neat, deliberate handwriting—Jonathan's voice stretched across more than a century, as steady and sure as the man himself. There were notes about weather, trail routes, hunting signs—ordinary things. But scattered among them were passages that made Lisa's skin prickle.

"There are moments when the air shifts, as if time itself is folding. I feel her near me then—Lawitha. Not in memory. In presence."

Lisa drew in a soft breath. "Jack… this sounds like—"

"I know," he said.

They read in silence for a few minutes.

Jonathan wrote about dreams he couldn't explain, about walking through the forest and smelling smoke from a fire he hadn't built, about hearing a woman hum a tune older than the trees.

And then one line that made Lisa press a hand to her heart:

"The mountain does not forget who has walked upon it. And it does not forget who belongs to it."

A gentle tremor went through her.

Jack noticed. "You okay?"

"Yes. I just…" She tried to find words. "Sometimes when we're on the trail, I feel something watching. Not in a scary way. More like… remembering me."

Jack reached for her hand. "That's why I wanted you to see this."

Before she could respond, her phone buzzed.

Wakanda.

Lisa smiled faintly and answered. "Hey. I'm with Jack. We're reading... something."

There was a pause on the other end, then Wakanda's voice softened.

"Are you feeling it again?"

Lisa closed her eyes. "Yeah. Stronger this time."

"Listen to it," Wakanda said. "Don't run from it. If something's rising up in you, there's a reason."

Lisa swallowed, moved by how easily Wakanda always cut to the heart of things.

"I'll call you later," she whispered.

When she hung up, Jack turned another page.

A sketch filled the paper—rough, but clear.

A cabin.

The old one.

The one that Running Horse built for Jonathan.

Lisa leaned closer. "Jack... that's the same ridge line we hiked below last fall."

"I know," he murmured. "I think Jonathan saw more than anyone realized."

Their eyes met—quiet, steady, and full of unspoken recognition.

Whatever lay ahead, the mountain wasn't finished with them.

And Jonathan's words were no longer just history. They were a guide.

Chapter Fifty-Six

The Chief's Blessing

"The heart that listens will find its way." — Lakota Proverb

The wind on Mount Hood was soft that morning, carrying only the faintest chill as Lisa and Jack followed the gravel path toward the small gathering circle near the edge of the timberline. The sky was a clear, pale blue—the kind that made the mountain look both immense and impossibly close. Even before they reached the lookout circle, Lisa felt a quiet hum in the air, something subtle but deeply familiar.

Wakanda walked beside her, hands tucked into her coat pockets, eyes wide as she took in the landscape. She'd never been part of anything like this, but she carried herself with an easy blend of curiosity and reverence.

"You weren't kidding," she murmured. "This place... it feels older than the clouds."

Lisa smiled, but she said nothing. Words didn't seem to fit the moment.

The chief waited near a low ring of stones, his hair braided neatly, his presence as steady as the mountain behind him. When Lisa and Jack approached, he nodded in greeting. Wakanda gave a respectful dip of her head, unsure if she should speak first.

"You honor us by being here," the chief said gently, his gaze settling on each of them. "The mountain remembers those who walk with intention."

Jack stood a step behind Lisa, quiet, attentive. The chief gestured for her to come forward, and she did, feeling the earth shift beneath her in a way that wasn't physical—more like recognition.

Wakanda stepped aside to give the two space but kept close enough to witness. She folded her arms, not out of tension, but as if holding herself still so she wouldn't disturb the moment.

The chief lifted a small pouch of sage and cedar, letting the smoke rise in a slow winding ribbon around Lisa. The scent curled through the air, warm and grounding.

"You carry two paths," he said. "One written before you were born. One you have chosen with your own heart. These paths are not separate. They are learning to walk together."

Lisa's breath trembled—not with fear, but with something like being seen.

He touched her shoulder lightly. "You are opening. Do not be afraid of what meets you."

Wakanda swallowed hard, eyes glistening. She wasn't sure why the words struck her so deeply, but they did.

When the blessing ended, the chief placed a small cedar sprig in Lisa's hand.

"Keep this until the wedding," he said. "Let it remind you that the wind carries memory, and memory carries strength."

Lisa nodded, touched beyond speech.

As they stepped back from the circle, Wakanda let out a quiet exhale. "Lisa," she whispered, "I swear... something in you shifted just now. I felt it."

Lisa squeezed the cedar sprig gently. "I did too."

Jack fell in beside them, slipping his hand lightly over Lisa's back in a quiet gesture of support. Wakanda walked on her other side, protective in her own way.

The wind climbed a little higher across the mountain slope, rustling the evergreens like a whispered approval.

Something had changed.

And all three of them felt it.

Chapter Fifty-Seven

Night Before the Wedding

*"The moon teaches us that light is strongest when reflected." —
Lakota Saying*

Lisa stood at the small oak mirror in the loft of the lodge,
brushing out the last waves of her hair. Outside, the wind
carried a soft hum across the mountain, a low, steady breath
like someone whispering through cupped hands. Timberline
Lodge felt wrapped in its own quiet tonight—fireplaces crackling, footsteps softened by old wood, an air of anticipation
settling into every hallway.

A gentle knock sounded.

"It's open," she called.

Wakanda slipped inside with a grin that was half-mischief,
half-tenderness. She wore deep cedar-green, a shade that made
her brown eyes look even warmer. "Well, would you look at
you," she said, leaning against the doorframe. "If Jack has any
sense left, he'll faint before you even reach the aisle."

Lisa laughed softly. "Please don't let him faint. I don't
think George can catch him anymore."

Wakanda stepped closer, rearranging a loose strand of Lisa's hair without asking. Her hands were gentle, practiced—the way only a best friend could touch someone without shifting their balance.

"Nervous?" Wakanda asked.

"Not really," Lisa said. "Just... full. Like everything that's been building is finally meeting me at the same place."

Wakanda nodded, studying her for a beat. "There's something different in your eyes," she murmured. "You've had this glow for weeks now. Ancient, almost."

Lisa felt a warmth move up her chest—not embarrassment, not pride, but something quieter. Something true.

"I think the mountain has been teaching me," she said. "In ways I didn't expect."

Wakanda tilted her head with a half smile. "Well, don't go turning completely mystical on me. I still need you to remember your vows tomorrow."

Lisa swatted her arm, but both of them ended up laughing.

For a moment, they simply stood together, the wind brushing softly at the windows like a familiar friend asking permission to enter.

Wakanda's expression softened again. "I'm proud of you," she said. "For choosing joy after everything. For letting yourself be seen—really seen. That takes more courage than people admit."

Lisa swallowed against the tightening in her throat. "Thanks."

Wakanda stepped back, sensing the shift without needing words. "I'll give you a minute," she said, squeezing Lisa's hand once. "If you need anything, knock on the wall. I'll pretend I wasn't eavesdropping."

As she slipped out the door, her footsteps faded down the hall.

Lisa walked toward the window and unlatched it, pushing it open just enough to let the cold drift in. The wind rose gently, threading through her hair, carrying the scent of snow, fir, and something older—something that felt like memory brushing against the skin.

She closed her eyes. The mountain hummed softly around her, a sound that wasn't quite a voice and yet felt unmistakably alive.

"Tomorrow," she whispered into the night, "I'm ready."

The wind curled around her hand as if answering. And for the first time, Lisa believed it.

Chapter Fifty-Eight

The Wedding on Mount Hood

"The heart, like the mountain, knows when it has come home."
— *Lakota Proverb*

Morning came clear and bright over Mount Hood, the sky washed in that pale, early summer blue that looks almost new. Snow still clung to the upper ridges, glowing gold where the sun touched it, while the lower forests shimmered with melt-water and the breath of awakening earth. The mountain felt alive—not loud, not commanding, but quietly welcoming, the way a long-kept promise finally steps into the light.

Lisa stood at the open window of her room at Timberline Lodge, holding her bouquet loosely, letting the cool breeze brush her face. It carried the clean scent of fir and distant snow... and something else. Something familiar. Something ancient. It had been with her ever since the chief's blessing, settling deeper each day until it felt almost woven into her bones.

A soft knock sounded behind her.

"You ready, mountain bride?" Wakanda's voice teased gently.

Lisa turned with a smile. Wakanda looked radiant—soft green dress, hair pinned just enough, eyes shining. But her expression held something quieter too, something reverent.

"You look... full," Wakanda said, searching for the right word. "Like you're carrying light."

Lisa swallowed the small knot of emotion. "I feel steady," she whispered. "More than I thought I could."

Wakanda stepped closer and straightened the small braid woven along the side of Lisa's hair. "Well. Let's go get you married to that trail-lost man before he starts pacing holes in the snow."

They laughed—soft, warm, easy.

Outside, guests were gathering on the terrace. Timber-line's stone arch framed the sweep of the mountain behind them, a view so vast it felt like standing on the edge of story and sky. The wind stirred lightly, brushing against Lisa's dress as if in greeting.

Jack waited near the officiant, hands clasped, eyes fixed on her the moment she stepped outside. He didn't blink. Didn't look away. His expression said everything—certainty, awe, and that quiet devotion he never spoke of but carried like breath.

Wakanda squeezed Lisa's hand once before taking her place.

As Lisa began to walk forward, the world seemed to settle into a single whispered moment. The voices of the guests softened. The wind quieted. Even the mountain seemed to listen.

Jack's eyes glimmered with something deeper than happiness. Recognition. As if some long-lost thread between past and present had finally been tied.

When they joined hands, the officiant spoke, but the words hardly mattered. What mattered was the feeling—solid as stone, soft as wind. Lisa felt it move through her, a warm current rising from somewhere older than memory.

During the vows, Wakanda brushed tears from her cheeks. She wasn't the only one.

For a moment after they spoke the final words, the world seemed to hold its breath.

The crowd blurred at the edges, the snowfield brightened, and the wind curled around them like something recognizing its own.

Lisa felt her pulse racing—until something else rose beneath it.

A second heartbeat.

Slow. Steady. Ancient.

Not external.

Not imagined.

But moving through her, as if another life—another memory—opened its eyes inside her chest.

Not frightening.

Not taking anything from her.

Just... settling in, like someone who had finally come home.

She inhaled sharply. Jack's hands tightened around hers, sensing the shift even if he couldn't name it.

The mountain listened.

The wind brushed her cheek with a touch that felt almost familiar.

And somewhere deep inside the silence, something old and gentle whispered: I am here.

Then the moment softened, folded itself quietly into her, and the world resumed its rhythm—just as the chief stepped forward to bless them.

And when Jack and Lisa finally stepped together into the sunlight, the wind rose gently—just enough to lift her veil, just enough to circle them like a blessing carried from someplace far beyond the present moment.

Wakanda leaned close as the guests applauded. "Told you," she whispered with a grin. "Something ancient was waking up in you."

Lisa squeezed her friend's hand. "It wasn't just in me," she replied softly. "It was waiting for us."

Far above them, Mount Hood shone bright and still, the old keeper of stories standing watch as two new ones began their life—rooted in the past, steady in the present, and carried forward on the wind.

A Note to Reader

I enjoyed writing this book, which was originally planned as a trilogy. The first novel was published in 2013, and over time I found myself returning to that story, drawn back to its characters and places. Eventually, I combined that original work with the other two sections and reshaped it into a single novel told in three parts.

Editing, as any writer will tell you, is its own kind of challenge. Early on, a friend offered advice that has stayed with me ever since: "Write drunk and edit sober." While the writing came from imagination and instinct, the editing required patience, care, and a clear head.

Although Whispers in the Wind is a work of fiction, I chose to ground it in real places and fragments of history. The Watlala people of the Hood River area are part of that history, as are the landscapes that shape the story — Elk Meadows (one of my favorite hikes), Mount Hood, the Columbia River, and the town of Hood River itself.

As for Portland — Portland is Portland. I grew up near the neighborhood that became Jack's home in the novel, and the city naturally found its way onto the page.

PATRICK TIMM

The twists and turns woven through these pages grew from a dream — the same one Jack experiences in the story. And yes, for those wondering, the box and the pocket watch do exist. They sit in my office as I write this.

Thank you for following this journey.

~Patrick Timm